PLOUGHSH  Y0-CBR-083

Fall 2008 · Vol. 34, Nos. 2&3

GUEST EDITOR
James Alan McPherson

INTERIM EDITOR-IN-CHIEF
DeWitt Henry

MANAGING DIRECTOR
Robert Arnold

FICTION EDITOR
Margot Livesey

POETRY EDITOR
John Skoyles

ASSOCIATE FICTION EDITOR
Maryanne O'Hara

FOUNDING PUBLISHER
Peter O'Malley

PLOUGHSHARES, a journal of new writing, is guest-edited serially by prominent writers who explore different and personal visions, aesthetics, and literary circles. PLOUGHSHARES is published in April, August, and December at Emerson College, 120 Boylston Street, Boston, MA 02116-4624. Telephone: (617) 824-8753. Web address: pshares.org.

ASSISTANT EDITOR: Laura van den Berg. EDITORIAL ASSISTANTS: Kat Setzer, and Sabrina Ramos. HEAD READER: Jay Baron Nicorvo. PROOFREADERS: Megan Weireter and Elizabeth Zdunich.

POETRY READERS: Simeon Berry, Jennifer Kohl, Grace Schauer, Kathleen Rooney, Heather Madden, Elisa Gabbert, Matt Summers, Autumn McClintock, Liz Bury, David Semanki, Chris Tonelli, Julia Story, Maria Halovanic, Pepe Abola, and Meredith Devney. FICTION READERS: Kat Setzer, Matt Salesses, Kathleen Rooney, Simeon Berry, Kat Gonso, Chris Helmuth, Leslie Busler, Jim Scott, Chip Cheek, Cam Terwilliger, Laura van den Berg, Sage Marsters, Eson Kim, Vanessa Carlisle, Brenda Pike, Wendy Wunder, Shannon Derby, Dan Medeiros, Sara Whittleton, Patricia Reed, Leslie Cauldwell, and Gregg Rosenblum. NONFICTION READER: Katherine Newman.

SUBSCRIPTIONS (ISSN 0048-4474): $24 for one year (3 issues), $46 for two years (6 issues); $27 a year for institutions. Add $12 a year for international ($10 for Canada).

UPCOMING: Winter 2008–09, a poetry and fiction issue edited by Jean Valentine, will appear in December 2008. Spring 2009, a poetry and fiction issue edited by Eleanor Wilner, will appear in April 2009.

SUBMISSIONS: Reading period is from August 1 to March 31 (postmark and online dates). All submissions sent from April to July are returned unread. Please see page 214 for editorial and submission policies.

Back-issue, classroom-adoption, and bulk orders may be placed directly through PLOUGHSHARES. Microfilms of back issues may be obtained from University Microfilms. PLOUGHSHARES is also available as CD-ROM and full-text products from EBSCO, H.W. Wilson, ProQuest, and the Gale Group. Indexed in M.L.A. Bibliography, American Humanities Index, Index of American Periodical Verse, Book Review Index. Full publisher's index is online at pshares.org. The views and opinions expressed in this journal are solely those of the authors. All rights for individual works revert to the authors upon publication. PLOUGHSHARES receives support from the National Endowment for the Arts and the Massachusetts Cultural Council.

Retail distribution by Ingram Periodicals and Source Interlink. Printed in the U.S.A. by Edwards Brothers.

© 2008 by Emerson College   ISBN 978-1-933058-10-8

CONTENTS

Fall 2008

Cover art:
Aqqr by
Eric Garnick
Oil on canvas, 48″ x 59″, 2007

Ploughshares Patrons

This nonprofit publication would not be possible without the
support of our readers and the generosity of the following
individuals and organizations.

COUNCIL: $3,000 for two lifetime subscriptions and
acknowledgement in the journal for three years.
PATRON: $1,000 for a lifetime subscription and
acknowledgement in the journal for two years.
FRIEND: $500 for a lifetime subscription and
acknowledgement in the journal for one year.

JAMES ALAN MCPHERSON

Introduction

As I was writing this introduction, a series of fierce storms began hitting sections of south central Iowa. Several weeks ago, an Iowa town named Parkersburg was completely destroyed, and the media focused on the efforts of the townspeople to contain the disaster. The storms persisted throughout most of Iowa, with extreme winds and torrential rains in Iowa City, where I live and teach. The university was shut down for at least a week, and major parts of downtown were flooded. During breaks in the weather, people—students, residents of Iowa City—worked in huge groups to sandbag buildings and roadways on the university campus and in the city.

As always, it was the human dimension of the tragedy that interested me. Many years ago, I learned here in Iowa City the local meaning of the term "neighboring." It evolved out of the frontier tradition of the rural landscapes: If a neighboring farmer could not take care of his planting or his harvest, or could not manage heavy rain or snow on his own, it became tradition for people living nearby to step in and offer assistance. Soon the word was abstracted from agriculture and employed to describe absolutely any helpful human gestures. In places like Iowa City, such "neighboring" gestures are normative. Paul Engle, who created both the Writers' Workshop and the Iowa International Workshop, had this tradition in his blood. In one of his many books, he wrote about growing up in a small town outside of Cedar Rapids. In his youth, a family of Orthodox Jews moved into the town. Because their religion prevented them from working on the Sabbath, Paul did the work for them on that day; he became their "Sabbath Goy." I believe it was this experience with an "other" that encouraged him to create a national writing haven, and then an international writing haven in Iowa City.

It might be said that the variety of young writers in this issue of *Ploughshares* are "neighboring." If there is a common thread in the stories here, I think it must be the communal effort to gain perspective on the highly complex areas of our fuzzy and fragmented American reality. We seem to live our lives against a backdrop of emotional fragmentation and failure of purpose: the economy, the various wars in the Middle East, the decay of rights movements (civil rights, feminism, economic help for those in poverty, sexual choice in marriage). In recent months, the media has been almost obsessed in its explanation of the appeal of Barack Obama. He seems to move beyond being black, a certified political liberal or conservative. His appeal seems to be spiritual but not necessarily religious. And he has inspired the enthusiastic support of a tremendous number of Americans, not all of them black or young. Many years ago, one of my mentors, the critic and novelist Albert Murray, coined a term that has kept inspiring me for the past thirty years. When the civil rights movement began drifting towards separatism and Black Nationalism, Murray argued in one of his books, *The Omni-Americans*, that black Americans derive from a very long and very deep association with the racial and cultural traditions of this country. Murray argued that the exploration of these influences might enable black people to look beyond nationalism and to recognize, if not embrace, the traditions of other groups within the American cultural environment. The result of this "integration" would be a newer and culturally complex kind of American. Such reflexive embraces would make members of the group more receptive to the mores of other Americans.

In his appeal to the political as well as to the emotional quests of people from a great number of groups, Obama is clearly the Omni-American that Albert Murray had in mind. One source of his appeal is that he thinks and operates beyond race and class and sexual orientation—beyond all the social categories that function as substitutes for a transcendent American identity. I believe that a great many people can sense this spiritual transcendence in him, and can project onto him their own desires for transcendence. I have read recently that former Supreme Court Justice Sandra Day O'Connor is trying to reach out to young people through computers and digital games ("games for change"). She hopes to embrace the internet and interactive digital media as essential tools for preserving American democracy, for attempting to "neighbor" with young people who are devoted to the culture of the internet.

The tradition of helping others was apparent in the supermarkets these past few weeks. The parking lots were full, and people rolled two or three carts full of food and bottles of water to their cars. People had moved outside of their immediate emotional concerns and refocused on transcendent communal needs. Securing essentials for others, like the act of sandbagging, became an Omni-American ritual gesture. Once during this period, my doorbell rang and there was a student, a young woman, with whom I had worked in 2001. She and her husband had brought me twenty-four bottles of water in a plastic case.

I am sure this gesture was being replicated all over Iowa City, and indeed all over Iowa. It was essentially the human thing to do. Something beyond race, sexual identity, or economic status. It was simply "the done thing" in a vital tradition of highly civilized manners.

I do not agree with Joseph Brodsky, in M. G. Stevens's "Sunday Morning," that America has become a decadent country. It seems to me that real decadence involves strict attention to non-essential matters, not the quest for something better. Most of the stories here dramatize some aspects of that quest.

Lady Fingers

Chi Chi inhaled the screen from her crack pipe."

I laugh and wait for Leslie to join in, but there is only silence on the other end of the line.

"You're serious?" I ask.

"You better believe I'm serious. That child gone and almost killed herself."

I want to apologize for laughing, thinking this was a joke, but I know Leslie doesn't have patience for polite chitchat.

"She's okay?" I ask. It seems absurd, the stuff of fiction. I didn't even know crack pipes had screens.

"She at Woodhull Hospital. Took her last night and she don't look too good." Leslie continues, "Her face was all sweaty and shit, but that could of been the crack. Thought you should know."

Leslie is the senior residential counselor at the group home and the vibrato in her voice leaves no one wondering who's in charge. Sometimes she takes the initiative to call me with updates about the residents. Update, I've learned, is synonymous with crisis. Leslie is fairly selective on what warrants a call: bodily harm, suicide attempts, hospitalization, physical assault on a resident or staff member.

Updates on Chi Chi have become more and more frequent.

I don't get the calls about prostitution or drug use anymore. Those incidents are too frequent and selectivity on Leslie's part saves me from information overload. I have fourteen other adolescents on my caseload right now with similar issues and Leslie knows that I can read all about the typical debauchery in the incident reports. No need to bother me with the petty stuff.

In a month Chi Chi will turn twenty-one. I was told that last year for her birthday she wanted a cake with lavender frosting and a Louis Vuitton purse. She got the cake and a gift certificate to Jimmy Jazz that she traded on the street for a couple of vials of crack. This year there are no questions about what she wants. Chi Chi knows what she gets on her twenty-first birthday. We've been trying to plan with her for this day for a while. In the State of New York, at age twenty-one, youth placed in foster care must leave the system. They call it *aging out.*

I worry about all the kids as their twenty-first birthday approaches. The weeks prior to the aging out date can produce the most stress they have experienced, even if they have a legitimate place to go. Typically, they act out. As their frustration mounts so does their dangerous behavior.

With Chi Chi I am particularly concerned.

When we met eight months ago Chi Chi wanted little to do with me. She was polite but rarely engaged me past a smattering of small talk and pleasantries. I was the new caseworker, the fifth one in the three years since the program's inception. My social work experience up to this point consisted of eight months as a residential counselor at a group home in Queens. How I arrived there I don't really know. All I was sure of at the time I applied for the job was that I had recently received my bachelor's degree, I was about to turn thirty and I was in need of a seismic shift in my life. I had effectively dwindled my days down to waiting tables at a Mexican restaurant and then, as pastime, drinking scotch after scotch until the blue of morning broke night. Often while lying in bed, midafternoons, under the heavy weight of a hangover, I dreamed of being plucked from my life like a chess piece and placed somewhere—anywhere—foreign, new. When I saw the job listing online one night in March, I told myself I had wanted to work with kids, in what capacity I wasn't sure, and here, before me, on my computer monitor, was an opportunity to push past the drudgery and seize something new for myself. It wasn't until I was actually hired for the position that I realized how underqualified I was. I'd never worked with youth before, never paid close attention to social welfare issues, or given a thought about the foster care system. And when asked by my friends who still clung tightly to aspirations of making it as artists, why I wanted to work in a group home, I answered, *because I need to serve something greater than myself.* It sounded good and I tried to fool myself into believing it was true. Really, I hadn't a clue why I wanted to work with marginalized youth in foster care and neither did the residents. They dismissed me immediately.

"A white caseworker?" I heard Shannequa say to Mush in the hallway as I entered the group home for the first time. "I give him two months." They knocked knuckles, laughed.

That day Chi Chi wore tight jeans and a threadbare halter-top. She sat on the living room couch watching TV on a lopsided entertainment stand with a missing wheel. The living room window blinds were bent; the bars on the window were bent, the floor sloped; two chairs against the wall sat unevenly. The Home Sweet Home plaque just over the kitchen doorway was intended to soften the institutional feel of the house; instead it seemed more like a reminder of what this place could never become.

Chi Chi's broad shoulders curled downwards, she crossed her right leg over her left and tucked her foot behind her ankle as she clasped her hands in her lap.

"I hear that you're back in a GED program, that's great," I said as I sat down beside her, hoping she would be impressed by the homework I'd done. She moved away from me to the edge of the couch and rolled her eyes. I was speaking first with Chi Chi because her situation was dire. We had seven months to set her up with the resources she needed. I was to work with her closely in hopes of establishing a discharge plan, getting her set up with employment, monitoring her performance in school and finding her a place to live after her twenty-first birthday. Chi Chi came into foster care as an adolescent, the only family was her grandmother who lived in Puerto Rico. Chi Chi was intelligent, having taught herself to be fluent in English during her brief time in New York. Everything I knew about her I learned from my supervisor. Of all the residents, Chi Chi kept to herself the most. As the oldest inhabitant in the house she claimed to want nothing to do with *these children*. I'd soon find out that it was common for her to sit alone in front of the TV watching a bootleg DVD of *Beauty Shop*, feeding her dream of stardom as the other residents played handball across the street or flirted with neighborhood *chulos* while smoking a blunt on the stoop of the Dominican church. She'd sit with her face swathed in Noxzema, sipping fruit punch in-between voicing her exasperation to the characters on TV. "You stupid," she'd snap at the screen. "Why you play yourself?"

"Well, I'm excited to work with you, Chi Chi," I continued. "I really want to make it a goal that you get a job. How does that sound?" As the words left my mouth I shuddered at their banality.

Chi Chi chipped away her nail polish for a while then looked up, "You finished?" she asked. Before I could answer she stood up and walked out the door.

The group home is called Keap Street. It houses gay, lesbian and transgender youth in foster care and is one of only three such programs in New York City. The kids are anywhere from fourteen to twenty-one years old. They've been placed in care because they were either neglected or abused by their parents or because their behavior was unmanageable in their homes. Most of them are here because when their sexual orientation or gender identity was discovered they were again abused. Maybe by a foster parent, maybe by a former group home staff member.

There are twelve residents. I read all of their files prior to meeting them. As we met I tried to connect their faces to their stories.

Blanca's sixteen, with long black hair. She styles herself in a tough way that is contradicted by her eyes. Her heroin-addicted mother died of AIDS when she was nine; her father was murdered in a gang dispute when she was eight. Junior (his real name is Sheadon) is a nineteen year old immigrant from Dominica. He was placed in care by the courts because he's a thief and a liar. He was raised in a one-bedroom apartment in the Bronx, with five siblings; tells people he's a doctor with homes in both Long Island and Florida. Donna, called Mush, because she gets so mushy with the girls, was placed at the home after a stint in juvenile detention for lifting some sneakers for "a shorty I was crushing on." In juvenile detention she got into trouble for flirting with another girl whose boyfriend found out and hit Mush in the head with a brick. Now she has periodic epileptic seizures. Nothing happened to the boy but Mush was labeled a sexual predator and removed from the facility. Now she's in love with Shannequa, the one with a trusting face and a dimpled smile, who prostitutes herself and uses sex in the group home to manipulate the other residents, namely Mush. Pimple-faced and slinky, Christina is a cocoa-colored, fifteen-year-old transgender Latina from the Bronx who thinks she's a white girl from the suburbs. Her Britney Spears impersonation borders on identity theft. Raheem, nineteen, thin and attractive, with full, bee-stung lips, was put into care because he was being sexually abused by his father and then by his foster parents. Both his mom and dad have since died. He's threatened to kill other residents and himself on more than one occasion. Celia is 5'4", 230lbs. She prides herself on not "being ghetto," slights the other kids' fashion style of Sean John, Timberlands and Akademics for anything black and adorned with skulls. Her hair changes color as often as her mood ring. On the day I met her she had a four-inch nail jutting out from beneath her bottom lip. She's a cutter, I read in her file, and as we talked I saw that her arms were dotted with tiny sliver-scars.

And there's Chi Chi.

I'm at the residence the day she returns from the hospital. When she invites me to see how she's arranged her room, I accept.

"Staff says I should be an interior decorator," she whispers, her Puerto Rican accent rolling her *r's* like pastries. She smoothes out her comforter with her large, calloused fingers that end in French tips. She shows me her Hello Kitty ornaments and porcelain cat figurines with real fur. The room is tidy and feminine. She has an eye for detail.

"Touch it, it's like real," she says, pointing to a fake cat. She giggles and covers her mouth with her hand.

Chi Chi wants to pass but she doesn't. With a quick glance you might not see what a closer inspection shows. She's constantly plucking, cinching, stuffing, bleaching, erasing. But she can't hide her Adam's apple, her broad shoulders, her large hands. She fills her bra with socks, tucks and secures her penis between her legs, tapes maxi pads together and stuffs them down the sides of her pants to create the illusion of hips. On the street she finds someone to supply her with feminizing hormones. Her regimen is uneven, only when she strolls enough can she afford it. The effects are wicked. Her voice rattles, her skin blanches. She works hard at being a girl and when a man pays her, I imagine, she feels the warmth of success.

"He likes my hands," she once confessed to me, "he told me so. He said I got lady fingers."

When she vanishes we don't hear from her until we get her call asking to be picked up from central booking. The charge is loitering with the intent to prostitute or purchasing narcotics. I'll go get her and she'll walk out of the men's holding area without makeup, clutching her belongings to her chest. She won't speak on the way home.

For months I've been trying to formulate a discharge plan for Chi Chi, scrambling to find anything that could work. She has no family members in New York, no appropriate visiting resources. Chi Chi has no adult figure in her life outside of her caretakers in the system, and, of course, her tricks. She can't keep a job; her addiction makes that impossible. Anyway, she can earn double, maybe triple a menial income strolling the streets.

I pat the fake cat. It's eerie, feels dead. I'm anxious because Chi Chi and I need to have a discussion. Time is running out and she acts as if the impending date is just another day, as if nothing is about to change. If my job is to prepare her in some way, to provide for her some basic tools of survival, I've failed. She's ready for nothing. The world will greet her on her birthday with indifference. When everything falls away, she'll have no place to go.

"Chi Chi," I say, "we need to talk."

She freezes, doesn't look up.

Now that I've started, I have no clue what to say. I'm lost. I suddenly feel like a hypocrite telling Chi Chi she needs to get herself in order, needs to start making healthier choices for herself. I wonder what she'd say if she could peer into my apartment window at night and witness me, alone in my mess of dirty laundry and empty beer bottles, chatting online at a safe distance from real rejection or scorn. I hear her laugh and say *You supposed to be telling me how to live my life? Least I got one.* She'd look at my place, so small and dank, squalor even by her standards, and then turn to me, with embarrassment softening her face, her head slowly shaking.

What option does she have other than calling her grandmother and letting her know the situation?

"I'm not going back to Puerto Rico," Chi Chi quips, flicks her finger in my face. "*Abuelita* don't want me."

"You don't have to go back," I say, "but maybe you should try to get in touch with her."

Chi Chi won't look at me. She smoothes the same spot on her comforter over and over. I know the parts of this story that I've read in psychiatric evaluations and in psychological assesments. I've read lists of events loosely threaded together that lead to diagnosis. In my head I've reworked those events and rubbed them smooth, like Chi Chi does her bedspread, to find something more, in hopes that not only the victim but also the person is revealed. I've thought about the numerous case histories in her file, the facts strung together so many times that I've begun to see her life as if I were there.

"I'm not going to Puerto Rico," she says and suddenly pushes me out into the hallway, slamming the door in my face.

In the beginning the name was Baldomero. He remembers his mother running past him like a crazy woman as he played in the island dirt. She was running, he remembers, her eyes shiny with tears. And screaming. He remembers her screaming, and *Abuelita* chasing behind her, a rock over her head.

—How can you do this to your child? *Abuelita* bawled and hurled the stone at his mother's back. You beast!

Baldomero dug his hands into the wet earth as his mother escaped into the thicket of pineapples. —I hope you die, *Abuelita* screamed. I pray that New York swallows you.

That is all he remembers of her leaving. He stayed on the island with *Abuelita;* there was no one else with whom he could live. Baldomero's father had disappeared a year earlier to San Juan and then was jailed on drug charges. Baldomero didn't remember anything about him.

Abuelita's drinking was always bad but when Baldomero was ten years old it worsened. The smell of rum reminded him of browning butter splattering in a pan as she barked in his face.

—You are such a *maricon, Abuelita* said. It's because your parents abandoned you, you have no man to look up to. Now it is my job to make you a man.

She corrected his posture, his effeminate speech, told him to act like a boy, play soccer with the other kids. She cracked a switch across his knees if he crossed his legs and sat like a girl. She hated when he giggled in a high pitch, covering his mouth with his limp wrist. She locked him in the bathroom as punishment where he stood in front of the splintered mirror, a t-shirt tied over his head that fell like a wig onto his shoulders. He pretended to comb through what he imagined to be long hair as he removed a hidden picture of his mother from behind the toilet.

At twelve years old, Baldomero stayed out until early in the morning, eyes traced with heavy black eyeliner, lips smeared red. Tiny bruises blossomed like violets around his neck and chest. Baldomero started growing his hair; he wore tight clothes he got on the street. He placed rolled socks in his shirts and sculpted them until they resembled small, perfect breasts. This is what pleased the men in town who met with Baldomero secretly in the dark anonymity of night. They praised their little girl, their little Chi Chi and spoke about love as they pressed him down on the wet dirt.

The marks he received from the men and those from *Abuelita* were indistinguishable.

—I will not have a fucking *maricon* living in my house, *Abuelita* said and slapped Baldomero across the face. Her breath, browned butter, her eyes, red candies. I'm sending you to see your real mother, she said, you two deserve each other.

That winter Baldomero stepped off the plane in New York. He left his mother's picture safely hidden behind the toilet where he could retrieve it when he returned to Puerto Rico in two weeks.

She looked nothing like he remembered. Her face was gaunt; her eyes sunk deep in her skull. Her skin was pasty and flaky, not bronzed and clear like on the island. When he hugged her she stood rigid. Maybe she was sick. The man standing next to her grabbed Baldomero's bag and walked to the terminal exit. He was thick and ugly. Serpent tattoos coiled around his forearms and bracelets collected at his wrists. Baldomero wanted to know who the man with tattoos was, but wasn't going to ask.

New York was not what Baldomero imagined. There was nothing glamorous or fantastic about this city. The buildings looked old and run down in the night sky, not unlike the crumbling shacks of *el barrio bajo* on the island. Exposed metal beams jutted out of junk piles along the side of the expressway and the horizon glowed in a rusting haze, a mix of street lamp flush and snow. The cab driver wore a cloth wrapped around his head and a wiry beard dropped from his chin. He spoke to the man with tattoos and his mother in what Baldomero suspected was English. Looking up at his mother he asked what the driver had said.

—He asked where we are going, his mother replied, her words were flat, her body listless.

—Where *are* we going? Baldomero asked.

—The Bronx.

It took four nights for it all to go to hell. He was in the bathroom testing his mother's makeup. Meringue and sour smoke trailed in from the other room. Baldomero spotted his mother's panties and bra on the tile floor. He put them on over his clothes and burst through the door, popping his hips to the staccato tremors of music.

—*Mira, Mama,* Baldomero said, I'm Chi Chi the dancing queen.

What happened next was like a spatter of paint.

Baldomero heard the tattooed man's voice but didn't see him coming.

—Your son is a fucking faggot.

Baldomero was lifted into the air, slammed back to the floor. Then his clothes were ripped from him; he felt a burning in the arm pinned behind him. Then the burning turned to numbness as something in his shoulder popped.

—You fucking faggot.

His face was flattened against the wood floor; a hand had a fistfull of his hair. He saw small vials strewn under the coffee table; he saw his mother's feet, motionless, as she watched from the couch.

The police spoke English. Baldomero didn't understand why they were taking him away. His mother was on the couch, her arms cuffed behind her back; she didn't look up as they opened the door and took Baldomero out onto the dry winter street. Snow clouds seemed to scrape the rooftops. He tried to stop crying, to quiet himself, but visible breath continued to spit before him in stuttering spasms. The lady officer rubbed his back, whispered calm down, calm down.

He was being taken to the hospital for the night. The next day he would be referred to the Administration for Children's Services, placed in foster care where he would remain.

I knock.

"Leave me the fuck alone."

I can hear her fumbling through her things. The sounds of rustling cloth, the hollow clink of porcelain against porcelain. I ask if I can come in, I ask if we can sit down calmly and have a discussion.

"Why everybody needs to talk with me? You, Leslie, Sherry, it's annoying," she says through the door.

"Because we're concerned, Chi Chi. We want to make sure you are as prepared as possible when you age out."

With this the door flies open. Chi Chi is now wearing tight low-cut jeans and a belly shirt that exposes the ring dangling from her navel.

"Fuck you and the future." Her voice has lost its feminine tone and settles into a kind of thunder. She pushes past me and down the stairs. I follow, calling after her until she passes through the front door, making her way into the clatter and trill of Brooklyn.

I collapse into the living room couch. B.E.T. is on the TV blaring out Fat Joe's shattered beats from blown speakers, Sincere and Mush are haggling in the hallway over who is better at fucking Shannequa, and Junior and Blanca stagger around the residence in a slow motion blur, glassy-eyed and dumb from the blunt they just smoked. I'm left in the center of the room; Chi Chi's probably crossing the Williamsburg Bridge now. I pushed too hard.

Back home, I'm flattened, drinking on the futon, smoking. I had quit years before but started up again after two weeks on the job with the kids. Unopened bills litter my desk; empty beer bottles line the counter and fill the sink. I haven't thrown away take out containers and pizza boxes amass in a corner. The air smells oily and stale. I should call a friend to go see a movie, just get out, but no one is available. Rachel has a baby, Meghan's working, Billy's preoccupied with his band. I stare at my bookshelf. My mind's restless and my body's sluggish. It's dangerous to just lie here. I'll think too much—or not enough—do something foolish. Under the futon is an old wooden cigar box where I stash my money. I count through it, relieved that there isn't even enough to pay my rent. A few months ago that wouldn't have mattered, I would have blown whatever was there. I tell myself this is progress. Working with the kids is helping. I'm wiser, I think, not making such desperate decisions.

I should clean up my apartment but somehow can't find the strength. At the home the kids are expected to keep their rooms picked up. We tell them it shows self-respect. Looking at my clutter, I think of how I fill my days trying to find order in the lives of the youth in my care. I work long hours at the office and the group home, busy myself with filing, with finishing reports, counseling residents, testifying in court, conducting home visits. There's always more to do. I told my friends I wanted *to serve something greater than myself* but I'm a fraud. I take care of others because it's easier than having to take care of myself.

After sucking out the last drag of the cigarette I reach for a nearby ashtray and stamp out the butt. A plume of smoke rises and hangs still in the air under the dull glow of my lamp. I pop two sleeping pills in my mouth and wash them down with my last swallow of beer, then, with the light still on, roll over and fall asleep.

Two days later and Chi Chi's back at Keap Street. Again a phone call from Leslie.

"Are you sitting down?" she says, not waiting for an answer. "Chi Chi's back and she's wiggin'. She locked herself in her room and had herself some marathon crack binge. Now she's tearing the place up."

When I arrive at the group home the front door is ajar, letting the screams out onto the street. Boys from the handball court are on the stoop trying to eye the action. Chi Chi has Blanca trapped against the wall in the living room. She looks a wreck. Her face is flushed and damp, stubble peppers her chin and the whites of her eyes shine with a manic light. Staff has separated the residents, barring them from ringside access. Leslie sees me, mouths to me that the police are on their way.

"I ain't playing, bitch, give it to me," Chi Chi says.

"You ain't gettin' nothing, yo." Blanca puffs out her chest, stares dead into Chi Chi's face. I notice that Blanca's left hand is bleeding, one fingernail ripped off.

The other residents are trying to wiggle past staff, chiding, provoking Chi Chi.

"Kick her ass!" cries Mush, and the room erupts into hollers. "Flat line her!"

Chi Chi presses her forearm against Blanca's chest, locking her in place. I'm shocked by her strength, rock solid, muscles twisting and sinewy beneath her skin. This is the first time I've looked at her and have seen Baldomero. So much energy is spent erasing all signs of her manhood in day-to-day life, that this rare glimpse, when her focus has turned outside of herself, is startling.

"Give me my fucking money," she hisses inches from Blanca's face.

Blanca is resolute. Says no, doesn't blink.

Staff are in all corners of the room prepared to take Chi Chi down if need be. She pushes Blanca with one final threat, grabs a chair and launches it against a wall, then retreats out the door. Sherry follows her but can't keep up and Chi Chi is gone.

By the time the police arrive it's over, the room has deflated into murmurs and drone. They ask Blanca what happened. She's tight-lipped. One officer takes down names, ages, while the other comments on the new paint job in the living room.

"This mauve trim is so much better than the red you guys had in here before. That was too...aggressive, this is much calmer," he says while surveying the room, his hands on his waist.

They leave and it's as if they never arrived. Staff starts to pick up the overturned tables, broken picture frames—all the remnants of Hurricane Chi Chi. The residents disperse, leaving the living room empty except for Blanca, who is sitting on the couch, clutching her bleeding hand, her chin pressed against her chest. Sherry gives her a cotton ball and some gauze to wrap up her finger. I ask her to go for a walk with me.

"Buy me a loosie?" She asks as we make our way beneath the elevated J train along Broadway. She stops outside the corner bodega and puts out her palm.

I dig in my pocket and extract two quarters. She plucks them from my hand and runs inside. Not that I make it a practice to provide cigarette money for residents, especially those who are underage, but Blanca is shaken.

She exits the store with a single Newport menthol, lights it, inhales deeply and offers a forced smile. When I ask her what happened with Chi Chi she becomes sullen and stares at her feet. Then it comes out like an irrepressible hiccup.

"She was fiending, yo," Blanca says. "She came into the house all high and shit and asked me to hold her money—two hundred coins—told me not to give it to her no how."

"Where'd she get it?" I ask.

"Some guy she sees on the regular gave her eight hundred and this was all she had left. She was afraid she was gonna blaze it all, that's why she told me to hold it from her. Then she went into her room and smoked the rest of the rock she had. Fifteen minutes later she came into my room asking for twenty, saying all she wanted was twenty, and I was like, hell no. I said she needed that money for an apartment or something. She needs to think about her future. That's when she started tearing up my shit."

Blanca and I stop on the BQE overpass and look out onto the cars racing beneath us.

"I hate when she smokes that shit," she says, and we let it rest there and make our way back to Keap Street. A train rumbles overhead, a homeless man cradles himself in the doorway of the abandoned movie theater on the corner. The doors are shattered, boarded up, the marquee above reads, C OSED.

"I'm proud of you," I say. "Chi Chi's going through it right now, you've been a good friend."

I place my hand on her back and turn the touch into an embrace, she smothers herself into me, doesn't let go right away.

The discharge conference. Our agency support team and the case planner from the Administration for Children's Services gather in the conference room to discuss planning strategies for Chi Chi. She doesn't attend. She's been AWOL from the program for days. Some of the other residents have seen her on the stroll. There are rumors that she's been staying at the Hotel Gansevoort in the Meat Packing District with a celebrity. We begin to talk about her functioning during the previous six months and her discharge plan. Each child goes through these meetings twice a year. Most of them refuse to attend although their participation is considered critical. They know from experience that they can be ugly, uncomfortable gatherings. Adults sit in a room and discuss their cases, offer suggestions, conflict resolutions, speak about the most private moments of their lives. Each incident still-framed, dissected, picked through. I don't blame her for not showing up.

The room is light yellow, maybe canary. There are pictures on the walls of sunsets, a snowy landscape, subtitled with "inspirational" sayings like, *Today is the first day of the rest of your life.* Workers sit around a conference table and half listen as I read from the narrative that I've prepared.

Chi Chi is non-compliant with program rules and regulations. She interacts well with staff and peers but refuses to do her daily chores. Residential staff reports that she AWOLs and breaks curfew with regularity. Chi Chi abuses marijuana and crack cocaine on a consistent basis and self-reports that she prostitutes intermittently although staff believes it is much more frequent. She was arrested three times during this reporting period for prostitution and once for purchasing narcotics. The agency has made concerted efforts to engage Chi Chi in therapy in order to address her history of family trauma and abandonment but she refuses to comply with recommendations. She also refuses to attend scheduled medical and psychiatric appointments. The Independent Living Specialist made efforts with the caseworker to find gainful employment for Chi Chi and an internship was acquired for her through the Silvia Rivera Law Project, an advocacy group for transgender rights. She attended the internship for one week and then suddenly stopped. Chi Chi will be turning twenty-one on August 30th and subsequently aging out of foster care. This caseworker has been working diligently to establish a permanency plan for Chi Chi but with little success. She has refused to attend meetings with aftercare programs and assisted living centers, she is unwilling to keep appointments to discuss housing subsidies and section 8 applications. She has no viable visiting resources and is unable to maintain employment past two weeks. The agency has attempted to place her in a detox program to address her chronic drug abuse but Chi Chi refuses.

And on it goes. The details of her life imparted by dry, curt language. Summing up her existence by a series of failures to comply with recommendations, exposing her tender spots like blisters. We pick, we pry and make our fingers sticky with the mess of her life.

"Are there any positive role models in her life?" asks the ACS worker. I can't place her accent. Not exactly Jamaican but definitely Caribbean. She is overdressed. A gold chain lies heavy over her blouse. She looks out of place. I'm suddenly reminded of when I went out with Chi Chi for the first time in public. She drew so much attention to herself that it made me uneasy. Sashaying down the street like it was her own personal catwalk. Boys walked by and howled. "You see that?" one said, "that was a dude. Nasty ass shit." She kept walking with her chin high. The boys passed us and one spat at her feet. I pretended not to notice, just buried my hands deep in my pockets, searching for some change I didn't have.

"The only adults in her life are from this agency and the tricks on the street," I say. Looking down at my report, unsure of my impulse, I continue, "I hate to plan this way, but I feel like we're out of options." I pause to try and frame it in my mind and make sure it comes out all right. "If we can get her to get tested—I know this sounds horrible—but if we can get her to get tested there are residential programs for people with HIV. She might qualify."

"We can't force her to get tested," Leslie says. "And she won't do it, we've tried."

"There's little recourse," the Executive Director says. "The only thing we can do is set her up for long-term drug treatment. She's knocked down all other attempts at permanency planning."

Despite the canary walls the room seems dark. The ACS worker scribbles down her notes, pen to paper, fingers clasped firmly around the shaft. Her nail polish is immaculate and loud. An imitation jewel is centered at the tip of each nail. She starts to make recommendations for Chi Chi although she's never even met her, doesn't even have a clue what she looks like. She talks strategy and planning, bank accounts, job referrals. She calls Chi Chi Baldomero, and I know she doesn't get the difficulties of planning for her. I want to explain that finding a job for Chi Chi has obstacles that a typical client doesn't have to face. An employer takes a look at her, glances at her state ID. *Baldomero?* Then, *I got nothing against you people personally, but we don't want to make our customers uncomfortable.* I want to explain that the allure of the stroll is more than just money. It's the only place where Chi Chi feels accepted. For a brief moment in the arms of a trick she's no longer a freak; she's desired. I look at the wall, the pale canary. The worker keeps spewing out words that have no relation to Chi Chi: family resources, secured employment. She might as well be discussing stock options, summer homes in the Hamptons. I imagine where Chi Chi could be now instead of this meeting. I picture her in a room near the piers, maybe with two other trans-girls. They've scored enough rock to get them roiling until the sun crashes into Jersey. Only a blow job a piece, fifty bucks a pop, thirty minutes out of their day, and they can blaze until their brains ignite, filling their lungs as the world fades away leaving them to forget all the things they never wanted to be. *Today is the first day of the rest of your life.* Hallelujah.

Finally she stops talking; the meeting is over. I make my way down the stairs and push past the door.

I meet weekly with Briana, the program therapist, for clinical supervision. Caseworkers and house managers in our program are offered individual sessions to air frustrations and grievances about the work in a confidential environment. I'm intent on not mentioning my personal life. I try to speak solely to the stressors of the job.

"How are you today?" Briana says, as she does at the beginning of every session. She's sprightly and always engages in talk with a puckish curiosity. At first I'm annoyed with her peppiness but then wonder if it is in fact envy that I feel. Each week as we begin I watch as the same blonde curl just over her right eye bobs as it did the week before. Her hair fascinates me. It's a bundle of controlled chaos.

She asks about my week, if I found anything particularly frustrating. I can't think of something specific and grab my water bottle as a distraction, swig from it, struggling to maintain eye contact. I need to answer her so I make up something about paperwork and the difficulties of meeting deadlines.

She nods gently and smiles.

"How do you feel you are acclimating to the position? It's a difficult job," she says, "feeling overwhelmed would make sense." She emphasizes that in this work it is important to take care of yourself. "Have you been going out with friends? Exercising?"

I can't remember the last time I did anything social. I seem to have forgotten how.

I manage to say that I'm unsure how to separate my work from my personal life. I admit that I haven't been tending to myself, as I should. Then all of a sudden I feel this swell inside me. I don't know how to fill my time when I'm away from work because work is the only thing that keeps me buoyed, and without it I'm afraid where I might sink. I'm unsure how to empower the young people we work with when I am myself weighed down with so much self-doubt. I have done things, too, things that, if ever found out, might jeopardize my credibility as a positive influence on the youth.

But I don't tell her any of this. Sitting back in my chair, I shove the desire for disclosure back down into my gut, keep it buried.

"You are no good to the residents if you don't take care of yourself." Briana brushes a drooping curl away from her forehead. It falls back in place. "You come first," she says, "then the kids."

I find myself instead confessing that I am overwhelmed and that, specifically, it is working with Chi Chi I find most difficult. In the past month I was just starting to get close to her. Her guard, finally, began to drop. She started speaking about her past, something she rarely did.

"Do you feel responsible for Chi Chi's failures?" Briana asks me.

"Of course I do, it's impossible not to." I suddenly feel self-conscious and don't know what to do with my hands. Chi Chi's failures—the part of her that can only accept affection from a stranger, the part that is restless, empty, that, if left idle, might wither all together—I know those parts of her; I've met them within myself. I reach for my water bottle, take a gulp, "It's my job to get her to a place where she'll succeed."

"Your job is to provide the tools that enable successful behavior and you've done that," Briana says. "The youth come to us fully formed. We can't undo their pasts. We can only hope to help them heal and move forward successfully. But we can't do everything for them; they have to meet us half way."

Briana looks at me gently until I meet her eye.

"Ryan," she says, "whatever happens to her, you've done your part. Now it's Chi Chi's turn," she continues, "now she has to come to you."

I can tell she's been up for days. She fusses, struggles to get comfortable in her seat. She's wired and sluggish at once. Taps her foot incessantly, props her head with her hand. Moves again, shifts around.

"I didn't have to come, you know."

Chi Chi is sitting in my office.

"I coulda just left out, never come back," she says.

We haven't seen her for almost two weeks. No phone calls, no visits, nothing. I was starting to think that maybe she hustled the wrong guy, he realized Chi Chi had a penis, freaked out and dumped her in some alley, off some pier. Turns out she found a thirty-year-old man from Hoboken who lives with his parents, his crack habit as chronic as hers and his delusions just as grand.

"He loves me," she says. "He gonna give me a car and an apartment. So you do you and I'll do me."

We're both uneasy with this conversation.

"You've known this guy for how long? A week?"

I want to ask if she's high but don't.

Her face scrunches. "So," she says, "you can love somebody that quick."

"Chi Chi, what happens if it doesn't work out?"

"He already showed me the apartment. A guy lives there now but he's moving out soon. It's in Hell's Kitchen. I told him I want new carpet and a wood bedroom set with the thing over the bed, how you call it?"

"A canopy."

"Yeah, a canopy." Her arms reach out as if she's touching it. "And I want nice dishes for dinner, too."

I lean forward and place my hand on her knee. She stops fidgeting. "Chi Chi, listen to yourself," I say. "This isn't realistic; it's fantasy. Time's running out. You have two weeks, two weeks. Something's got to change or you're going to end up on the street."

Chi Chi becomes motionless as my words fill the space between us. Her legs are pressed together; her arms fold over her chest. Her head is now turned away from me as she stares out the window. In the muted Brooklyn light filtering through the window she almost looks like a silent screen star waiting for her close-up.

"Can't you just let me have my dream?" she says.

Note: In certain cases names and physical characteristics have been changed in order to respect the confidentiality of all involved.

The Incurables

When Adam "Drew" Drewshevsky, a.k.a. Dickie DeLong, returned to his hometown of Sherman, Ohio, his old friend Barry Borkowski took him out for a beer at Don's Underworld and raised a glass to the Prince of Porn. There was truth to the title: In the past decade, Drew had made more than three hundred erotic films of varying length and quality. But his career, he told Barry, was over.

"I need a new life," Drew said.

"Can I have your current one?" Barry asked.

Drew didn't tell Barry he had herpes, which no medicine he'd taken and no diet he'd tried had prevented from erupting every couple of weeks like chicken pox of the penis. And he didn't confess to Barry his more troubling problem. Even after near-overdoses of Viagra and every one of its pharmaceutical competitors, even after sucking back blenders full of supposed cock-hardening concoctions—*green bananas,* the woman in the Oriental scarf and red eye-patch had told him; *sperm whale eyes,* said the man with three gold rings on his lower lip—even after six trips to a specialist in erectile dysfunction (which one of his former co-stars and former girlfriends, Misty Moans, called erectile dishonor), even after praying to all the gods and all the false gods he knew, his penis remained paralyzed.

Drew hoped to find something in his hometown that would return him to the man—the boy, really—he'd once been. But three minutes into their conversation, Barry reminded him about how, when they were twelve years old, they'd stolen *Playboy* magazines from Reeves' Drugstore and had simulated intercourse with the centerfolds on the floor of Barry's basement.

"You were born a porn star," Barry said.

Drew's father had died of a heart attack when Drew was ten years old. His mother found Jesus soon after Drew told her what he was doing in California. She'd moved to Georgia five years ago in order to live closer to the television preacher whose show, she believed, had changed her life. Drew's paternal aunt, his only living relative left in Sherman, set him up with a job at the Sherman Public Library. He was in charge of stacking books, cleaning the bathrooms, vacuuming the rugs, and rebooting the four computers in the children's section whenever their screens froze.

In his first week on the job, no fewer than three library patrons asked him if they'd seen him before. "I grew up here," he told each of them, but two were recent arrivals to Sherman and the third said he was positive he had seen Drew on TV. Drew's blindingly blond hair was hard to forget. It made him look Danish, thus his casting as Hamlet in *Ophelia, Nymph in Thy Orgasms.*

In his second week, a woman who recognized him—and obviously knew why—grabbed her red-hatted toddler and fled the library as if he'd exposed himself, herpes and all. During his third week, he wore sunglasses. The head librarian, who, per the cliché, was bespectacled but had a body most of his former co-stars would have taken out a second mortgage on their souls to acquire, chided him for looking like a Secret Service agent and scaring the children. "Besides," she said, "you shouldn't hide such a pretty face." Two days later, she invited him to dinner.

Before he'd finished his salad, she smiled at him and, as her feet crawled up his legs, said, "I know what I want for dessert."

He told her he was considering joining the priesthood.

"But you're Jewish," she said.

"I'm hoping they're desperate," he said.

During his lunch break the next day, Drew did go talk with the priest at Our Lady of Perpetual Tears. Like the librarian, the priest pointed out the problem of Drew's religious affiliation. "And I'm not sure I understand your reasons for wanting to join the priesthood," said the priest. "Could you restate them plainly?"

All Drew could think to say was: I'm in a pit and I'm reaching toward whatever light I see above me. Instead, he said, "I've forgotten."

"Well, if you remember, come back," the priest said. "And why do I have this feeling I've seen you before?"

On a Wednesday of his sixth week back in his hometown, Drew was supposed to meet Barry for drinks at Don's Underground. He was going to tell him everything. But Barry had left a message with the bartender saying he wouldn't be able to make it. After Drew finished his fourth beer, the bartender asked him if he was planning to drive home.

"I'm on foot," Drew assured him, although he felt obliged to look down to make sure his feet hadn't deserted him.

As he drank his fifth beer, Drew recalled, for perhaps the two hundredth time, a conversation he'd had with one of his former co-stars. In *The Good, the Bed, and the Naughty,* she had played Mabel Syrup. She was what all the cowboys had with their breakfasts.

Her screen name was Amber Waves. Before performing the climactic scene, a shootout followed by an orgy in Betty's Bordello, they'd sat half-clothed on a red velvet couch. The smile she'd worn every time he saw her, on camera and off, vanished. She stuck out her hand and said, "My name is Erin." After he'd introduced himself, she said, "You remind me of my stepfather. He had hair like yours—like he'd stuck a paintbrush into the moon and swirled the color all over his head."

Her voice, high and childlike—like a cartoon duck's—made everything she said seem frivolous and inconsequential. "Well, let's not say the moon," Erin amended. "I love the moon, and I didn't love him."

Erin gazed into his eyes. He was shocked by the intimacy of the gesture, and he bowed his head to look at his bare feet. "When I was twelve," she said, "my stepfather raped me. It wasn't the last time. I've never told anyone."

When Drew looked up at her, she was staring at him with the same fierce, shocking intimacy, and although neither of them moved, he felt the distance between them disappear. "What do you want me to do about it?" he said, although this wasn't what he'd wanted to say.

She didn't reply. A moment later, it was time to shoot the scene.

One morning soon thereafter, Drew woke up to find his penis inert and covered with raging, red blisters.

"I'm on foot," he assured the bartender when, after finishing his sixth beer, he stumbled to the door of Don's Underground. He turned and waved. The bar had recently banned smoking but nevertheless seemed suffused with a gray-green haze, the color of a Los Angeles rush hour. Drew decided he wouldn't miss any of it.

A minute later, he was standing in the middle of the pedestrian walkway on the Main Street Bridge, staring over the edge, wondering how far the fall was.

Far enough, he decided.

With both hands, Drew grabbed the topmost bar of the railing, which was a little higher than his chest. Slowly, he lifted his right leg and positioned his foot parallel to his hands. He looked like he was either preparing to kill himself or was warming up for a role in *The Nutcracker*—or *The Nutlicker* (he'd played the Mouse King).

"Goodnight," he said to the night.

A hand clasped him on the shoulder. "Hello," said a man's voice. "I can't let you do what you're about to do."

Drew, who hadn't noticed a police car pull to a stop in the middle of the bridge, returned his foot to the ground.

"I think you could use some help—don't you agree?" said the man, who introduced himself as John Lewis, Sherman's sheriff.

"You'll hear no argument from me," Drew said.

The sheriff looked like Santa Claus without the beard. "Do I have your permission to take you to the hospital?"

"Permission granted," Drew said. "But I'm incurable."

In the Matthew A. Dunkirk Psychiatric Ward of the Ohio Eastern University Hospital—known, the nurse who registered him said without irony or apology, as the MAD—Drew would be identified only by his first name and his photograph, which the nurse snapped in a red-curtained booth behind her desk. Despite his months of misery and tonight's drunkenness (a condition Sheriff Lewis said he would ignore because of rules prohibiting the inebriated from being admitted to the psych ward), his snapshot showed him looking raffish, even, given the Valentine-colored backdrop, romantic.

The nurse who did Drew's intake survey was named Herman. "As in Herman's Hermits," Herman said. "But I don't suppose you know who I'm talking about."

Drew did—one of his first film roles was as the drummer of The Kinky in *The British Invasion (Our Music Wasn't All That Made 'Em Scream)*.

"So what in your mind or spirit brought you tonight to the brink of welcoming eternity?" Herman asked.

Drew named the reasons, although as he did so, they seemed insubstantial. They didn't, anyway, appear sufficient enough to warrant a dive from the Main Street Bridge. But Herman nodded and nodded again. "Loss," he said. "Of virility. Of career. And your herpes is a recurring reminder of both."

Herman had gray streaks in his hair and wrinkles at the edges of his eyes. He might have been old enough to be Herman Hermit himself, if there was such a person. "You have work to do," Herman said, "and drugs to take."

Herman handed Drew a ham sandwich, which Drew ate in the ward's dayroom. The dayroom looked more suited to a childcare center. The wallpaper featured a circus motif, with pink elephants and baby blue lions. In the front of the room were a table with six chairs and a bookshelf with two dozen Bibles, a deck of jumbo playing cards, and five board games, three of which were Chutes and Ladders. At the far end of the room, below a window with a view of the hospital's parking lot and, beyond it, Ohio Eastern University's football stadium, was a wide-screen television.

Sitting cross-legged in front of the TV was a woman about Drew's age, in pink pajamas, watching "Winnie the Pooh." He focused on her hair, a color between blond and brown. It had hundreds of corkscrews and was as short as a man's.

When Eeyore, the donkey, appeared on the screen, the woman turned to Drew with exasperation and said, "You know what he needs, don't you?"

Drew shook his head.

"Electroshock," said the woman. "ECT. Like me." She laughed. "I have my sixth treatment tomorrow." Her voice was a whisper: "Don't tell them, but number five put me in a mania. I'm feeling good right now. Are you single?"

Drew knew he should be attracted to the woman, who was pale and slim and had small, strawberry-colored lips. Any heterosexual man in his right mind, and with functioning and unsullied equipment, he decided, would be. "Yes, I'm single."

"Well, I'm not," she said, shrugging. She turned again to the TV.

She diagnosed all the characters: Piglet needed anti-anxiety meds, Tigger was manic-depressive. "And Pooh's a honey junkie," she said. "Sugared up but always thinking about his next fix."

A nurse popped into the room to tell them it was ten o'clock, time for lights out.

"I'll see you tomorrow," Drew said to the curly-haired woman.

"Only if I haven't escaped."

"So this place is locked?" he asked.

"Where do you think you are," replied the woman, smiling, "the Four Seasons?"

Drew discovered he was sharing a room with Rusty, a dark-bearded man of uncertain age and enormous girth. Drew imagined that Rusty owned a loud motorcycle and a pit bull. Rusty apologized in advance for his snoring.

"My last girlfriend said it was like a Bach fugue," he confided with a grin. "His face clouded over. "I didn't know what the fuck a Bach fugue was, so I beat her again."

At midnight, Drew woke up. From the bed next to his issued a sound not unlike what might play outside a haunted house at Halloween.

After a breakfast of eggs, toast, and orange juice the next morning, the patients had an hour to themselves. Most of them opted to return to their rooms and sleep, although at least two signs posted on the walls of the ward discouraged napping.

Drew remained in the dayroom, anticipating a conversation with the Pooh woman. But as she reminded him, she was scheduled to have her sixth electroshock today. She returned to her room and emerged wearing a blue hospital gown. Her feet were bare.

"You'd think I was about to give birth or have my appendix removed," she said. "My name's Erica, by the way."

Drew introduced himself, and they shook hands.

"You have cold hands," she said. "You know the saying about cold hands."

"Cold hands, warm heart?" he said.

"Oh," she said, "is that it? I thought it had something to do with vampires."

Presently, a nurse came for her. "When I come back," Erica told Drew, "I may not remember we had this conversation. So I hope you don't mind if we have it again."

Erica walked beside the nurse toward the double doors to the left of the nurses' station. Before departing the ward, she turned and blew Drew a kiss.

"Are you Adam?" a woman's voice asked.

He opened his eyes. "I go by Drew," he said.

"Follow me, Drew," the nurse said, and she led him out of the dayroom to a small conference room at the back of the ward. Inside was a man whose peach-fuzz hair made him look like a cancer patient or the singer of a punk band. His skin was as white as his doctor's coat, and a scar ran diagonally from the far corner of his left eye to the left corner of his lips. He introduced himself as Dr. Ramshide.

"And please call me Dr. Ramshide rather than by my first name, which is Sebastian, or any of my nicknames, one of which is Rambo," he said.

"Will do," Drew said.

"You forget to add something."

"I did?" Drew said.

"Yes, you forgot to add my title and my last name."

When Drew said nothing in response, the doctor said, "Dr. Ramshide, remember?"

"I haven't forgotten," Drew said, sitting in a chair across from Dr. Ramshide's oversized desk.

Dr. Ramshide asked him the same questions Herman had, and Drew answered the same way. After a pause, Dr. Ramshide said, "I want to start you today on ProPax. It's an excellent anti-depressant. Unfortunately, we won't be able to gauge its effectiveness for six weeks. And there's one major potential side effect."

"What's that?" Drew asked.

"Impotence," Dr. Ramshide said.

Drew opened his mouth, but couldn't find the words to convey his incredulity. At last, he managed, "Haven't you read my..." But there was a knock on the door. It was the nurse with another patient.

Lunch was followed by dead time. As Drew sat slumped in one of the dayroom's chairs, he saw Erica return, a nurse escorting her. Erica moved slowly, her shoulders sagging. She looked like she was about to collapse. When she saw him, she stopped but gave no sign of recognition. He lifted his hand, a tentative wave.

"All right," said the nurse, who was as dark as Erica was fair, "enough of the *One Flew Over the Cuckoo's Nest* routine."

Erica laughed and stood straight. "They're no fun here," she said, winking at Drew.

Despite her apparent cheerfulness, she returned to her room to sleep and didn't reappear until after lunch, during Art Therapy class. She found a spot next to Drew on the floor.

"How was your treatment?" he asked her.

"Shocking," she said.

The art therapist, a short, round-faced woman from India, asked the patients to paint their worst nightmare on one half of a sheet of paper and their happiest dream on the other half. For Drew, the nightmare was easy, a collision of reds: engorged body parts, blood, herpes. The happiest dream was harder to conjure.

During his first months in California, he'd dated a woman named Barbara, from Santa Barbara. He'd teased her about this, as if he'd been the first person to make this joke. Her face was appealingly asymmetrical (her right eye was larger than her left) and she enjoyed fiddling with words. They would play late-night games of Scrabble or, as they drank a bottle of wine on her couch, rewrite the lyrics of pop songs so they'd all mention dandelions or flatulence. He never worked up the courage to tell her how he really made a living, although she must have discovered the truth. She stopped returning his calls.

He held his paintbrush over the blank right side of his paper, wondering.

"How does it feel to be back in kindergarten?" Erica whispered to him.

"I was thinking preschool," Drew said.

"Five more minutes," the art therapist said.

Drew began painting without intention. He ended up with a dark landscape. The art therapist said she was certain she saw a serene moon emerging from behind black clouds.

Erica had painted a picture of the Devil sword-fighting with the Easter Bunny. "It's always war with me," she said, sighing.

In bed that night, Drew wondered if he should try to masturbate. But he imagined there were sores on his penis, sores as prominent as moguls on a black diamond ski slope. Besides, on the rare occasions he'd tried to pleasure himself, the nude women he summoned from memory and imagination inevitably dissolved, distressingly, into their prepubescent selves. They even spoke to him in age-appropriate voices. One blond-haired girl—six years old maybe, her pubis as hairless as glass—said, "I want to be a veterinarian when I grow up, but I'll probably end up sucking cocks." Another girl, even younger and with curly black hair and rose-red lips, said, "For me, self-empowerment will mean allowing anonymous men to fuck me four ways to Friday so other anonymous men can watch my DVDs and videos and pretend they're fucking me six ways to Saturday. I also like ponies and rainbows."

In the next morning's Re-Entry into Society group, in which patients were expected to share their fears and hopes about returning to their lives on the outside, no one said anything.

"Would anyone like to speculate about why we're so silent today?" asked the group's leader, a social worker named Bradley, whose six gold earrings—three in each ear—shone like circles of fire against his ebony skin.

After another few minutes of silence, a new admit, a woman in her late forties who constantly chewed on her lower lip, said, "Were you on the Ohio Eastern basketball team about five years ago?"

Bradley sighed. "Yes," he admitted.

"I knew it!" she squealed. "I knew it was you!" She turned to her fellow patients, as if hoping to find similar enthusiasm. No one said a word.

The silence continued until the same woman turned to Drew and said, "And you look familiar too."

Eyes turned to him. He swore he heard a growing murmur of recognition. But the silence returned and prevailed.

"Why isn't anyone talking?" Bradley asked.

Five minutes later, he asked the same question.

When the session ended, Drew idled in the dayroom with the rest of the patients until he was called in for his session with Dr. Ramshide. He made certain to address him as Dr. Ramshide three times within the first minute, figuring if he could appease the doctor's need to be addressed formally he could question him about his treatment plan. But the doctor was more interested in hearing details of Drew's film career. Dr. Ramshide mentioned the names of porn actors with the casual expertise of a baseball fan reciting the starting lineup of his hometown team.

Drew tried without success to change the subject.

In the afternoon, the patients had an hour of Recreation Therapy, in the first-floor gymnasium. They were led in calisthenics by another former Ohio Eastern basketball star, who, given his enormous height, must have played center.

During sit-ups, Drew held Erica's feet. "Let me warn you, I'm still in a big-time mania, so take everything I say with a tablet of lithium," Erica huffed as he softly counted the number of her sit-ups. "But I think you're cute."

"My dick doesn't work," he whispered back.

She didn't break her sit-up rhythm. "For how long?"

"Eight months."

"Winters in Siberia are longer."

"And I have herpes."

"So did my grandma," Erica said. "And when she died, of a heart attack, she was with a UPS driver who certainly knew how to deliver a package."

Erica laughed in a huffing way.

"I used to be a porn actor," Drew said.

"There are worse ways to make a living," she said. "If I could have a hundred dollars for all the loveless sex I've had, well, I'd be right where I am today—only richer."

He tried to smile and half succeeded.

"I still think you're cute," Erica said. "Have I done fifty yet?"

The next morning, Drew was promoted to Level Orange, which gave him the right, twice a day, to follow one of the nurses into the hallway, down two flights of stairs, and into a fenced-in courtyard. At the end of it, in the middle, was a locked gate. It was made of the same black iron as the rest of the fence except its lock was red. It seemed, Drew thought, like a fairy tale door, like something you'd walk through to enter a new world.

On his most recent outing to the "Cage," as even the nurses referred to the enclosure, Drew wore only a T-shirt and blue jeans, but he could see his breath pour out of his mouth. It was about nine in the morning, but what month was it? he wondered.

When Drew returned to the dayroom, Erica was sitting cross-legged in front of the TV, which was off. "Good show?" he joked, but she didn't reply. Erica was only at Level Red, which meant she couldn't go outside. The risk of her escape, or her suicide, was too great, even under supervision.

Level Red also meant she couldn't have any visitors. Drew was allowed this privilege, but when Barry called Drew before lunch and asked if he could come see him, Drew said he would prefer to recover in anonymity. "It's just as well," Barry said. "If I showed up, they'd probably want to keep me."

After lunch, Erica again sat in front of the blank TV. Her eyes were closed and she was whispering something.

"Meditation?" Drew asked.

Erica opened her eyes. "No, something more ambitious," she said. "I'm trying to communicate with aliens. I'm begging them to take me away from this sad, sad world."

A moment later, Drew was called in to see Dr. Ramshide. But Dr. Ramshide had been replaced by Dr. Salvador Hernandez, a man in his sixties with a lean, freckled face, a silver mustache, and a gap-toothed smile. The desk, too, had changed—from gigantic to medium-sized.

"What happened to Dr. Ramshide?" Drew asked.

"Rambo?" Dr. Hernandez said, shaking his head. "He's been transferred to Food Services."

Drew couldn't tell if he was joking.

"With your permission, I'll be changing your meds," said Dr. Hernandez. "The idea of throwing ProPax on top of erectile dysfunction is like treating heat rash by sending the patient to a tanning salon."

After they had talked for a while, Dr. Hernandez said, "I think your herpes is both a real affliction and a form of self-punishment."

"Self-punishment?" Drew asked.

"Even if you wanted to resume your sex life—and your impotence, I'm convinced, is a problem of desire, or lack thereof, rather than anything physical—your herpes, by its near-continuous presence, would keep you celibate. It's your superego. It is saying, 'Never again.'"

They talked more, and Dr. Hernandez suggested Drew might write to a few of the women with whom he'd had intercourse on film and now thought of with regret and guilt. Specifically, he could write to Erin.

"What would I say?" Drew asked him.

"You could tell her you remember her," Dr. Hernandez said. "You could tell her you hope she's all right."

"That's it?"

"I don't know," Dr. Hernandez said, smiling. "Throw in a wedding proposal. See what comes back."

"Why don't you try acting in regular movies," Erica said. "You know, the Hollywood kind."

They'd finished their twenty-eighth game of Crazy Eights. The dayroom was empty except for Rusty, who was snoring in front of a football game on TV. It was late. The nurse would soon tell them to go to their bedrooms.

"I'm not convinced I can act," Drew said.

"I can," Erica said. "Watch."

Erica dropped her head onto the table and began to cry.

"That's good," he said.

She lifted her face. Her cheeks were red and damp.

"Very good," he said.

Drew waited for her to stop crying, to wink. When she didn't, he felt a rush of anxiety, and he turned to look for the nurse. But instead of going to find her, he put his hand on Erica's shoulder. Still crying, she leaned her head against it.

"You get the part," he said.

She didn't smile, but she stopped crying.

In his next meeting with Dr. Hernandez, Drew talked about all the women he'd been involved with romantically and how, two years into his movie career, he'd given up dating anyone but the women he worked with.

"Why?" Dr. Hernandez asked.

"I was lazy, I guess," Drew said. "I knew them already."

"Did you? Did you really know them?"

"I thought I did. Or maybe I told myself I did so I didn't have to know them."

For Drew, evenings now had the feel of a slumber party in which he left the boys in order to sit with the host's sister in the den and play cards and talk. If there was anything good about the MAD, it was this, even when, as now, Erica stared up at him from her cards with a look so drained of emotion, so stripped of life, he doubted he could reach her with even the most outrageous declaration.

He wanted to say something to her, something kind, but every phrase he conceived seemed as stilted and unimaginative as a line from one of his movies. So they played cards without saying anything at all.

In their next meeting, Dr. Hernandez said, "Are you aware that the Ohio Eastern University Hospital has one of the most well-respected sex addiction clinics in the country?"

"Are you suggesting I'm a sex addict?" Drew asked incredulously.

"Not at all," said Dr. Hernandez. "But after your discharge, you'll walk past the sex-addiction waiting room. There's a chance you'll be recognized."

"It won't be the first time," Drew said, smiling.

Dr. Hernandez touched his silver mustache. "I think you're ready to go home."

"But the antidepressants haven't had a chance to kick in," Drew said.

"We'll have a thorough outpatient treatment plan in place for you, but you've done much of the important work already. And you're telling the truth when you say you don't feel like jumping off the Main Street Bridge now, correct?"

"I don't think I'd even stop to look over the side."

"I've seen only one porn film in my life," Erica told Drew.

It was night, and they were playing their fourth game of Chutes and Ladders. Erica had won the first three, and when Drew said she must be cheating, she said, "No, it's because I've had hours of practice. Every stay-at-home mom learns to become a Chutes and Ladders all-star."

Drew had asked her about her children and husband once, but she'd told him she didn't like to talk about them—it made her too sad, she said—so he hadn't asked again.

"My brother and a friend of his found or rented or stole a porn video," Erica said. "They were watching it late at night in the base-ment of our house. My parents were sleeping—or maybe they were out of town; my brother might have been old enough to look after both of us. When I walked in on them, they pretended they didn't notice me."

Rusty, sitting on the couch, was snoring, the noises he pro-duced at once comical and funereal. In the lone window, the lights of the hospital parking lot looked like fluorescent heads on thin black stakes.

"Were they watching hardcore?" Drew asked. He didn't think he would have been old enough to have appeared in the movie, although he braced himself to discover he had.

"Hard enough," Erica said, "although, to the movie's credit, there was a plot, which had to do with a knight, a princess, and a sex-crazed stepmother of a queen."

Drew relaxed: He hadn't appeared in the film. He hadn't even heard of it, although he could guess its title: *A Knight in Shining Ardor*. No, he thought, too soft, too sweet.

"They didn't try very hard with the setting," Erica continued. "It was supposed to be a medieval castle, but I could see a washer and dryer in one scene. I guess we weren't supposed to notice much besides the screwing, which I did find interesting. At first. But not even halfway through the film, I saw how mechanical it all was. It reminded me of a cuckoo bird in a cuckoo clock—in and out, in and out—with plenty of nonsense cuckoo noise." She paused. "I'm sure your movies were better."

"I never watch them," Drew said. This had been true, anyway, for the past year.

"I guess I'm a romantic when it comes to movies," Erica said. "I want there to be courtship, kisses—poetry, even—before the clothes come off."

Drew glanced out the window and saw that the stadium's lights had been turned on. There could be no game at this hour, so the stadium crew was probably testing the lights. But Drew preferred to think the lights had come on by themselves, fulfilling a sponta-neous desire to shine.

He turned to share the scene with Erica, but she'd buried her head in the crook of her right arm and was softly sobbing.

A nurse announced it was ten o'clock and time for bed.

In their last meeting, Dr. Hernandez told Drew, "There's one more piece of advice you need to accept."

"All right," Drew said.

"It comes in three parts."

Drew nodded.

"First, forgive yourself. Second, forgive yourself. And third—"

"Forgive myself," Drew cut in.

"Third," said Dr. Hernandez, "look at your case of herpes as an occasional annoyance, a permanent but manageable affliction acquired in a job and a life you have outgrown. Do not see it as a sign from God or fate of your complicity in the continued suffer-ing of human beings—unclothed women in particular. Mean-while, look at your impotence as temporary, a holding pattern you've put yourself in as you establish a new balance in your life between sex and love and trust."

"And also," he added, "forgive yourself."

At midnight Drew was awoken by a soft whisper: "Let's get out of here for a while." It was Erica, her face moon-bright in the dark of the room. In the bed next to Drew's, Rusty's snores sounded like a clarinet concerto played in a garbage can.

Erica, who was wearing blue jeans and a brown T-shirt, watched him dress. In his old life, he would have felt at ease with this; he wouldn't even have noticed her presence. But as he stood in his underwear and a short-sleeved, button-down blue shirt with yellow pinstripes, he felt self-conscious. He caught her eyes, and she smiled before turning her head. He finished dressing.

"Where are we going?" he whispered.

"To breathe," Erica said.

The nurses' station was empty. But to the left of the station, sit-ting slumped against a wall, was Herman. He appeared to be talk-ing to himself.

"We'll get caught," Drew said resignedly.

But Erica kept walking. From up close, Herman looked like a koala bear in the wake of a eucalyptus binge. He lifted his right hand and formed a peace sign.

"What's wrong with him?" Drew whispered.

"Ecstasy," Erica replied. "Not the drug, but the state of mind." A few more feet down the hallway, they reached the locked door. *Here's where the adventure ends,* Drew thought, but Erica produced a ring full of keys.

"Did you steal them off Herman?" Drew asked. He knew he probably shouldn't be so interested in the nuts and bolts of their breakout; he might be called on to testify to his part in it.

"Herman and I agreed on an exchange," Erica said. Before Drew could inquire, she added, "Desperate times call for blow jobs."

Drew thought he'd heard the line before, in *The Postman Always Comes Twice.*

As Erica pushed the key into the lock, he caught a glimpse of the key chain. It was a mini-replica of Freud smoking a cigar. Erica saw him looking at it. "This is what passes for humor around here," she said. "Now show me a replica of Freud with a cigar up his ass and smoke blowing out of his ears, then I'm laughing."

Drew wondered what would happen to him if they were caught. Would he still be allowed to return home tomorrow? Or would his return be postponed indefinitely and his unit status reduced to Level Red?

They walked down two flights of steps, pushed open another door, and found themselves in the Cage. Drew thought their journey was finished, but Erica marched to the iron door at the far end. After several keys didn't fit the red lock, she held up a gold key. It looked as ancient as a key to a treasure chest. She inserted it and the door sprung open.

A few hundred yards in front of them, the football stadium looked like a diaphragm for a giantess.

"Wow," Erica said, breathing in the cool air, "we could do anything now. We could even kill ourselves." She turned to him. "Do you want to?"

Walking at even a leisurely pace, they could be at the Main Street Bridge in an hour. Or they could climb onto the stadium's roof or to one of its high corners, with their easy-to-scale guardrails, and jump. But death held only a faint appeal to Drew now.

"I didn't think you did," Erica said. "Too bad. I guess we'll have to go to the fifty-yard line and fuck like high school kids on prom night."

Drew sighed. He was about to speak when Erica said, "Herpes isn't an obstacle." From her pocket, she removed a batch of condoms, in silver, red, and baby blue packaging. A couple of them trickled out of her palm and fell to the asphalt. She didn't bother to pick them up.

They headed across the empty hospital parking lot toward the stadium. The lights of the parking lot were enormous, white-yellow balls.

"You're married," Drew said.

"And my husband is a beautiful, kind man," Erica said sincerely. "He's the vice principal of an elementary school over in Sheridan. We have two beautiful children, a boy and a girl. They're ninety-nine percent perfect, which is about forty-nine percent more than a parent has a right to expect. All three of them write me every day. I used to have visiting privileges, but the last time my husband came to see me I tried to hang myself with his belt.

"You're luckier than I am," she continued. "At least you have something to pin your condition on. You have the whole porn career, your venereal disease, and your abusive father."

"How do you know about my father?" Drew asked, not with anger but out of startled curiosity.

"I guessed. Find me a white coat, and I'll be part of your treatment team."

They left the parking lot and stood at the locked gates of the stadium. Again, Erica produced her ring of keys. On her first try, she opened the gate.

"I don't understand," Drew said.

"You mean why Herman would have keys to the football stadium? He's sixty-five years old—he's held every job in this town twice. I think he was even mayor once, back in the mid-seventies."

There was something awe-inspiring, Drew thought, about football stadiums, later-day Coliseums. The near goalpost, shrouded in mist, looked like a redesigned crucifix. And Drew swore he could hear echoes of voices swirling around the concrete stands and aluminum seats.

Drew felt Erica's hand in his. "Don't worry," she said, "we won't do anything you don't want to do. I know you're concerned about my marital status. I'm sure that plenty of the ladies you worked with were married and you probably didn't care, but I respect that you're in a new stage of your life."

They stopped at the fifty-yard line and Erica let go of his hand. He immediately missed her touch. She began to undress, lining up her jeans, T-shirt, and shoes on the grass as if outfitting a reclining mannequin. He hesitated before doing the same with his clothes.

"That's right," she said. "Let it go." She unsnapped her bra, releasing breasts larger and less firm than he would have thought. She covered both of her nipples with her index fingers. "A year and two months," she said. "I nursed my oldest—the boy—for a year and two months. But my daughter, I barely nursed at all. After she was born, I had postpartum depression so bad it was like the Devil shoved his pitchfork in my head. I haven't been the same since." She lowered her underwear to her knees. "I had the perfect life and what did I do with it? I huffed and I puffed and I blew myself right out of it."

"It's waiting for you," Drew said.

"It won't be the same."

"It doesn't have to be. What's there is more than enough."

"All right, doctor."

He wanted to say more, to jolt her in a way her electroshock treatment couldn't. He wanted her to be happy, wanted to make her happy. When had he last felt this impulse?

"You're still wearing your underwear," Erica said.

"Right," he said, and he lowered it solemnly. His penis was flaccid, but in the darkness his herpes sores, if he had them, were disguised. If the night was cold, he didn't feel it.

Erica took his hand again. "Onto our beach blankets," she said, gesturing to their clothes, and they lowered themselves onto them. Above them, blue-gray clouds dominated the black sky. Here and there, like cats' eyes peering from a closet, were stars.

"I've always thought the Big Bang really was a big bang," Erica says.

"What do you mean?"

Erica laughed softly. "God's beautiful orgasm."

They were still holding hands.

"I think I'm getting better," he ventured.

"I know you are," she said. "And you're leaving tomorrow. Were you going to tell me or just leave me heartbroken?"

"I have mixed feelings about it," he said.

"It's normal to feel ambivalent about leaving a secure place. Even prisoners are ambivalent about going home when their sentences are up," she said. "But I wish you had told me."

"I'm sorry."

"You're forgiven." She squeezed his hand and sighed. "I wish I was getting better. But the chemistry experiment in my head went wrong and all these drugs and electroshock treatments are doing is confirming my hopelessness. I'm incurable."

"I thought I was too," Drew said. He breathed in. The air was moist and fragrant. The grass smelled like flowers. Or perhaps the smell was Erica. He breathed out. "But the problems I told you about are still problems," he said.

"I think you need a new fantasy," she told him.

He waited for her to explain.

"After you hit puberty, I bet you became fixated on the standard heterosexual male fantasy—probably involving two or more women, right?"

"That was fantasy number one," Drew admitted.

"But you've actually lived out fantasy number one as well as fantasies two and three and three hundred," she said. "And turning these fantasies into reality depended on the participation of certain kinds of women, most of them with histories you wouldn't wish even on a girl who'd broken your heart a hundred times. So now your fantasies make you sick."

"True," Drew conceded.

"Anyway," Erica said, "it's time for you to fantasize outside the box." She giggled. "I meant that metaphorically, but I guess it applies literally as well."

"All right. What should I fantasize about?"

"Anything besides a menage-a-tois or an orgy or anal sex," she said. "Anything besides legs glistening with baby oil and boobs as big as volleyballs. Anything besides women—or men, for that matter. Fantasize about the sky, the clouds, the moon."

"You're kidding."

"There's nothing sexier than a moonlit night. I've had some of my best orgasms looking up at the stars, thinking about nothing but how gorgeous they are." She paused. "Look, you can see a little edge of the moon, like her pale foot. But the cloud is keeping her mostly covered."

"Yeah," he said, "I see it."

"Isn't mistress moon lovely tonight? Isn't she just the prettiest thing you've ever seen?" She squeezed his hand.

He felt his heart pump, felt blood dance to other parts of his body.

"And now she's shedding more of her cloud clothing. She's letting you see more of her—she's letting you know her."

"Sure," Drew said, and feeling something return to him below his waist, he added, "She's beautiful. She's beautiful and she's lonely."

"She isn't lonely now," Erica said. "She has you."

He couldn't say it was only or even mostly the moon and the star-speckled sky that made him feel what he was feeling. He felt Erica's blood throb against his palms; he felt how warm her hand was. He'd never known how sensual a woman's hand could be.

"She's beautiful, isn't she? She's splendid in all the darkness."

"Yes, beautiful," said Drew, thinking of the moon, thinking of Erica. "Beautiful."

Now the moon was fully revealed, clouds dispatched to the sides of her. The stars burned bright. He held Erica's hand as if he was about to fall. At the same time, he held himself, and he found himself growing. Her hand, the moon. He felt a rush of pleasure—more—of joy.

"Yes," he said, the word springing from somewhere primitive and essential within him.

"Yes," she echoed, her hand burning his, the moon burning in the black sky.

"Yes." Again: "Yes." As his body surged with sensation, as it rushed toward orgasm, he wondered if Erica was pleasing herself. He wanted to be part of her happiness, however small it was, however fleeting. He opened his mouth to speak to her, but his pleasure, as intense as any he'd ever felt, silenced him. In the delirious waves of his orgasm, he didn't feel her hand disengage from his.

A moment later, he heard feet strike across the grass, and he looked up to see Erica racing toward the stands and, he was certain, the stadium's dark heights. He pictured her on one of the stadium's perilous edges, pictured her leaping into forever. "Erica!"

He sprang to his feet and chased after her, her bare ass brilliant and moon-white. He stumbled against a deflated ball or abandoned cleat, and for a second, he thought he was going to fall. He knew falling would mean losing her. But he righted himself and continued running.

She bounded up a set of wooden stairs from the field to the stands and climbed toward the right corner. Between the stands and the roof there wasn't even a guardrail but only sky and a fall of at least five stories onto concrete. She was at least two dozen stairs ahead of him, and he feared she would beat him to the edge. But he continued to chase her, and soon he halved the distance between them.

She was two steps from the unguarded corner when he caught her, his arms wrapped around her waist, his head pressed into her corkscrew curls. She resisted, slashing her elbows into his arms and the sides of his face, her strength surprising and scaring him. He thought she might break his hold, slip from his tiring arms. But at last, she relaxed. They were both hot and damp. From their breathing and nakedness, they might have just made the most intense love of their lives.

"Let me go, Drew," she said.

"I will," he answered, knowing there might be mercy in doing so. But he didn't let her go.

Are You Passing?

When Paul Loy was ten years old, watching the movers unload the Allied Van Lines truck at his family's new house in upstate New York, all the white kids on Ableman Avenue materialized. When his parents told him he'd have to learn to get along, even though he didn't understand the concept of passing, that was what he began to feel like they were asking him to do. Why replace Paul's Chinese friends? The ones he'd grown up with? Why were his parents encouraging him to know white *gui*, white ghosts? He felt betrayed. Resentment burned in him like a flaring match. Who cared if his family had to relocate because his father had a better job?

The feeling of making sacrifices and giving up pieces of himself continued his first day at Guilderland Elementary School when he heard only English being spoken. Paul realized he wouldn't be able to speak Chinese in a lunch room or on a playground again. If he couldn't speak his own language, did that mean being Chinese wasn't good enough? What was this new life saying about him? Doubt swirled like a gale through his mind. Homesick, he wanted to go back to the city, to New York.

Still the feeling of pretending, of being asked to put aside who he was, continued at neighbors' houses whenever a new friend invited him over for dinner. The mothers served casseroles, boiled meat, pastas, well-cooked steaks with baked potatoes, steamed green beans, lima beans, or yellow squash, the food always tasting plain, cooked far longer than anything Paul had eaten growing up in Chinatown. Did everyone eat such bland food in the suburbs? Would he only eat what he wanted at home now or constantly have to wear a mask of politeness?

And at age twelve, when Paul returned to the city, sitting in the back corner booth at a restaurant on Mott Street, he poured black pekoe tea for his grandfather from a white ceramic pot encircled by a blue dragon but couldn't understand everything his grandfather was saying. Paul realized he was losing his Chinese because he no longer went to Chinese school. There weren't any to enroll in upstate. So the feeling of giving up too much of himself had intensified. He felt ashamed, like he'd turned his back on his childhood and the years his grandfather had spent speaking Cantonese to him.

A year later, how far Paul had strayed from Chinatown felt worse. His parents asked him to be confirmed and pledge his faith to the Lord and Savior Jesus Christ, whose face was white on every painting at the McKownville United Methodist Church. Paul's parents had been forcing him to attend services each Sunday. He felt hypocritical, pledging what were supposed to be his deepest spiritual beliefs to a man of a different color. He went through with the ceremony for his parents' sake. He wanted to run away or live with his grandparents, and would have, if they weren't becoming too old.

Then the feeling of passing reached its height when Paul was with Karen Evans, the first girl he ever dated. Was he raising his status by dating her? Proving himself because she was white? She was seventeen like him, and there they were that October in 1978, parking at midnight in a Volkswagen Bug on a turnoff along Grant Hill Road. They were high in the foothills near the Heldebergh Mountains, so far from the main streets of Guilderland that no police cars ever bothered to patrol there. They were completely alone. To the left, a thick wall of spruce trees blocked out any moonlight, and to the right, a huge drop-off overlooked a National Guard training site used for firing munitions into sandy hillsides, though only during daylight hours.

Since Paul had shut off the engine the night's cold chilled their bodies, but then he and Karen were kissing. She was the first girl he'd ever made out with, and when he glanced up and saw how their breaths were fogging up the car windows it was a surprise. He'd seen it in movies and on television but had never known if it actually happened. Rain began to fall and bleared the windows—he felt safer, further wrapped in privacy—but there was still the slightest doubt in his mind, the lingering feeling that Karen might be with him for some misguided reason. A bet perhaps? Maybe a dare?

She played soccer and claimed to have noticed him running by as he trained for cross country. Then she approached him in the school lobby after practice, whispering in his ear that she thought he looked nice. He admired her sassy short brown hair, the cheerfulness in her eyes. She smiled and had the whitest teeth, her light brown eyes warm and inviting. He'd heard other boys talk about wanting to be with her but never succeeding. And now, as improbable as it seemed, she was speaking to him. "Why don't we go see a movie," she said, more like a direction than a question. That year *Grease, Animal House,* and *Superman* were playing, but she told him she wanted to see *The Buddy Holly Story.* He'd agreed, believing it would be better for a date; she'd know he was sensitive if they watched a story about love and tragedy.

Paul had wondered if they could be a couple, wanting to know if her parents would object, or if he or Karen would be hassled at school. "Don't give me a hassle," was what everyone said in those days. When he pulled up to her house she ran out to the car; he asked if her parents wanted to meet him, but she told him her father was a math professor who said she could date anyone within reason and that Paul was within reason. He knew she meant his being Chinese-American was good enough, and he wondered, What if I was black? Would that be all right? He sensed that it might not have been, but couldn't tell for sure. So there was a small unspoken doubt between them. And as they made out in his Volkswagen that night, because he had never felt white, he still felt like he was passing, getting away with something, treading where he shouldn't—only now she was kissing him harder.

She had a quick tongue. He tasted lip gloss and peppermint gum; he would remember that she tasted sweet. They kissed for so long that he began to feel passionate towards her. They learned how their mouths matched and fit and entwined their tongues, withdrew from each other and affectionately whispered how much they liked each other. They resumed kissing, and at some point she inhaled deeply and stole his breath. He liked learning that, and suddenly he understood more of the real implications of phrases like making out or French-kissing.

He dared sliding his left hand over her sweater and cupped her right breast, felt its suppleness in his fingers and palm. It was what he'd heard he was supposed to do—to go for—but he shared a pleasure and an intimacy with her that he'd never felt with anyone else. She let his hand stay there and kissed him harder, and how complicit she was moved him to want more of her and lower his hand and reach up under her shirt.

"Wait," Karen said. She reached back, unfastened her bra, and as they kissed again his hand felt the smooth curve of her breast from beneath, his fingertips finding her nipple. As she moaned softly his breath quickened, and he knew that he wasn't passing with her, and didn't have anything to fear.

They kept on that way, the car a sanctum of pleasure; for another fifteen or twenty minutes he was as astonished as he was happy.

His hand lowered for a moment—he meant to touch her other breast, to see where that might lead, even though he wasn't prepared enough to initiate anything more—but then she put her hand on his right knee and slid it further up his jeans. He already had an erection, but as she rubbed him there he felt unsure. Was she moving toward offering all of herself on their first date? Was that why other boys had talked about wanting to be with her? He felt embarrassed by his own lack of knowledge, as well, and because he hadn't brought a condom. Suddenly he was passing again, uncertain if life would have led him to such a night with such a girl if he'd stayed in Chinatown. And he was no longer was sure if they belonged together.

His confusion made him pull back, and he said, "It's getting late. We should go." She nodded and smiled, but what was she really thinking? Did she think he was shy, or too boyish for stopping? He wondered if she was going to make fun of him, or if she would gossip and embarrass him all over their school.

That year at Guilderland High there were the Jocks who stayed after daily for sports practices, the Bardhols who worked on cars, their name inspired by Bardhol Motor Oil, the Heads who smoked cigarettes, pot, and did all kinds of drugs, and the Nerds who studied hard, played instruments, or performed in plays or musicals.

Paul had run cross country which wasn't thought of as a hard core sport, so he didn't feel like a Jock or that he belonged to any of the other groups. But he didn't feel like he was passing, sitting outside on a clear cold morning two days after his date with Karen, because he was with his best friend, Tommy Chang, the only other Asian male at Guilderland. Tommy was a senior, a year ahead of Paul, and no one gave Tommy a hassle because he stood six foot-two and held black belts in three different martial arts. He even taught at a Kung Fu school. His body was limber muscle, his hair onyx black and parted in the middle like a calling card for precision. When he walked down the hallways, the toughest football players whispered with disdain that also revealed their fear, "Here comes Bruce Lee." And Tommy drove a nineteen sixty-eight Pontiac GTO that had been painted canary yellow. When he stepped out of the car wearing his black leather jacket, faded Levi's, black t-shirt and steel-toed boots, heads turned and necks swiveled, everyone afraid of what he might do.

Tommy had accepted Paul on the basis of race alone, their minority commonality providing them with an instant bond. Paul thought he was domineering, stubborn, sometimes too crass, but also looked up to him for how tough and decent he was. Tommy never picked on anyone, in spite of all his fighting skills, and there was always the knowledge that no one would ever threaten Paul for as long as he was Tommy's friend.

On this morning, in front of the West Building, the Jocks stood in the shade beneath the columns by the door. The Bardhols lingered out by their cars, engine hoods raised, and the Heads were smoking cigarettes or weed to the left, standing beyond the yellow line of paint that was the no-smoking boundary. To the right, the Nerds clustered tightly in their own little cliques for what safety could be had in small numbers. Six black kids, two boys and four girls, stayed together between the Jocks and the Heads. And near to Paul and Tommy, on a small bench, sat Sandra Lee and Charlene Moy, the only Asian girls.

Paul knew their parents were feeding them the same type of lines his parents were telling him. It was either "Find a nice Chinese boy," or "Find a nice Chinese girl," the encouragement really about racial purity, about not mixing, and the idea had made Paul feel claustrophobic and a little sick inside. As he and Tommy sat on the picnic table that was unofficially theirs—because of Tommy's presence—they kept watch over Sandra and Charlene, largely because Sandra was Tommy's girlfriend. They also passed the time by commenting on who was who.

"You see that Bardhol, the one over by the red Firebird with the cast on his arm? He called me a chink two days ago, so I slammed him up against a locker and broke his elbow," Tommy said. "Do you think he'll ever try that shit again?"

"You did that? I bet he'll keep his mouth shut for a little while."

"He deserved what he got. Do you see that cheerleader, Patty O'Connor?"

Paul looked over at the Jocks and saw Patty. She was a tall, statuesque blonde who everyone called Barbie. Her hair fell past her shoulders like flaxen gold. She saw that Paul and Tommy were looking at her, and she blushed. Paul had been her lab partner in Biology and realized that she was actually incredibly smart. "What about her?"

"She told someone she had a crush on me. I hope Sandra never hears about it. That's the last thing I need. Have you ever seen two women fight?"

Paul shook his head.

"If it's in a schoolyard, they fight dirty. I'd hate to see Sandra get mad. I can't wait to graduate. Someone always has to say something around this place. I heard that you went out with Karen Evans. Is it true? Did you know she's telling people about it? What were you thinking? Are you passing?" Tommy laughed. "Did she give you a badge that says you're an honorary white person now?"

"No, it's not like that—"

"—I'll tell you what. You should ask out Charlene. She's quiet, but don't let that fool you. She's into you. There's no selling out when you date an Asian chick. I hate how this country makes you think you have to ask out white girls like Karen Evans. White girls aren't any better than Chinese girls. Hell, why do you think there are a billion people in China?" He slid his right index finger back and forth between the circle he'd formed with his left index finger and thumb, and winked. "You be careful. Karen Evans will betray you. I bet she'll tell everyone you weren't like this white guy or that white guy, or she'll say she had a thing for you because you're Asian. Was it like that? Did she already tell you she's into Asian guys?"

"No, she didn't. Who told you about our date, anyway?"

"She's telling all of her friends that you went out. It sounds like she's bragging, or looking for admiration for breaking the rules, or just trying to get attention. You shouldn't play her game anymore. Did you talk to her about Homecoming yet?"

"No."

"Ask Charlene, and you can double date with Sandra and me. I'll drive, and I promise you'll have the time of your life."

"What if I want to go with Karen?"

"Look me in the eye and tell me that her being white never made you nervous. Just tell me that thinking she was white might be better for you never crossed your mind."

Paul couldn't answer, and Tommy's expression became more smug the longer Paul stayed silent.

"I knew it. Man, you need to drop her. Just drop her like a bomb, and get away from her as fast as you can. I'm telling you, we'll have a great time at Homecoming. You'll forget all about her. I've got something special planned. After that, you won't even remember her name."

Paul sat there thinking. The dance was in three weeks. He looked over at Charlene and tried to see himself with her and Sandra and Tommy on a double date.

Sandra had long black glistening hair and a lively face with flawless skin, full lips and wide beautiful eyes. She wore stylish denim skirts, taut blouses with short sleeves, or jeans and a black leather jacket with the orange and black Harley Davidson logo stitched across the back. She had a grown woman's curves and looked down at almost all the other girls for being childish and immature. She and Tommy were always driving away from school each afternoon, heading off to be alone.

Then there was Charlene, who had always struck Paul as determined. She was trim and lean and wore denim skirts and pink, white or light blue button-down shirts with matching monogrammed sweaters looped around her neck, the sleeves knotted so the sweaters hung loosely like fashionable scarves. Her shoes were prim, brown or black leather with buckles, and she always had a maroon Ane leather pocketbook hanging from her right shoulder. She carried her books pressed tightly against her chest as she walked—he could picture her in that classic schoolgirl pose—and she was his height. He liked how clean and put together she was, her hair always gathered back, held neatly in place with a brown plastic headband.

Karen? Charlene? Tommy's cautionary words echoed in Paul's mind, and as the bells rang signaling the start of classes, as the wind blew colder off the nearby mountains and seemed to remind him of how little time there was before the dance, Paul got up, slapped Tommy five, and hurried inside, believing there was only one choice.

Paul found Charlene that same day between Chemistry and English as she kneeled by her locker. His guilt and his nerves almost stopped him, but he asked, "I was wondering if you'd like to go to the dance with me?"

"I'd love to," Charlene said. There was such willingness in her voice, and she smiled at him like they'd shared a secret. He wondered why he'd ever been too shy or too intimidated around girls before. It was like a window had suddenly been opened, allowing him to look forward and see more of his life. *He* could ask a girl out? *He* could be the one to initiate a date, or a conversation, unlike how it had been with Karen?

Should it be that way with intimacy too?

Charlene blushed, and told him, "I'll talk with you later."

She moved off quickly as if neither of them were supposed to linger after such a moment; Paul wondered if there was some unspoken rule that said they weren't supposed to talk, and that she was immediately supposed to tell all her friends about being asked to the dance.

When Paul saw Karen later that day from across a hallway, she wouldn't maintain eye contact with him. She frowned, then glanced away at a friend who she'd been talking with, and kept looking at the friend, so Paul knew she'd heard about him asking Charlene out. Would she stay upset and distant? Or demand an explanation? Part of him wanted to talk with her, although he didn't know what to say.

Two days later, Paul still had not spoken to her, and he heard a senior named Jimmy Grimes was taking her to the dance. He was a gangly kid who was always brushing the long brown bangs out of his eyes. He'd played the lead role in the school's productions of *Brigadoon* and *Oklahoma* and was constantly striding down the hallways with his shirt hanging out of his jeans and his hair awry, singing at the top of his lungs like his life was a heart wrenching drama. Paul admired him for his individuality, but the kid could never shut up. As much as Paul tried not to think of it, he couldn't help wondering if Jimmy had asked Karen to the dance, or if she'd spoken first.

The night of the Homecoming dance Paul wasn't passing; no, not with Charlene sitting close beside him in the back of the Pontiac GTO while Tommy and Sandra leaned against each other up front. They were a sleek quartet, so cool, fashionable, everything that was right with being Chinese in America. Paul and Tommy wore navy-blue polyester suits with cobalt silk shirts, and Sandra and Charlene wore short black dresses with spaghetti straps and dark green sweaters over their bare shoulders, high heels on their feet, the orchid corsages Paul and Tommy had picked up at the Bloom Flower Shop pinned to the fabric above their left breasts. Leaving the florist, before climbing back into the car to pick up their dates, Tommy had reached into his wallet, withdrawn a condom in its neat square wrapper, and thrust the prophylactic into Paul's hands, saying with a grin, "You might need this." Paul had laughed at Tommy's presumption; he was just glad to be taking Charlene. Then Tommy showed him a flask filled with Jack Daniels.

On the way to dance, to Paul's surprise, Charlene sipped from the flask as readily as Sandra, so Paul drank too, excited, caught up in being cool. The gymnasium was festooned with red and white streamers—those were the school's colors—and because the theme of the Homecoming was *Imagine,* psychedelic rainbows and glittering silver stars hung everywhere in a tribute to the enduring spiritual presence of John Lennon. Paul felt like he was passing, as a disc jockey spun disco hits like *Get Down Tonight* and *Last Dance;* he felt silly dancing with Charlene as they grooved beneath a revolving mirrored disco ball that spun light in every direction, a smoke machine sending out drifting red and green clouds. When a local rock band called *The Resisters* got on stage and played songs like *Smoke On The Water, Help!, Lucy In The Sky With Diamonds, A Hard Day's Night,* and *Satisfaction,* the Bardhols and Heads crowded the floor. Paul and Charlene sat and rested and drank Cokes spiked from Tommy's flask, but toward the end of the evening, when the disc jockey returned and played slow songs, Paul clasped Charlene's hand and led her out into the throngs of swaying teenage bodies. Holding her close he smelled her perfume, apple-scented shampoo, lavender soap, and she nestled her head against his shoulder and pressed her body into his, as if expecting the hard on it gave him, saying, "I've always liked you." He held her in a blissful haze until the last song, Lennon's *Imagine,* started playing.

Paul hadn't seen Karen all evening; Charlene had kept him from thinking about anything else. But now he saw Karen with Jimmy, and they made an awkward looking couple. Jimmy wore a powder-blue polyester suit, and he was hanging onto Karen, his tall, thin frame draped over her, clinging yet bending with his arms around her waist. He kept trying to kiss her and wouldn't stop even though she was turning her face away. Her eyes were red, bleary and tired, as if she was drunk or high, and Paul felt guilty. When she looked up and saw him, she tried to smile; it was a faint, half-hearted attempt at being kind, in spite of the awful time she was having. But then the facade crumpled, her eyes conveying hatred and loathing, as if she blamed him for all of her misery.

What had Tommy said? You'll forget all about her? But no one had ever looked at Paul like that, especially not the first girl he'd ever dated or made out with, a girl who'd let him touch her bare breast. So holding Charlene, he almost felt cruel. He was having a good time while Karen was having the worst time; it was like he'd chosen and survived, but not without having doomed her to a worse fate, like he'd decided her extinction in some kind of Darwinian struggle. Was that what love in America was about?

"Paul, it's time to leave. Let's get out of here," he heard Tommy saying, and then Tommy and Sandra led him and Charlene away. As Paul left, he wasn't passing, not at all, but he still felt uncertain; he felt like he should have pushed Jimmy away and stayed with Karen, as if he might have belonged with her.

Then they were the sleek Asian quartet again—it was only them—and the Pontiac GTO roared out of the parking lot and swerved left down Route 156, although a right hand turn would have taken Sandra and Charlene home.

Where were they headed? Paul knew Tommy had someplace in mind because of how deliberately he drove through the sleepy town of Altamont, then up the steep twisting roads into the Heldebergh Mountains. Charlene gripped Paul's hand, clasping it tightly as they sped through the turns, and he liked how it seemed as if he were there to protect her. Tommy's right arm was around Sandra's shoulders, and she laughed when he said, "I have to show the lights to you two kids in the back."

Soon they reached Thacher Park. Tommy pulled into a parking area marked by a sign that read *Scenic Overlook*. He stopped the car beside a stone wall, and from the backseat Paul and Charlene could see the twinkling lights of the city of Albany far to the east. Everyone was quiet for a moment, and then Tommy started to kiss Sandra, but she pushed him away and said, "Not here. I'm not doing it in front of anyone."

Tommy sighed but started the car, whispered into her ear, and steered back out onto the road.

"Are you all right?" Paul asked Charlene.

"I'm fine."

"Do you have to be home?"

"No. My parents trust me. They know I'm with you," she said, and laughed.

Tommy drove fast, taking turns Paul couldn't keep track of. After a time, the car turned onto a dirt road that led to a cabin on a lake. Tommy held up a set of keys and jingled them triumphantly, and as everyone stepped out of the car he opened the trunk and held up two brown shopping bags. Paul heard bottles clinking.

Tommy laughed and said, "This is my surprise. We can have a party here. A friend of my father's owns this place, and he said it could be ours for the night."

The air in the cabin felt cold and drafty, but there was a stone fireplace in the main room, and Paul noticed there was a kitchen, three adjoining bedrooms, and one bathroom. After Tommy arranged kindling and logs in the fireplace, he lit a fire with his silver Zippo lighter. The whole place soon grew warm. In the meantime Sandra had unpacked the shopping bags, setting the bottles on a Formica table. "I want to make everyone vodka tonics first," she said.

Charlene drank, and Paul drank. He felt glad she was enjoying herself. The four of them sat on couches by the fire, drinking until they would laugh at anything, then Tommy lit a joint and passed it around. Paul had never gotten high before; the top of his mind felt like it was all over the place, which made it easier to keep being silly. Soon Tommy tried to kiss Sandra again, and she said, "I told you, not in front of anyone." Her expression was stern, but when Tommy stood and pulled her toward one of the bedrooms, she laughed, going willingly, the door shutting quickly behind them.

Paul wondered what Charlene was thinking. She smiled at him, and as they finished their drinks, he thought she looked pretty with the firelight flickering on her dark hair and her smooth face. He wanted to kiss her, and when he did she kissed him back. Nothing was wrong, the issue of passing forgotten, as if it were a part of someone else's past.

"We should be in our own room too," Charlene said.

Paul nodded, and they went into one of bedrooms on the other side of the cabin. Shutting the door behind them, he saw there was a double bed. He felt nervous but excited to be with Charlene there, instead of in a car. She sat down on the bed and kicked her shoes off, smiling. She still wore a dark green sweater over her bare shoulders, and as he sat down next to her he tugged the sweater off and started kissing her.

Charlene's mouth felt different. Did it fit his as well as Karen's? Did that matter? She kissed slower, more deliberately. Soon she was beneath him, on her back. They started taking each other's clothes off, moving under the sheets and covers. He had always liked her—that thought flashed through his mind for a second— and after her bra was swept away he kissed her breasts. They were firm, small, and she didn't hesitate or stop him at all. He told her, "I haven't done this before," and she said she hadn't either but she wanted to. Then he moved away from her and retrieved his pants, and after fumbling through one of the pockets he found the condom Tommy had given him, and struggled to remove it from the wrapper.

Paul rolled the condom on before returning to Charlene. He kissed her, and the way she closed her eyes and waited, letting him know she trusted him, made him feel she was the right girl to be with—the one he should be with—and she gasped once he was inside her. He would never forget how good moving within her felt, and how despite their inexperience she came, crying out. There was the shuddering and pleasurable release of his own orgasm soon after. But there was still the vague sense that something wasn't as it should be, and he realized only weeks later, when Charlene told him she cared for him but didn't want to date steadily because he wasn't right for her, that passion was what had been missing. The kind of ardent passion he'd felt with Karen a month before.

In the following days Paul didn't apologize to Karen because she looked at him too accusingly, as if her awful time at the dance had been entirely his fault. But he hadn't forced her to go with Jimmy. Could she really blame him for that? As the weeks wore on, she continued to frown or scowl at him because he didn't say anything, and he only wanted to avoid her.

That summer Karen moved away; Paul heard she'd ended up somewhere in Arizona or New Mexico. He finished high school, went to college at Columbia in New York, and moved on with his life. He married Lisa Hu, a Chinese woman who'd grown up in Canada, and they stayed in the city. No one stared at them when they were out walking. No one questioned Paul like Tommy Chang had. He didn't fear anyone objecting to their being a couple. And although he and Lisa had arguments about vacations or investments, they happily raised two children, a boy and a girl, telling them they were free to date or marry whoever they wanted. Paul worked for an insurance company—his life was demanding; he lived in the moment, his memory never troubling him or waking him at night. He didn't feel like he'd ever betrayed himself, or that race, in his personal life, had ever mattered.

But one evening he was driving on I-10 near Jennings, Louisiana, heading east from Houston, Texas to Cape San Blass, Florida. He was towing a boat on a fishing trip, and almost thirty years had passed since he'd been a junior at Guilderland High School. His fifteen-year-old son, Thomas, was in the SUV with him, and they stopped for Chinese food just off the highway at a place with a red neon sign that read, Jade Garden, Cantonese Cuisine. Paul figured the food wouldn't be nearly as good as in Chinatown, New York, but it was almost seven in the evening. He and his son were hungry.

As soon as Paul pulled open one of the restaurant's heavy red twin doors, he sensed something was wrong. Perhaps it was the

nearly empty seafood tank that should have been filled with highly oxygenated water and many saltwater fish, live crabs and lob-
sters. Only one fish swam in the murky water, and upon closer
inspection he realized it was a catfish. Then he stared at the proprietor behind the front counter. From growing up in Chinatown,
Paul had always been able to tell if someone was really Chinese or
not, and he discerned from the shape of the man's eyes and the
bone structure of his cheeks and jaw that he wasn't Chinese. He
was either Vietnamese or Korean.

Paul scrutinized the features of two of the waiters, and of the
hostess who came out to greet him and his son. She was attractive,
her hair cut in a sexy bob, her mouth a sultry shade of red, and
she had a heart-shaped face and the nicest smile. The idea of passing had nearly been lost to him; he hadn't felt that way for so
long. But he knew for sure now that that all of the people running
the restaurant were Korean. Yes, they were passing, probably
because Louisiana was no hotbed for Korean food. Asian ingredi-
ents could be cooked and called Chinese cuisine though, then
sold anywhere in America to unknowing customers whether the
food was authentic or not.

"Would you like a table or a booth?" the hostess asked.

Paul couldn't speak. At that moment Tommy Chang's predic-
tion, "You'll forget all about her," became so very wrong and
untrue, because Paul's memory suddenly returned him to the festooned gymnasium as *Imagine* was playing, and Karen Evans was
staring angrily at him, blaming him. He felt an unsettling wave of
guilt rise within him now—it was only slightly muted by time—
and he could have been thirty years younger, bearing the intensity
of the accusation her eyes had cast long ago. His heart quickened,
he felt dizzy, and he regretted not apologizing. He'd been a fool.
Too untrue to himself. How could he have been so impressionable, and then so cold?

"Dad, what is it?" his son asked, and Paul could have called out
all the workers for pretending to be Chinese and not serving
authentic Chinese cuisine. He could have profaned or derided
them for passing, with the same adamancy Tommy had spoken to
him with.

But Paul wanted to be kind now, as he should have been to
Karen. He wanted to be better than he'd been long ago. He didn't

want to react as harshly as Tommy had. These Asians needed to make a living. Needed to survive. Who was he to call them out, when no one else knew the difference? What did it really matter? What was the harm? America was all about being whoever you wanted to be now. Chinese kids were even dyeing their hair blonde. What was passing but another way of saying you weren't happy with what life was giving you?

"Dad, what's the matter?"

"We'd like a booth," Paul told the hostess, and then he turned to his son. "Nothing's wrong," he said. His voice was wavering a bit, but he wanted to sit down and enjoy a meal. He thought of tipping the waiter well. "Don't worry," he said to Thomas, "I'm just hungry. I'd like some soup, maybe some seafood. I bet the food is good here. What do you think?"

DAVID GULLETTE

Fort Macon

a novel excerpt

Well OK, let's see: start with the climactic moment and my father wearing his regulation State Trooper iridescent mirror shades so I could see a pair of shrunken images of myself but not his eyes and he stood there in the marl-paved parking lot beside his truck with the red light still flashing legs apart pistol on his hip doing his Rod Steiger sheriff thing: *I never thought I'd live to see a white man stand up for a nigger.*

Of course I knew almost instantly that the words coming out of my mouth were the wrong ones, not *Well you damn well better get used to it* or *I'm not the first, I won't be the last* or *If she goes I go* but:

If it's good enough for her it's good enough for me
which of course was completely meaningless. But I was so trembling with years of stored-up rage I could have been speaking Urdu and he'd've got my drift. It was as though we'd been rehearsing this scene ever since my freshman year at Chapel Hill when I came home for Spring Break and told my mother I'd visited a Negro Church in Carrboro and heard this wonderful sermon about Civil Rights and I could hear him clearing his throat and stomping around in the next room, telegraphing *I'm here, I know what crap you're talking about, you two, you don't fool me.*

What I was was Chief Life Guard at the State Park over on the Outer Banks. And what he was was my boss, the Super. He'd lost his shrimpboat in a storm a couple years before, stupid, he should never have gone out, damn near drowned, search party, Coast Guard choppers, the whole shebang. I remember waiting up all night with my mother and my aunt her sister drinking bourbon (I drank RC Cola) and after a while playing gin rummy until just as the sky got light the phone rang and my mother said, I guess that means he's safe, I reckon I'll go to bed now.

After that he did some deputy work with the Sheriff just to make ends meet which aside from fishing was about all he knew aside from turning out the best flat-bottomed cypress-plank skiffs in Beaufort County. Deputy meant he knew how to wear a uniform and pack a gun so when the Super job opened up over at the Park he applied and got it without knowing that I'd applied that winter from Chapel Hill for the Chief's job, that the last decision by the outgoing guy was to say hell yes why not. So there we were, both of us new hires, and when the State looked into it nobody in Raleigh could figure out a way to make it look like nepotism so they just let it stand.

He and I pretty much left each other alone, which was nothing new for us. He had his rules which me and the other guards had to toe the line on—clean white shorts and shirts, police the beach, wash out the dressing rooms at the end of the day, women's too, Tampax Kotex and all, keep the swimmers out of trouble so you don't *have* to rescue them, no girls or liquor in the guards' quarters which was a little strip of six rooms with its own kitchen, like a sort of minimalist motel in the dunes. There was a park-wide speed limit of 35 and he used to wait in a little turnoff and flip on that goddamned siren we could hear all the way out on the beach and nail those poor suckers if they went 37. He loved that part of the job and he did it whole hog, the reflector troopershades, cowboy boots, tooled leather holster, man you didn't want to look in your rearview and see him swaggering up to bust you, nosiree.

He went back to Beaufort at night, no doubt to eat in silence with my mother before retiring to his "den" to watch tv.

I had a good team of boys for the week, kids from Morehead mostly, one from New Bern, but on weekends and holidays we had to hire extra hands from Cherry Point, tough-talking wiseass crewcut Marines, lifeguards from the pool at the base and before the extras arrived he'd say to us as a group although I knew it was meant for me *Be careful I don't catch you gettin too friendly with them gawdamn pimplyfaced whorehoppers from Havelock.*

But I actually liked those guys. Me and my boys would meet them Saturday nights at the Pavilion down Atlantic Beach and we'd drink a lot of Schlitz or Blatz and dance the Twist with the summer girls or go out to the railing and watch the phosphorescent waves break out of the darkness and talk trash and maybe smoke a Pall Mall and they'd tell tall tales about all the women they'd fucked in all parts of the world. I guess we were all of us pretty much the same age, but we were just Joe College and they were Men With Real Lives so while we kidded them a lot I think deep down we really wouldn't mind having those real lives of theirs.

April came to the beach every day with her two boys. Her husband was at the Duke Marine Research Institute in Beaufort, a visiting biologist from SUNY Buffalo. She was an educated woman stuck for the summer in this sleepy southern port so naturally she had prepared herself to be, and was, bored stiff. But when during a casual conversation (I'd been showing the oldest, Duncan, the rudiments of body surfing) she learned that I loved Camus and was reading Melville's short fiction her wonderful brown eyes lit up like someone lost in the desert spotting an oasis.

I had to be careful. The old man had a way of popping up unexpectedly on the boardwalk to scan his immaculate beach. I'd come down from my roost up on the chair and stand near her blanket facing the water and the swimmers, arms crossed, pith helmet and zinc oxide and whistle on its lanyard all in place, for all the world the very model of the vigilant all-American lifeguard. And so we talked, for hours. Books, ideas, politics, her house in the country where the deer came at dusk into the back yard, her girlhood in a small town in South Carolina, her very serious (and, she made clear, far from passionate) husband.

She was tall and gorgeous and in her mid-thirties and as the summer progressed and her Yankee-winter paleness turned a golden brown the untanned whiteness of her cleavage (although somehow her bathing suit managed to ride a little lower week by week) began to drive me crazy. Despite the cute and available and lifeguard-loving girls at the Pavilion, I was still technically a virgin. So sure, I dreamed: My Ideal Older Woman would teach me everything, everything.

It was my practice to take my lunch break at a shaded picnic table at one end of the boardwalk, and after a while she and the boys joined me (triangles of ham and Velveeta, chocolate milk, ice cream sandwiches) and then Duncan and Kyle would go romping and shouting off into the dunes and we would sit there side by side staring out to sea until at last one day she put her hand on my thigh—not squeezing, just resting there, that perfect hand, the one without the ring—and said, "Harry's going off to Newport News for an overnight, can you come over to the house later on?"

It was a rented bungalow just off US 70 in Morehead City. We sat at the kitchen table with only the light from the stove-top on, sharing a Bud. She had also put out crackers and cheese. As we spoke she kept stroking my arm the way I had seen her stroke her boys when they got hurt or were falling asleep collapsed against her.

The gist was something like this: She had never met anyone like me in her life—so sensitive, so attuned to literature, so alive to emotional nuance. She was suffocating in this marriage, he was draining the very lifeblood from her soul. When it was not icy neglect it was forcing her to have sex—*forcing her!* She had to escape. She would shrivel up and die otherwise. I want you to save me, she said, please, save me. Imagine us, you and me. And the boys, they love you, they really do. Oh, I know, I'm older than you are, but you have a man's mind and (her hand now between my legs, massaging ever so gently) and a man's body.

I managed to blurt out something like: But I still have another year of college.

That doesn't matter, she said, the boys and I will move to Chapel Hill. I love Chapel Hill. We'll find a sweet little house, and I'll get a job and the boys will go to school and you'll work on finishing your degree and when you come home at night I'll be waiting for you. The boys will be asleep in their own room and I'll be in our bed and you'll come to me, oh Jesse, you'll come to me. My hero. You'll save me and you'll come to me, won't you?

She took my head in her long cool powerful fingers and began to kiss me. It was like nothing I had ever begun to imagine, given the frantic amateur slurping and tonguing that had passed for kissing in my adolescent life up until then. It was slow, deliberate, unrushed. It was the kiss of experience.

I had a pretty good boner going, that's for sure, and somehow without unlocking her lips from mine she swiveled herself around until she had my head bowed and she was kissing upward like a baby bird being fed and then somehow she was kneeling before my chair, and still, still our lips together as she fumbled with my belt and expertly popped open the stud on my jeans-shorts and unzipped me and drew out monsieur and at last withdrew her lips from mine (ever so slowly, nothing sudden, everything's fine) and dropped her head and took me, which is when we heard the snuffling shuffling sound of one of the boys staggering sleepily out of his room.

Mommy?

She drew back so quickly she banged her head pretty hard against the table, spilling the beer.

What is it, honey? Bad dream?

And then she was up and herself again heading toward the door and I managed to put the car back in the garage and zip up and started mopping up the beer with a paper napkin.

She brought Duncan into the kitchen with her. He was really more asleep than awake, eyeing me with groggy indifference—no surprise, no curiosity.

Jesse came by to say hello. Let me get you some water.

Duncan sat in her chair, his eyes still on me, but droopy, droopy, as though I were some familiar slightly boring stock character from a repeated dream-sequence.

She stood next to him. He drank some water.

OK, kiddo, back into bed with you.

Lie down with me, he said, putting his arms around her waist, burying his head in her belly, his eyes closing. Please.

Well OK, sure, why not.

She led him out of the kitchen, pausing at the doorway to give me a Sorry, what can we do, expression. It was then I saw the trickle of blood coming down her left temple, and I sign-languaged her to touch it and she did, tasted the blood, smiled, shrugged, blew me an air kiss and disappeared into the hallway, Duncan in tow.

I drove back to the barracks stunned and oscillating like an out-of-tune guitar string.

Save her. My hero. Chapel Hill. Waiting. For some reason I kept seeing myself opening the front door of one of those old Quonset huts in Victory Village the university had thrown up after the war for the GI Bill flood of married students. Opening but not entering. Honey, I'm home.

Wednesday was my day off. The old man was in court with his speeders and litterers. I went home to do a week's dirty laundry and see my mother. She was in bed, again, surrounded by her books and papers and pills, looking as though she hadn't slept in days. But we had always been thick as thieves since as long as I could remember, co-conspirators, and if she didn't have energy, she just faked it, so we had a good talk over tea and ginger snaps. After a while I told her I thought I was in love with an older woman, and not just older but married, and with kids. And that she was unlike any woman I'd ever met. And that she was in a bad marriage, a really bad marriage. And how her face lit up every time she saw me. And how she made me feel like a man.

My mother sat up in bed and fluffed her pillows a bit and smoothed her hair back before she spoke.

Have you told me this because you want my advice?

I said I figured she'd give me some advice whether I wanted it or not but that yes, I wouldn't mind hearing what she thought. She closed her eyes for a spell and then opened them and looked right at me.

Ever since you were knee-high to a grasshopper (she said) you've been headstrong and done what you felt you had to do. Sometime that's got you into a heap of trouble, and other times it's worked out pretty well. But sometimes you've also actually listened to your old mother. So listen now. Nobody knows better then I do that Jesse Pelletier's got a big heart. Maybe too big. But this woman, she sounds needy, too needy. It isn't how you're so much younger than she is or that she's already married that bothers me. It's that she's using you like a rope to get out of a burning building. That's no way to start up on something that needs to last. So if I could give you one piece of advice it would be not to put her out of your mind, but to put her *in* your mind, to really think about her and what her being so desperate *means* and what it *could mean* down the road. Think. Think about it hard. Imagine you and her five years, ten years from now. And imagine yourself as father to those children. That's all I ask, that's my advice: use your noggin.

A few days later the 4th of July weekend began: I hired extra guards from Cherry Point and even two from Camp Lejeune. Overflow crowds expected.

Of course this was still what we may as well call the Apartheid South. And ours was an all-white beach. Black folks wanted to go to the beach, they had to drive through the woods to a swampy

creek beyond Swansboro, wait in the swarms of greenhead deer-
flies for the maybe twice a day ferry out to an abandoned Lejeune
gunnery range and then walk half an hour through more green-
heads to a beach with no facilities. As for our beach, Fort Macon
State Park, which boasted the remains of a breakwater designed by
a young officer named Robert E. Lee, the old man had already
turned away a carload of black college kids from Greensboro who
wanted to test the limits. There was supposed to be a court case or
something. But I hadn't been around when it happened and he
wasn't exactly open about it, just some grumblings of the Give 'em
an inch and they'll take a mile variety. But I could tell the race
thing was on his mind and what with Johnson pushing the Civil
Rights Bill my father had made up his mind, and that made-up
mind of his was getting set in some kind of bitter concrete.

I did have one real friend among the regular guards, a kid from
New Bern named Timmy Eustler—"Useless" for short. We shared
a passion for body surfing, and one of the happiest days of my life
up to that point had been when a hurricane passed offshore and
we closed the beach and Useless and I spent the day riding these
Waikiki-sized combers made all silky by the pouring rain. He was
the only one (beside my mother) I had confided in about me and
April getting chummier and chummier. As there had in fact been
no sex I could tell him with a straight face that ours was essentially a Platonic affair. But Useless was no dummy. He guessed how
hot the soup was getting. He told me one night (we were drinking
beer at Atlantic Beach, leaning over the rail in a fine drizzle,
watching the big waves come breaking through their white foam
out of the darkness) *Man, that woman gonna eat you up you not
careful.*

How the thing happened was this: it had rained for two days
straight after my visit to April's bungalow, so she and the boys had
not come to the beach. But on Sunday the sun came out and the
crowds just swarmed. The old man had to open up the half-fin-
ished auxiliary parking area. I caught a glimpse of him during
one of my breaks: he looked pretty flat-out and herky-jerky, but
you could tell he was watching everything like a hawk.

The couple was prosperous looking, plump and what passed in
those days for stylish. The wife had horn-rimmed sunglasses with

sequins and the husband wore a straw hat with a feather and both of them settled into beach chairs and promptly got lost in their Best Sellers. The baby, about two, was being looked after by a portly midlife black woman in a white maid's uniform. She had decided not to take off her white nurse's shoes, which meant they were soon soaking, especially after she had to pick up the kid when a wave came in.

I sauntered by and smiled.

Nice day for the beach.

Yessuh, shore is.

Looks like she's having fun.

Oh that li'l thing just love the water.

About 11:30 April, Harry and the boys arrived. Kyle came running toward me *Jesse! Jesse! Look at my new goggles!* Duncan went straight for the water without looking at me. April fussed with the blanket. Harry came over, cool and dapper. I'd met him once before, a previous Sunday when his lab was closed. We exchanged inanities and then he waded in to watch Kyle disappear in the shallows for long bubbly stretches.

After a while April came over and we stood side by side, arms crossed like a pair of caryatids, watching her husband watch her younger son. *I've fallen deeply in love with you,* she said, smiling blandly at the sea as though we were discussing the weather, *and it hurts like hell.*

For some reason I turned around. Sure enough, there was the old man up on the boardwalk, legs apart, shades glinting, and *his* arms crossed. Was he looking in our direction? Who knew? And (I said to myself) who the fuck cares?

A group of people had begun to flounder about in the waves beyond the NO SWIMMING BEYOND THIS POINT sign, so I just mumbled *Likewise, excuse me* and set off jogging and gesticulating down the beach, my whistle in my mouth, relieved to be in motion.

During my lunch break, knowing my beat-up old two-tone Pontiac would be like a furnace, I hitched a ride back to the barracks with Luther, who drove the Park maintenance and garbage-pickup truck. I wanted to get the collection of Dylan Thomas poems April had lent me. Luther said he had about a half hour's work to do up at the fort, a lopsided pentagonal 1812 and then

Civil War—era earthworks, complete with moat, sunk in the dunes at the tip of the island. Aside from the beach, the fort was our main—our only—attraction. So I sat at the barracks kitchen table eating cold leftover meatloaf and reading Thomas until half an hour had passed and no Luther. So I took the book and walked out to the road, thinking I might catch a ride up to the beach entrance with one of the guys from the Coast Guard Station. But nobody came by for more than ten minutes, and then it was Luther.

When I returned to the beach Useless came up to me looking a little guilty. He stood beside me and spoke in almost a whisper.

Look, Jesse, I don't want to get in between you and your Daddy but he is my boss, so look: after you went on break he called me up to the boardwalk and told me to tell those people with the old nigger lady in the white dress that she couldn't be on the beach because it was Park policy and it came down from Raleigh and so I did it. They left. They weren't happy, but they left.

He's a fucking coward, I said also very quietly.

Around us were shouts and laughter, the cries of children. A lot of white folks having fun. We kept our eyes on the swimmers out in the green and white mixed chop.

He knew I wouldn't do it, Useless. He waited till I was off the beach.

Sure looks that way.

I can't take this, I said. I can't go on working for that man. Just can't do it.

I thought you were working for the state of North Carolina.

Hey, wake up, buddy. My Mama didn't raise me to take no shit, even from him. Besides, in case you haven't heard, the Civil War? It's over. It's history.

So does this mean you're quittin?

What say we don't call it quittin, OK? Quittin is like when you give up and slink away. I'm gonna resign is what I'm gonna do.

This is stupid. We got half the summer left.

It's not stupid. It's something I gotta do.

But why?

He saw, rightly, the end of our friendship: my telling him in detail entire plots of novels, our skinny dipping by moonlight in the bioluminescent surf, our skimming together down the frontside of the same wave, turning our heads to lock eyes and scream with joy.

I have to find him, I said.

But why? said Useless. A mixture of grief and exasperation.

I started to walk up toward the boardwalk. April was perhaps asleep on her blanket, face down. Harry and the boys were elsewhere.

BUT WHO'LL BE CHIEF? his voice mixing with the roar of the sea and the other tangle of voices and Little Richard from somebody's portable and the cry of gulls.

So I stalk off toward the parking lot and of course he's waiting for me (although where was he hidden when I arrived with Luther? I've never figured that one out.)

I've relived the showdown itself so many times it's like a cartoon or like some favorite scene in an old movie.

He's all so Mister Law The Man and I'm all so Mister Righteous Indignation Hero, and so it's *You waited until I was off the beach* and *I'll run this park as I see fit* and *You're a coward, you've always been a coward* and *You watch your lip, boy* and even as I'm pumping up my anger I realize that I'm standing there barefoot on the sharp marl under the blazing sun dressed in little more than underwear and he can see my eyes but I can't see his and despite the fact that he's my father he's got a gun on his hip and all I've got is a book and it's *I can't believe you went behind my back and forced that woman off the beach* and then the old standards *I never thought I'd live to see* and *if it's good enough for her*

And *I can't go on working here with you, you know that*

And *So don't. You got half an hour to get your shit outta here*

Back on the beach, furiously stuffing my things in a canvas bag.

Useless: You quit. You fuckin quit. I knew you would. What's the matter with you?

Harry: I was dumbfounded when I saw it. *So* unnecessary. And such an insult to the family!

April (livid): The family! Who the hell cares about the family? What about the lady herself?

Duncan: What happened?

Me: I'm leaving.

Useless (almost in tears): Asshole! Deserter! You just did this to show off!

As I was throwing my stuff in the car (all the doors open to let it cool down a bit) April appeared out of nowhere, winded from running.

What will you do? Where will you go?

I don't know. I can't spend another night on his turf.

But will you be... nearby?

I don't know. Probably not. Probably Chapel Hill.

How can I reach you?

(There was a blank page at the back of the Dylan Thomas, which I was still carrying around. I scribbled the address and phone number of the apartment on Franklin Street. Then she wrote her address in New York State but not the phone number and carefully tore the sheet out and tore it in two. She didn't try to hold back the tears, they were all over her face, she was a mess, she held my face and kissed me very slowly, her lips were cool almost clammy as if she'd been swimming, it was a touching moment but I had to pee like crazy.)

April: It wasn't supposed to end *like this*.

Me: I know. I'm sorry.

April: Don't be sorry, lover. Never say you're sorry.

One last embrace and then I was gone.

Back in Beaufort I brought my mother a glass of orange juice in bed and told her what had happened and that I had to leave, that if anybody asked she could say I was "just going back to school a little early" but she and I both knew I would never put a foot inside this house again and so in a very real sense this was our farewell. I went into my room and made a lot of noise packing up some things and banging the screen door on my way out to the car.

When I came back into the bedroom she wasn't sad, or if she was she masked it pretty good. If anything she seemed sharp and bright-eyed and mischievous.

Well! I guess it's lucky this opportunity came along.

Lucky?

Oh yes. It allows you to solve two problems at once.

What two?

Him. And her.

I don't know what you mean.

Oh you don't, don't you? Hm! Well why don't you just think about it at your leisure. Now come over here and give your Momma a kiss. And you be sure to call me the minute you arrive safe and sound in Chapel Hill.

Chapel Hill in July was sleepier than sleepy. I got a job waiting tables at the Rathskeller. The only one of my roommates around was Butch, who was drinking a lot and flailing away at his paintings of lopsided naked women in impossible poses.

The story of my resignation was in the papers for a while. Charles Craven did a piece about it in the *News & Observer,* and some guy from AP managed to track me down for a phone interview. I told him I had quit as a matter of principle. And what was the principle, he asked. Well, I said, racking my brain, that our public parks are for all the citizens of the Great State of North Carolina. And was the lady in questions a citizen? Well I didn't know for sure, but that was beside the point, yaddada yaddada. I have no idea if the story ever made it out onto the wire.

I talked with my mother three or four times a week. April never called, or at least Butch wasn't aware that anybody had called when I was at work. But then what *was* he aware of but the taut and silky arms and legs dancing in his head?

That fall I got involved in the local Civil Rights movement: went to meetings at that same church in Carrboro, gave out leaflets, stood on picket lines outside redneck cafes, ducked a couple of beer bottles tossed in our direction, met a lot of intense people and slept with a couple of them. Things were looking up.

In January a letter arrived from April. She hoped I was doing well. She said it was a relief getting back to her house and garden. The boys were fine. Things were slightly better between herself and Harry. Still, she missed me, *especially at night.* She wanted me to know how much she treasured our time together. There was a snapshot of the view out her kitchen window: a jungle gym up to its knees in snow, then a long white field falling away toward a line of black trees.

I look out across this frozen field and think of you. That warms me up.

That Spring my mother got worse. I called my father, ready to argue ferociously blue-in-the-face that we bring her up to Duke, listen, it's the best goddamn cancer treatment in the state, you can't deny her this. But he just said, Yes, right, we'll do that.

He and I managed to stay out of each other's way. And it was on my watch, early one morning that she slipped away, her hand in mine. He and I didn't speak at the funeral. That was my last trip to Beaufort. Not to the region. The old man remarried and moved down to Wilmington. I went to Boston, got a teaching job, and married Anna Cataldo. Some years later Anna and Suzy and I made a trip to Atlantic Beach. The Pavilion was closed, gone. We swam at the (now integrated) State Park. And by then there were even girl lifeguards. The New South. But the spirit of Jesse Helms was still abroad in the land.

> *I'm a Tar Heel born*
> *I'm a Tar Heel bred*
> *And when I die*
> *I'll be a Tar Heel dead.*

Well why don't you just think about it at your leisure.

Salk and Sabin

A year after my father was called before the McCarthy subcommittee, the acne began to appear, and nothing I did prevented the blotches from rising and spreading like a small red army over my cheeks and chin. I tried calamine, witch hazel, all seven lotions from the pharmacy on Sixth Avenue, and finally a paste my mother mixed from powdered roots and soil—something she knew from her childhood. Perhaps my skin wasn't ruined enough for her medicines and already too rough for the soft, white creams the other girls used.

We'd just moved to Bleecker Street from the Upper West Side, mostly at my mother's insistence, though it was Father who decided. My mother hated the way the people stared at her uptown. Whatever she wore—solid, print, cotton or silk—was always too loose or too short or too bright. She didn't roll her hair or iron her skirt; she didn't hold my little brother's hand when they crossed the street. "They can see that I'm foreign," she complained, though she'd been a foreigner her entire life: a child of French diplomats in Cuba who grew up to dance for the German ballet. She'd met my father at a performance on Broadway, given up the stage for another foreign world of streetlights, sirens, the scream of New York.

Now my mother offers private dance lessons in our living room, which is why we have no furniture, just mirrors, dozens of mirrors, hanging on nails at different heights. I use a gold-framed rectangular one to study my skin, where I count seventy-eight distinct pimples and forty-two red blotches that will certainly develop new dimensions. My mother asks me if I was smoking reefer. "You can tell me," she says, eyes appraising my skin. "I see the signs." She wears pink and orange with a cloth flower in her hair. Dark eyes, dark lips. I almost feel she wants me to admit to it. "No," I say, and she says, "Do I have to talk to your father?"

My father has the last word on everything, though since we've moved, he's become more accommodating—allowing a small

black-and-white TV, the orange and blue molding Mother painted despite the no-alterations clause in the lease, and several late
dinners at nearby restaurants. I like to think he is trying to make
things better for us, but his allowances feel so fragile, I don't want
to consider them for fear they will disappear.

For a while, right after the hearings, Father wouldn't allow us
out at all. But that was before we moved, and long before Jack. My
mother only sees Jack when Father's working. It's her secret, and
ours, me and my brother. My father has his work; we have Jack
Steenwycks, or someone like Jack. First we had Uncle Stew, later
Uncle Nathan and then—my mother stopped using prefixes—
Walter, Scott, and Jack. Each one came with presents: ice cream
sundaes, trips to Coney Island, a card trick where twos turned to
aces and aces became queens, a box of hard candies, a carved
wooden train we still keep hidden beneath my brother's bed, a
cloth doll I left out in the street. Jack has the debates, which he
moderates himself, pitting my brother against me on topics like
syphilis and malaria: which is the worst disease? Or medical care
during wartime: should the soldier or general receive care first?
He asks questions, and Mother asks questions, too. Simple things
like "Is blood blue," or "What if we had no bandages"—things
that could never be true, and thus make us feel smarter.

When Jack comes over today, he wears a soft leather jacket and
wide-brimmed hat that make him look like a cowboy. He still
smells of shaving cream even now, in the late afternoon. He
brings flowers, purple irises, which my mother likes, though they
have no scent, and he carries the ragged journal he sometimes
pretends to read from, though it's filled with nothing more than
geometric scribbles. My brother and I looked through the book
once while Jack and Mother were in the bedroom.

My mother takes Jack's hand. "We're going walking," she says.

I'm scraping the pink chewing gum from the cover of my alge-
bra book. In English class, I found a second wad under my desk,
where it was sure to stick in my hair during the next air-raid drill.
The note didn't surface until history class, when I found it
wedged between my almanac and the wooden back of the desk.
"Communist" was all it said.

I've never told anyone about my father or his party meetings,
though I know he is right, that the government needs to change,

that food and shelter and a share of the wealth is every man's right. I've seen my father say it hundreds of times: at rallies, union meetings, strikes—even at the university, where he teaches, despite the fact that communism's forbidden there. He's given me his articles to read, pages that compare whole economies to ailing human bodies; gangrenous hands, legs crippled from polio. How does such a creature live? he writes. How, when the limbs that support it have no health, can the body function? Yet people fear his cure. They reject it, as if health itself were a disease, something to avoid at any cost.

I couldn't answer when Mr. Wharton called on me; I didn't even hear his question. I was folding the communist note in my palm, imagining how I would reinvent myself, how my skin would clear, and how one day I'd return to this school, and who-ever had done this would seek me out and beg me to teach about the unions and strikes. The reason communists weren't more popular, I believed, was entirely aesthetic. Even I acknowledged that my father, with his long chin, thick brows, and hairy nose was particularly unattractive.

Mr. Wharton tapped his pointer on a wooden chair, staring at me, his jacket missing a button, his trousers so short that his socks showed. The chalkboard was covered with notes I noticed only then: battle diagrams and years, without any indication of significance.

"I don't know," I said.

Katherine, who sat behind me, laughed.

"Joanie's wet her underpants," she said softly so that only I and a handful of others heard. I realized then that she'd scrawled the note and placed the gum in my textbook. Her tone revealed it, and the fact that she knew I was upset. I can picture her placing the gum between her lips, cheeks wide and fat as a pregnant belly. People think she is beautiful, but she laughs like hard change in a beggar's cup, her pale hand sporting Walter Thompson's class ring. I know she lets him touch her. Secret places, dark places. After school, after she lingers at the back of the room to apply the red lipstick my father forbids me to wear, I follow them to Central Park and watch as Walter slips his hands under her skirt. She's never seen me, but he did, once. He was kissing her, but looking at me. He was watching me and I him and for the first time I was equal. I, too, had a chance at winning his heart. I'd felt such a thrill then, I'd turned and run.

*

At dusk, before Jack and Mother return from their stroll, the light in our flat becomes forgiving. My skin looks softer, almost a single, coherent red hue. I write my compositions in my ledger book and help my brother with arithmetic. He doesn't need assistance, but he always asks for it. I think he gets lonely. When we talk, lying side by side on the living room floor, he rubs his bare feet together. "How was school?" I say, or "Were they mean to you?"

We are accustomed to talking across empty spaces. When I was his age and he only ten, we'd promised never to marry and live together in a house in the middle of Central Park where no one would call us names or whisper behind our backs. He still believes we will do this, though I have committed myself to a newer, secret love: Walter Thompson.

Through the open window, I hear the sizzle of laughter. Crowds have begun to form on the streets—the night crowds, who dress in black or clashing colors, orange and purple, yellow and blue, and drink coffee until breath reeks and hands tremble. I know the Bohemians. They define themselves as outsiders, but outsiders who belong. I've been an outsider since the day I was born. I have no interest in proving that.

When footsteps sound on the landing, my brother runs to the door. He stands on his toes to kiss Jack on the cheek. Later, perhaps after Father comes home and we all lie in separate rooms (or sit—Father types till late into the night), I will tiptoe into my brother's room and tell him that he is too old to be kissing men. But my brother loves Jack. He has decided to become a doctor, like Jack. I like Jack, too, but he is only twenty-two, and not really old enough to be any of the things he professes: a world famous surgeon, a poet, a politician, a father of a baby girl. He says that his grandfather was a famous surgeon, and his father before him—all the way back to the *Mayflower*. I don't think Jack is even a doctor, or that he belongs with my mother, with his fair skin and hair, straight shoulders, torn leather coat. He speaks loudly, just as my father does, but he never seems angry, and he never speaks of politics or revolution, though I know he's a communist.

I've seen him reading Father's newspapers, and when he realized I noticed, he didn't try to hide it.

The first time I met Jack, he pulled up his trouser cuff so I could see his pale left calf. I was surprised when he later told me he displayed his crooked leg to feel closer to children. Like sharing a secret. He'd nearly died, he said. And he'd been so jealous of his twin brother, who was healthy and strong and smart. "He's a doctor," Jack confided, and then added quickly, "a doctor, too." He looked sad, but only for a moment, and then he smiled. Had it not been for the long months in bed, he would never have read so widely or learned the poems he'd used to "infect my mother's heart."

"Infect?" my mother asked him.

My brother fell in love with Jack that first day, and Jack still listens to him and nods as if he agrees with everything my brother says: that the trash can in the corner is not big enough, that one day he'll have a car like the blue Ford that drives past our apartment each morning, that he prefers milk to ice cream, as ice cream is too cold, that his favorite color is red, his next favorite, green. He won't stop talking, and Jack won't stop nodding, and my mother always seems delighted by the whole thing. She really likes Jack, though she's not herself when he's around. She laughs too easily, her smile foreign. When Jack's around, mother forgets that she's an outsider and that people stare or that life is hard and she's isolated—all things she complains about to my father, who explains again and again that she feels so precisely because it's her nature. "If you insist on being miserable, you will most certainly remain so."

If my mother were with Jack, only Jack, he would have to become more like my father before she could really be herself again. Jack would have to eat with his mouth open, refuse to bless food, forget my mother's birthday, and mine too, for that matter. He would have to have admirable passions, selfless ones, like ridding the world of misery. He would have to forego walking so as to have more time to read, or read as he walked, and thus arrive late to most engagements. My mother can only be with a man like that, which is why all the others have come and gone.

Jack pinches my cheek, rests a hand on my shoulder. His hair is still matted from the hat he no longer wears. "No kiss from you?" he says. I feel my dress, too small, pull against my back.

Mother glides across the living room, stops with her heels facing each other and slightly apart. She wears a long strand of glazed beads and a dress that resembles our lace curtains, loose and transparent. It flows around her like a necklace or bracelet, something she wears for decoration.

Jack takes my brother's hand and leads him to the far end of the room. Usually, now, we'd have the debate. I am too old for the game, but Jack always makes it fun, so much fun that the hours pass, and Mother forgets to pour drinks, and my brother forgets the kids who have beaten him, and I forget the taunting and Walter, or rather, I imagine that Walter is Jack, or Doctor Jack as my brother calls him.

Today's topic is polio, which I know about. Four boys in my first year class were stricken, and two now walk with metal leg braces and brown high-top orthopedic shoes. Audrey, a blonde with perfect small teeth, died, but I never knew her well. I've seen iron lungs with emaciated children tucked inside. I've heard stories of children quarantined in hospital rooms, with parents who visit once a week to speak through cloth masks. During polio summers the pools close and the movies stop showing. And my brother and I are slapped—by any passing grown-up—when we step through the mud puddles we now know are really dark pools of polio, polio, polio.

Jack says that we will discuss vaccines, which he has to explain to my brother. "The body makes antibodies when it's injected with dead virus," he says. "The antibodies protect against disease." He says that vaccines are the science of life and that there is no more noble pursuit than the search for a cure to man's greatest foe. He speaks fondly of Salk—I've had two injections of the Salk vaccine, as has my brother, though he doesn't remember. Then Jack mentions Sabin, and I pretend to have heard of him, too.

"Who's Sabin?" My brother asks, and Jack tousles his hair and says something like—I don't know for sure because I am more interested in his hands; he has one on my brother's shoulder, and the other folded loosely over his own stomach, but I realize that his nails are long and dirty—Jack says something like Sabin is developing a vaccine with a live virus, a weak virus that doesn't grow in the nerves, just the gut, the intestine, where it can't hurt us.

I still don't know what we're debating. Usually Jack's debates have a single question and two sides, one of which I argue, the other, my brother. Two sides, with a clear winner and loser and ultimately, a single truth. Jack always states the truth, at the end, before he leaves: malaria is worse than syphilis; you should save the soldiers first.

My mother lights a cigarette, removes her walking shoes, turns on the radio, a soft jazz piano. She's wearing her good jewelry—an opal ring she's promised me, and a bracelet that once belonged to my father's grandmother. We both hear the key in the lock, though my mother doesn't look away from Jack until Father closes the door behind him, his gray three-piece suit and hat nearly the same as the brown ones he wore yesterday. He sets down his briefcase. He usually carries it into his study before we sit down to eat Velveeta cheese over toast or cream soup, something prepared quickly.

"I'm home," he says. He should not be here. He should never be home when mother's lover is. He is not part of our afternoons, and I sense that he feels this, that he imagines he stands on the tiled landing, waiting for us to answer the door. He must wonder why he returned at all. I wonder, too, and look to see if anything is different about him. I look and look, but don't see anything.

My mother starts walking, slowly, her hair falling loose over her shoulders. She should be carrying something, a box of chocolates, a plate of sandwiches, a pair of dance shoes to return to a young pupil. But her palms are open and empty. She has nothing to explain Jack's presence.

Jack says, "But the live virus—Sabin's virus—can travel. We'd infect each other with a polio that would never hurt us, and once infected, we'd become immune. Isn't it wonderful to think: a virus spreading to save our lives?" He seems untroubled by my father's arrival. If anything, he speaks louder than usual.

My mother brushes Father's chin with a kiss so brief, it seems like a whisper.

"What are you doing here?" my father asks Jack, and I realize that the two know each other, perhaps from party meetings.

"We're discussing polio," Jack says. "Salk and Sabin."

"Sabin?" my father says. "I've not heard of Sabin."

"His work is only known abroad."

"Ah," my father says, but he is watching my mother. She has moved to the window, where she gazes two stories down to the street. My brother is still asking questions, "Wouldn't an infection kill us? Won't we kill everyone?"

"Comrade." Jack rises and extends his hand to my father in belated greeting. "I am having an affair with your wife."

*

My mother retires as soon as Jack leaves, and my brother, who senses but does not understand what has happened, complains of a stomachache and lies in bed. I make dinner, bread with cut apple and cheese, and pour two glasses of water.

My father rests his chin in his hands and stares across the table at me. The empty seats to his right and my left don't seem to bother him. In fact, the way he sits and looks at me, I feel like dinner has always been just the two of us. That I am his wife, not his daughter, the woman who cooks and cleans and enforces his rules, at least when he is home. I will clean his dishes, as I do every night, and then take a stroll where I'll meet Jack and have a cigarette or a drink, or whatever it is Mother usually does when Father retires to his study. I can be an adult with my father because he has always treated me so. Even before I started school, I went to his meetings, where I helped take attendance and pass out stacks of printed fliers.

My father chews. "How was school?" he says.

I stare behind him, to the one small stretch of bare wall in the adjoining living room. I've never told him about the bullies at school. I've never mentioned the taunts or the jeers. But the silence around the table, the fact that we are sitting together while Mother lies alone in her room, the fact that I feel like everything changed today in some way I do not yet understand, makes me bold. "Jonas came home early," I begin.

"His stomach," my father says, with his usual authority.

"They hit him." I pull the crust off my bread. "Like they do all the time, because he's a communist."

"They hit him because they are ignorant," my father says.

"No one likes us," I say.

"Don't be a fool," my father says, the same words he spoke to Jack only hours before. I wait for him to order me to leave the house, too. I remember how Jack reached for my mother, how she didn't move, and how much greater his limp seemed when he walked alone from the apartment.

My father takes another bite of his meal.

*

I decide to stay home from school—to take care of my brother, I say, though he doesn't really need me around. Mother is here, even if she doesn't leave her bedroom.

I spend the morning rewriting my homework assignments and the afternoon reading *Jane Eyre.* I make sandwiches. I listen to the telephone ring. My brother lies under the dining room table, his ledger open, yesterday's homework not yet begun. He only speaks of Salk and Sabin; Salk who killed the virus, and Sabin, who spread the live one. "I still don't understand," he says. "Why would we take a virus?" I pretend I understand and call him a fool.

At two o'clock, I slip out of the flat and take the subway north to the park.

Walter and Katherine have chosen the south shore of Central Park Lake, close to the place where the Vaux's boathouse once stood. Last fall I watched the construction men pull it down, the sagging roof and pillared porch and balustrades. I watched the new boathouse rise as well. Saw the limestone and brick before it was set, the gabled roof, the new dock and boat ramp. I know the lake intimately, each landing and path, and where to hide to secure the best vantage of every small clearing.

I pull a branch of new growth maple, spreading the leaves enough that I can see.

Walter, his trousers collecting around his ankles like folds of soft skin, sprawls on top of Katherine, who lies with her eyes tightly closed and the red of her lips spreading outward over her chin and onto her teeth. She jerks when Walter does, but only after a moment. She draws a sharp breath, and I think she might cry. I've seen her call out once or twice on previous days. I've watched Walter kiss her. I have to imagine his tongue, but I know it finds hers. I can hear the sticky sound of moist bodies meeting. I can smell bitter sweat. I watch his legs. He presses his toes into the ground, his calf and thigh becoming one long muscle that collects in a flattened mound before giving way to back. He holds his shoulders up, like wings.

Their meeting ends abruptly. Walter stands and stretches, allowing me to examine the dark hairs around his groin and the other parts—the ones no girl is meant to see without a wedding ring. Katherine, more modest, straightens her skirt and brushes her hair. Silently, they stroll along a pebbled path and then part ways.

The clearing becomes mine: the matted grass, the dents where toes or heels or fingers pressed. The cherry trees are beginning to bloom. The yellow-green lake reflects only darkly. The grass is still warm. I sit where Katherine had and try to imagine myself beneath Walter. If he closed his eyes, as he did with her, he would not see my skin. I lie back and, with only emptiness above me, think of Jack.

Things will go back to how they were before he arrived and after mother left her previous lover: She would give dance lessons; three of her old students had followed her from uptown. She'd schedule them for the afternoon instead of the morning. She'd sleep late and my brother and I would make breakfast. Nights, when Father worked or went to party meetings, we'd go on city walks, me and my brother, searching for salt cod or fresh ginger root. We'd pretend not to notice our neighbors, too (though perhaps people would be kinder here in the Village). My brother and I could make dinner and clear the dishes. And after, when no one was looking, we could steal cigarettes from the cloth sack Mother kept full and guarded when she was sober, and trade them for hard candy or respect in the school playground. We'd start a new school, closer to the Village, start over ourselves.

I run my hands through the grass where Walter and Katherine had lain. The air seems different, thicker somehow, and beginning to darken, though it is not so dark that I can't see her dropped lipstick. I open it, note the curve her lips have pressed into the pigment. It is mine now. I can paint her desk with it, tall letters advertising that she is a whore. Dark red marks on her books and chair. Red, as she's marked me. Or maybe, I stand and turn homeward, I can summon the courage to paint my lips, just like a grown woman, and spread my red smile.

Ostracon

Katya is searching for her glasses. They were just here. One minute ago, on the counter, the big brown glasses. Without them, everything is waxy. She lays her hand on the cool Formica and makes a brushing motion. Keys, coffee mug, phone book. Two different pens. Why are there so many pens? She has never bought even a single pen.

Katya squints to see the table, pats various spots. The sisal placemats are crusty with stale crumbs. The Shabbos candles are dribbly stumps. Another pen.

She's had these glasses for so long. Decades probably. They are chestnut brown and shiny like a stone you pluck from the shore. They fit her face just right.

Now Katya is in the den. She is overturning newspapers and envelopes. She would like to throw them out, but what if they are new? Without her glasses, the headlines are smudgy glyphs.

When Joe comes home from work he finds his wife crouched on the floor, her sweater frosted with lint. She looks up and smiles.

*

Workmen have cut a hole in the living room ceiling. Apparently there was a leak in the roof which Joe said was causing some kind of damage. The men are short and brown and smell like the inside of a taxi. They smile at Katya, but she is suspicious. She is protectful of her space, this home she has spent half a century grooming and curating. Clods of who knows what are caked to the treads of their boots. One of them is smoking outside. *A choleryeh ahf dir.* He had better not leave the butt on the porch.

*

Writes the Russian neurologist, Alexander Luria: "I shall never forget a case in which a man wounded in the temporal region could easily read his surname 'Levsky' written on an envelope addressed to him, but was completely unable to read the much simpler word 'lev' (lion), which was not fixed to the same degree in his memory."

*

Joe is becoming impatient. He is inspecting a spoon Katya has scrubbed—she is certain she scrubbed—and making angry whispery grunts. He grabs a fistful of silverware from the drawer and hastily examines each utensil. He is shaking his head, glowering. He dumps them in the sink, which makes an explosive clang, and walks away. The ringing lingers in his ears like a tuning fork all the way back down to his office.

*

The workmen have left for the weekend. They said they needed to order a special tool to refasten something to something else, and that they would be back on Monday. In the meantime, there is a jagged half-moon gouge in the ceiling which looks into the dark crawlspace above. Katya is uneasy. She dislikes all that translucent tarp over everything, the little flakes of paint and plaster clustered in its folds. Will the men remember to wash off their dirty fingerprints from the ceiling once they've sealed it up?

*

Katya appraises her teeth in the bathroom mirror. How did they get like this? Each tooth is a pale, caramelized beige and emplaqued with creamy filament like dried-up caulk. Her lips are crackly and sallow. Is someone playing a trick? *A farshlepteh krenk.* She touches her hand to her face but it too has gone bad. Her flesh is slack and splotched with moles. Her fingers are too small, the veins too big. She traces the brittle etchings in her hand, remembering briefly the tender pink palm of a monkey that grasped her finger through its cage during a childhood trip to the zoo.

*

The noun *reflex* made its way into the medical vocabulary during the 17th century, having derived from *reflexion*. It was believed at the time that spirits in the nervous system were "reflected" into the muscles in the manner of light bouncing off a mirror.

*

As a younger woman, Katya illustrated books of Jewish folktales. One tells of a young student who has been traveling with his rabbi for many days. Each day they roam the land, study the Talmud, and sleep at a village inn. Tired of spending all his time with the rabbi, the student one night decides to continue his travels alone. He instructs the innkeeper to wake him extra early, so that he may take the first train before the rabbi wakes. The next morning the student stealthily gropes around in the dark for his clothes and, in his haste, dresses himself in the black robes of the rabbi. He rushes to the station, buys the ticket, boards the train, but is startled when he sees his reflection in the compartment mirror. "What a fool that innkeeper was," he says. "I ask him to wake me and instead he wakes the rabbi!"

*

During the Han Dynasty, Chinese soldiers wore mirrors over their breastplates to ward off wicked spirits. If these mirrors broke, the warriors would grind up the shattered glass and ingest it, so that its magic would protect them from within.

*

The men are back today. Katya is surprised at how glad she is to see them. Why shouldn't she be? The men are friendly. They smile and call her "meesez."

The living room is even less recognizable than it was last week. Thick orange cords, navy blue sound blankets, pails, toolboxes. It's like a crime scene, or a fabrication shop. The men are wearing thick gloves and gauzemasks.

The sound of the drilling is savage but also fascinating. It's like a dentist's drill, high-pitched, metallic, and loud enough to be inside your mouth. It growls through the resounding crawlspace, sending specks of fiberglass across the rafters in jangling spurts.

What are the men doing in there? They've set up a yellow-caged lamp so they can see their way around. Katya is curious to look, but something seems perverse about the open cavity. Too intimate. Like looking into somebody's guts.

*

Of particular concern is the fate of the armoire. As a piece of furniture, it is not much to speak of—a clunky oak display case enswirled with scratch-marks—but its contents are delicate and irreplaceable, protected only by a thin sheet of glass. Atop each of the four, dimly-lit shelves sit a selection of rare items Katya and Joe have collected over their many travels.

Fragments of pre-Columbian textiles, a beetle entombed in a bulb of amber, a lock of Madame Curie's hair. There is a vial of perfume recovered from a sunken barge, an opened letter postmarked to a Ukrainian village which no longer exists. On the top shelf, a jar of gallstones sits beside a splinter of Katya's coccyx salvaged from the surgery last year—as foreign as an ancient mollusk.

Each year at Passover, the grandchildren ask Katya to identify these curiosities, and each year she enchants them with tales of adventure and magic. A bullet casing from one of the revolvers used to shoot Grigory Rasputin. A diamond smuggled from Kiev in the stomach of a boy who'd swallowed it in a ball of wax.

As the children grow older, they become more skeptical of Katya's stories, though the objects remain radioactive with mystery.

*

In 1873, a young Italian anatomist named Carmillo Golgi discovered a revolutionary method for viewing nerve cells. He'd converted a small hospital kitchen into a makeshift laboratory where, in the evenings, by candlelight, he would carefully impregnate microscopic samples of neuronal tissue with silver nitrate. Laboriously, he experimented with various chemical baths and exposure times until one night he observed what he called *la reazione nera*, or "black reaction." The silvery-black clusters of neurons were suddenly crisp and vivid, the gossamer stain sharply articulated by the luminous yellow slide.

Thirty-three years later, the German physician Dr. Alois Alzheimer used this same technique to investigate the neurological roots of senile dementia. What he found was an almost literal correspondence between the pathology of the disease and the resulting affliction: nerve fibers were gnarled and pasty, synapses were clogged with proteins like a grimy sink drain.

*

It was about this time last year when Joe found the checkbook. The bank had called asking all sorts of questions. Why hadn't the amounts on the deposit slips matched those on the checks? Whom had number 3601 been made out to? Why hadn't these four been endorsed? Joe was flummoxed. Katya had always handled the money. She was good with numbers, with the planning and organizing. Her parents had run a textile business back in Poland, and had trained her to run the accounts since the age of nine.

Joe went to the study and fished through the drawers. Already something was off. Calculators, envelopes, typewriter ribbons—all were piled into heaps. Loose staples were scattered about. Had the maid carelessly dumped everything together? When he finally discovered the mint-green checkbook with its marble saddle-stitch, two thoughts entered his mind at once. The first was the hope, the fantasy: *clearly, one of the grandchildren defaced it.* The second was the fear, the reality: *clearly, my wife has lost her mind.*

The carbons were ablaze with gibberish. The penmanship was a dance of curlicues, like a roll of barbed wire. But the scribbles were neither childish nor methodical. They were discernibly Katya's, hers alone; they contained both the impulsive, half-cursive jabs and drags of her handwriting and the needlepoint slopes and slashes of her drawings.

*

In World War I, fighter jets were first becoming equipped with machine guns. They were initially crude and imprecise. A tail gunner needed the flexibility to swivel his gun along a 360 degree axis in order to follow a moving target, yet this increased the odds of accidentally shooting his own propeller. Bullet proof propeller blades were no solution—they simply deflected the bullets back towards the gunner. Finally, in 1915, an ingenious instrument was engineered by Anthony Fokker which synchronized the rate of the machine gun with the oscillation of the propeller, such that the trajectory of each consecutive bullet would be interleaved between the microsecond windows in the spinning blades, like a beam of light through a movie projector.

*

On the bottom shelf of the armoire is a shattered limestone ostracon, each segment propped up with small Lucite sawhorses. The paint is pale and chalky, the accompanying text jagged and pocked. There is a narrative of some sort running across the grid of panels, though the events aren't clear, not with so many sections missing. A czar, a bride, a lake. Rust-colored figures strafe this way and that. Bare-breasted women carry baskets through fields of maize. A fire. A dance. A gift.

*

Katya is at the osteopath for her hip. She has been coming here ever since she fell down the front steps and shattered her coccyx. Dr. Mallah is a short, gym-built man almost exactly half her age, with furry black forearms and slow walnut eyes. He is, of course, Jewish. She would never think to trust a gentile with her health.

On the walls are laminated pictures of skeletons and organs, the same ones that adorn every doctor's office. Such a mess the insides of bodies are. All that cartilage, all those valves and wires.

*

The term *synapse* was introduced by Charles Scott Sherrington in 1897. He'd taken it from the Greek verb *synapsis*, meaning "to clasp." Synapses, the connection points between neurons, were essential to Sherrington's conception of the brain. They were like docking stations in a vast network of stockyards, transferring or withholding cargo from one freight to another.

*

It is dusk and Katya is inexplicably agitated. She is getting up and sitting down. She is licking her finger and rubbing away tiny stains on the glass coffee table. Joe is demanding to know what's wrong.

A gesheft hob nicht, she keeps muttering. *What do I care.*

*

In 1963, a peculiar article appeared in the medical journal, *Brain,* authored by a former student of Sherrington named Wilder Penfield. Entitled "The Brain's Record of Auditory and Visual Experience," Penfield described a series of intracranial experiments he and his colleague, Phanor Perot, had performed on patients with severe epilepsy. Before operating, the surgeons applied local anesthesia and stimulated the exposed brain areas with tiny charges of electricity while the patients remained awake and fully conscious on the operating table. The results were startling: subjects reported sudden flashes of dreamlike imagery, many of them accompanied by a deep sense of familiarity. Some spoke of nightmarish visions, like being chased by robbers, while others reported quotidian episodes from the past, such as hanging up a coat or boarding a train. One claimed to hear voices in the dark, coming from "around the carnival somewhere—some sort of a traveling circus."

*

Where is the camera? The Seder is tomorrow evening. Her grandchildren will be there. Everyone is counting on her to capture the event like she always does. They are expecting her to develop the pictures and send them to each family. The precedent has been set by years of tradition. She can't let them down.

What will happen if there are no pictures? No one will remember the party. They won't remember the laughter and the children's games and the magnificent feast she is preparing.

Without a document, who will remember?

*

One of the men descends the red ladder holding a slender, forearm-length strip of wire. He shows it to the other men like he has just caught a great fish! It is warped and steel and strangely sculptural, with rusty perpendicular brackets clamped to the ridges like vertebrae. Was this the problem? Have the men solved the problem? Katya is excited. She would like to keep the metal wire for the armoire but worries it may be impolite to ask. After all, they were the ones who excavated it.

*

Joe stares up at the ceiling as Katya sleeps beside him. He is thinking of Matisse. *My lines are not crazy,* the artist claimed, *for they contain an implicit verticality.* The words loop in Joe's mind like an incantation, half soothing, half maddening.

*

Katya's parents were moderately wealthy, enough so to buy their daughter a ride overseas just before the occupation. There is a slightly over-exposed picture of Katya boarding the ship in a grey peacoat with big white buttons and white gloves, looking not unlike Anne Frank.

A maidel mit a klaidel, is the name Joe has given this photograph. A Yiddish expression meaning, approximately, "a pretty maiden showing off her fancy clothes." He has a name for all his favorite pictures of Katya.

Who could know what was going on inside her at that moment? Children never appear traumatized. Here is the thirteen-year-old refugee, buoyant and alert, her shoulders angled into a sort of lopsided shrug, like she is concealing some private joke.

*

"There are no specific recollections in the brain," writes Israel Rosenfield, "there are only the means for reorganizing past impressions, for giving the incoherent, dreamlike world of memory a concrete reality. Memories are not fixed but are constantly evolving generalizations—recreations—of the past, which give us a sense of continuity..."

*

New York was strangely welcoming to the fourteen-year-old Katya. Her wizened and soft-spoken uncle, who had taken residence in the Prospect Heights section of Brooklyn a decade earlier, converted his attic into a small bedroom. A single window, diamond-shaped, sepia-stained, faced the bustling intersection of Washington Avenue and St. John's. The vaulted ceilings and exposed beams in the space were both rustic and cathedral-like, hidden and holy. On her first day of school, Katya was shocked to receive a compliment from her homeroom teacher. *That's a pretty dress*, said the woman. Katya assumed it was a trick—friendly language between teachers and students was unthinkable back home.

*

It is Tuesday and the men are still working on the ceiling. Katya is growing anxious. What if they do not finish in time for Passover? The possibility quickly forks off into a host of attendant worries. Is there time to reschedule? Could one of her children host the Seder this year? How hard would it be to serve dinner outdoors? She's overwhelmed. There are too many fires to stamp out. She is pacing about the house, tending to various minor tasks without actually committing to any of them. *A foiler tut in tsveyen.* She sweeps the dust from the kitchen floor into fluffy grey islands but forgets to collect them with the dustpan. She scrubs the bathroom but leaves the filthy sponge in the tub.

*

Again, the glasses are missing. Every spot of light is plied out into fuzzy radial threads.

*

"I sit at my worktable, a still world around me, and stare at the wall, empty of decoration," writes the gardener, Thomas DeBaggio in *Losing My Mind.* "I become lost in the vocabulary of silence. Thoughts squiggle and writhe into sentences that disappear before they can be acknowledged."

*

A mighty storm had lashed the roof in the spring of 1940, causing a smattering of leaks in the attic ceiling. Within hours, the beams were soggy and dripping. Katya was at school while her few belongings were soaked. Her pretty white dresses, which hung from an iron dowel, were jaundiced about the shoulders; her shoebox full of letters from home became a cloudy palimpsest of multicolored inks. Katya's uncle had managed to rescue three of her paintings, but most were soiled beyond recognition.

Of the three, one has survived the intervening decades. It is a humble yet darkly evocative composition, a capricious earth-tone sketch of bustling shoppers and vendors cramped in the Prospect Heights thoroughfare.

Something in its hasty, boyish contours suggests an immediacy, an urgency, held at arm's length. There is also a murky, gauzed quality, a faint glow smeared into the weathered flax canvas reminiscent not of fallen tears but a world seen through misting eyes.

In her adult life, Katya has now and then returned to this painting, adding texture, dynamism, gradually threshing the implicit verticality from the adolescent craziness.

*

There are moments when Katya's youthful beauty reveals itself. The mid-April light casts a sudden sheen to her pewter hair; an impromptu smirk betrays a girlish sneakiness otherwise lost.

*

Katya is dusting the piano keys with the feather brush. She swipes in gentle curls up the octaves—*plink-tink-dink? piddi-tunk-tonk?*

The piano has not been played in a while. It must be clean for the Seder, when the grandchildren will stage a little recital as they do every year. She bends over the bridge to dust the strings like a mechanic under the hood. Each swish sends a thrum of crystalline whispers through the birch chamber.

*

The party is underway. Children are performing handstands in the den. Katya's nephew is showing off copies of his latest book to the in-laws. Rain-flecked peacoats and scarves are piling up on the guest room bed.

Katya is thankful that no one has noticed, or at least commented on, the hole in the ceiling, which has been sealed with a makeshift slab of cardboard. She makes an effort not to look up, fearing that the duct tape might peel under the weight of her fretful gaze. She is not normally superstitious, but why push her luck?

Soon the Seder will begin. The family will take their seats at the long oak table. Katya's son, Ben, who is now twice the age she was when she married Joe, will read from the Haggadah with his nicotine baritone. Her nieces will serve the salty parsley, the bitter herbs. The youngest children, Jennifer and Rebecca, will skitter about the house, searching for the *aficomen*. After the Seder, they will beg their grandmother to read one of her books to them, either *The Train to Kiev*, or *The Czar's Magic Mirror*.

Dusk is early to arrive this year. The windows are foggy and lusterless in the waning violet light. The muted scent of frost and peat leaks into the living room from the thawing backyard garden.

Who will remember?

Bless Everybody

They'd been led to our land. The woman, Meredith, was far along in her pregnancy, and the coincidence of her name being close to "Mary" struck me, no place to lay their heads as they awaited the birth of their child. We—I—owned two hundred acres, cut out of the red rock along the Wyoming-Colorado border. Indians had long ago run stolen horses into the box canyon at the end of our property, and after them, rustlers had done the same thing with cattle. I'd poked around in the red dirt and once dug out the shoulder bone of a bison as big as my thigh. Arrowheads, spear points, and shards of clay pottery I'd turned over to the local museum; rumor had it that this was as sacred ground as any that ran along the Front Range from Colorado to Wyoming.

Peck Foster, my neighbor of the adjacent two hundred acres to mine, had given the couple my name and number and told them to call me about the one-room cabin on our property. The young couple had parked outside the gate and took it upon themselves to walk the land and see if they could find the person who presided over this "magical" place. It seemed like a good story, this being "led" to the land. I didn't believe in providence, but I was retired and had time on my hands to be amused by such notions and told them I'd meet up at the gate to our property.

That "our" is misspoken. I'm divorced and Rosalyn took her share of the property in a cash settlement. I used a chunk of my retirement money to buy her out—I'm sixty-eight years old, and I'd worked as an inspector for the highway department thirty-nine of those years. I'd always wanted a piece of property as fiercely beautiful as this one. Every time I passed it on the road at sunset it glowed like hot coals in an evening fire—a view of the openhearted earth. When it went up for sale, I talked Rosalyn into putting our money down. I was land proud, no doubt about it, and a little stream called Watson Creek ran through the valley and turned the cottonwoods leafy with shade in the spring, as they were now.

They were waiting for me by the gate. When I'd spoken to the husband on the phone, he described their lifestyle as "migratory," but he certainly didn't sound like a dangerous drifter. I'd have put the man in his mid-twenties and the woman a few years younger and their Volkswagen bus older than the both of them combined, rusted on its fenders and painted a robin's-egg blue with a bumper sticker on the back that said BLESS EVERYBODY. NO EXCEPTIONS. The van's tires were bald and its grill had picked up a couple of tumbleweeds and was chewing on them like too much spaghetti in a child's mouth.

"Thank you, sir, for meeting us," Calvert said, sticking out his hand. He was a thin man with a big toothy grin, and blond hair down to his collar, his eyes all afire at hello. He tipped his hat to me, a brown felt fedora with a white feather tucked in the band.

They showed me their wares: ceramic leaf earrings and beaded hemp necklaces; tiny "sweetheart" notebooks no bigger than the palm of my hand with paper that still looked like the wood it came from; sassafras and strawberry scented drip candles in day-glo colors. They went to craft fairs and sold what they could, and took temporary jobs. "We're realistic people," Calvert said. "You can't live off today what you did in the Sixties."

Sixties or not, they didn't look like they had a practical bone in their bodies, not with that baby in their future.

"Sir, we'd just like to stay here a few nights," Calvert said. "We want our child to absorb some of this"—he spread his skinny arms in a panorama over the expanse of my land—"*holiness,* before we move on." I thought: people really talk like this?

He patted Meredith's swollen stomach. She looked as if she were due any day now.

"Where you going to have the baby?"

Calvert clasped his hands together. "Wherever we may be."

I looked at Meredith, hoping I wasn't hearing what I just did. But she had that dreamy come-what-may look. "There's a good hospital in town," I said. "You should check in with them."

"No need," Calvert said. "We'll be taken care of."

"Uh-huh."

"We just followed our hearts here. We came over the pass and looked down and just knew. Isn't that right, Mer?"

Meredith nodded, still that dreamy look.

"I'd feel much better if you saw a doctor or midwife while you were here. We got a clinic in town that helps those in need."

"You *are* a kind man," Calvert said, as if my reputation preceded me. "Your hospitality will not go unnoticed."

Meredith's stomach made a shelf of the long dress she was wearing, a thin faded shift of yellow daisies, not cut for pregnancy, just oversized. Her ankles and toes had a film of dirt, and I wondered how long it had been since they'd had hot showers.

Before she retired a year after me, Rosalyn had worked in the public school system, first as a teacher, then a district administrator. She appreciated the threat of liability. I did too, working as an inspector for the highway department. She'd moved out to Peakview Estates (I still had our old place in town) and her backyard sloped down thirty yards to an artificial lake with her own dock.

"You haven't heard the best part," I said.

"I can't wait."

"The wife is pregnant." I suddenly realized I'd been calling her "the wife" with no good reason. They'd never said they were married. "I tried pushing them to see a doctor while they're here."

"Wait...did you say *'pregnant'*? As in living-out-of-a-van *pregnant*? How many months?"

"I'd say seven. Not being the best judge of such matters. She's pretty ripe, though."

"Oh, Charlie, what have you gotten yourself into."

"Maybe nothing. They just want a couple days to rest their bones. I'd be more worried if there was anything there to *get* into. It's still the same empty one-room place with a bed and stove and a hard tile floor. Nothing to lose, nothing to break, and nothing to disturb. They want to walk the land, that's fine with me. Soak up the vibes or whatever they believe. Anybody breaks a leg, blame it on nature. I'm not running an amusement park up there."

"Anything happens, especially with her being pregnant, they could sue you."

"I'll take my chances."

I'd come over to get Martin. Rosalyn was going to Atlanta for a week. We shared custody of Martin, our golden retriever, going on twelve years now. Before that we'd had Betsy, a springer spaniel, and when we first married, Noah and Victoria, a couple of dachshunds who fought like the brother and sister they were. It wasn't lost on us that we always gave our dogs dignified people names, no Bandit, Snuggles, Nugget, or Lady for us. These were our children with hopes for their futures, limited as they might be. Rosalyn traveled every month or two working part time now as an educational consultant. Last month she'd gone to Hawaii. She didn't travel alone either; she had met a man when she was in Cleveland. He was a VP at a large educational testing company, and all I knew about him was that he was divorced with three grown children. She'd put a picture of him on her dresser. I suppose it was her way of introducing him to me since she knew I'd be over to take care of her plants while she was away. Her new man had blue eyes and a tennis tan that he wore like a good suit. His hair was graying around the temples—mine was almost all white. He was closer in age to Rosalyn, who was thirteen years younger than me at fifty-five, the new thirty I was hearing. Nobody said that about sixty-eight, not yet anyway.

Rosalyn put down her iced tea on the marble patio table. She'd fixed up the place with abstract paintings that reminded me of geometry problems (we'd had pictures of those grinning dogs of ours hanging in the old place—I still did), plush white sofas (she was always chasing Martin off of them), and long drapes.

"I'd better be going. I got some painting to do on the basement."

"Almost finished?"

"I'm getting there." Rosalyn hadn't been inside our old house for months. I was fixing it up to sell. We still owned it together, free and clear, our one common possession if you didn't count Martin. Just to keep it fair, I paid her a little rent every month until I could get it sold and move out. I was going to live up on the land. I'd priced running electricity from the utility poles at the road, and it would cost me three thousand dollars. Right now all I had was a well that pumped out rusty water. I'd warned the couple not to drink from it. Nothing would happen to them, just the poorest tasting water around from all the iron in it. They said that wouldn't bother them, the water was still purer than any that came from a faucet.

Rosalyn had spit out that water when we first went to look at the land. "Ugh," she'd said. She'd spoken with such vehemence that we got into an argument.

"Well, you don't have to make such a sour face," I said.

"It's terrible. It tastes terrible."

"You coming or not?" I had asked her.

"I'll wait here," she said, standing by the cabin that had a padlock on it. She had looked in the windows and shaken her head. It was clear she didn't appreciate the place. She wanted some mark of human existence up here, or maybe she just couldn't imagine endless days with me and my thoughts and nothing between us but open space and sky above. And those thirteen years that separated us in age.

When I got back from walking the property, I asked her, "Are you going to complain every time we come up here if we buy the place?"

"Maybe."

"Then maybe you shouldn't come up here," I told her.

"Maybe I won't."

I looked at her. "What's that mean?"

"It means I'm not going to sit around and warm my feet by the fire and watch golden eagles nest and pretend to be happy." A dust devil had come up and was spitting dirt in our faces. Rosalyn shouted through it. "I'm going to continue working part time, I'm going to volunteer more, I'm going to the health club, the malls, the museums, I'm seeing friends, eating out, and traveling. I want a life, not an *afterlife*. I don't want to close up shop. It's all right if you want privacy, Charlie, but that's not what I want. This fucking dirt!" she said and swatted at the dust, then ran for the car. I got in after her, walking slowly.

"And does this busy life of yours have any room for me?" I asked.

"We should get back," she said. Which was answer enough.

It's a terrible thing to get to the end of a marriage and run out of good will about the future. Once you stop talking about what's ahead—or start talking about it separately as we had done—it makes you feel as if you're on a train platform waving goodbye to the departing life you used to have. I always wondered if she agreed to sign the papers for the land just to have a reason to divorce me—two years ago now—and if I'd made her sign them because I honestly believed the place would bring us closer, like people do in a last ditch try to stay happy by having a child.

"I'd be a little more concerned about letting those people stay up there if I were you," Rosalyn said now. We were sitting on her dock. She didn't own a boat and didn't want one. But she liked to come down here and read a good mystery and have me join her for a drink. "It's your pride and joy," she told me. "I'm surprised you don't make them produce a passport to step on it." We could joke about what it meant to me now. And she was right, I could have planted my own flag up there. She wore white slacks and a low-cut pink sweater that I wanted to believe she'd put on for me. She'd never looked better. It all agreed with her, retirement, this big house, the traveling, the new man, the freedom—even me being here to always depend on. I would come over as long as she needed me, and not a moment longer than she wanted me to. That she knew this should have made me an object of concern if not outright pity in her eyes, but all I saw was gratitude when she put her hand on my stubbled cheek and said, "I don't know what I'd do without you, Charlie."

Over the next few days, I finished painting the house, replaced a couple leaky windows, and pulled up some soiled carpet beyond cleaning in the dining room where we never could get Victoria's and Noah's markings out—always fighting for dominance, those two. Martin followed me around, seeming to enjoy the liberty of jumping up on the old familiar couch without getting shooed off, and made a few half-hearted attempts to chase rabbits around our backyard. He was good company, and I would have liked more of it, but we were pretty fair about sharing him, and Rosalyn said he still liked to stretch out his front paws for a dive into the lake when she threw a stick, like the excitable puppy he used to be. So it was good to shuttle him between us. Just like a kid, he had his own bag packed and ready to go with his special food, blanket, and medicine for his arthritis.

I was pulling some unidentified boxes from the crawlspace in the basement when the phone rang. I ignored it at first, let the voice mail pick it up. But it rang insistently again, and I went upstairs and answered.

"Charlie?" It was Peck, my neighbor up at the land. "You better get up here," he said without any preliminaries.

"What's going on?"

"Those people, the ones you let stay..." Peck sounded mad as I'd ever heard him. "That fella shot a deer. With a *pistol*. Half shot!"

"I'm coming." I got my rifle and was in the truck in seconds. Martin jumped in the back. I still had paint on my hands.

You would have thought a wounded mule deer shot in the leg couldn't get that far. That would be a misconception. A deer on three legs can outrun any man on two. This wasn't the point, of course. The point was that this crazy fool had tried to shoot one out of season with a pistol and without a hunting license and with No Hunting signs posted on both our properties. That made him a poacher in the eyes of the law, even if I lied and said I'd given him permission. His van could be impounded, his gun taken away (a good thing, in my view), and the both of them fined more than they were worth.

"What the hell got into you?" I said when I drove up. I was jumping out the truck before the engine had stopped coughing. "Are you nuts?"

"Sir," said Calvert, "I...we needed food." Where was Meredith? Down by the creek I suspected, maybe washing clothes in the stream.

"Food?" Peck was standing there red-faced. His family had owned a thousand acres of this land going back a hundred years until they divided it up. Peck and I had worked out a lease to let his horses graze on my property, and between our parcels the animals found plenty of room to roam. I'd gotten a better offer for cattle from the sprawling McDonald ranch to the east, but cattle tore up the place worse than horses, and frankly horses were just prettier. I'm sure Peck was thinking the same thing as me: this fool could have shot one of his horses. "What gave you the idea you could hunt up here?"

Calvert, all twenty-something years of him, let out an exasperated sigh. "I was just trying to feed my family."

"You ever heard of a grocery store?"

"I thanked the land for its bountiful offering," said Calvert. I looked at Peck, who screwed up his face in disgust. "I thought you'd understand."

"Here's what I understand. You leave that deer out there to die and it's wanton waste, not to mention cruelty. I'm obligated to report this to the game warden, and if I don't, I'm up my own damn creek. Any way you look at it, you've committed a crime on my property."

Calvert mumbled something. He had the fedora pushed down over his forehead, his eyes darting around under the brim. I asked him what he said.

"Nobody has to know."

"*I* know."

"We're wasting time," Peck said. "Let's go. We'll argue about what to do later."

We went in three different directions. I told Calvert that if he found the deer first to stay with it, and we'd be by eventually. I mapped it out so we'd circle the perimeter and move toward the center, gradually tightening our radius. We'd end up in the upper canyon where I suspected the deer had gone to bed down, if it were still alive. The shot could have hit more bone than blood depending on where it went in the leg. I won't lie and say I didn't enjoy getting off a double lung shot. You could drop a bull moose with a clean shot like that, and I'd always been taught that was the fair shot you took—and you didn't take it until you were sure. I'd been hunting in Wyoming with an old friend and the wind had been blowing—though I won't blame it on that—and I got an elk in my sights. I squeezed the trigger and watched the animal crawl fifty yards with his legs splayed out in back before I could get there and put a bullet through his head. I'd hit him in the spinal column and paralyzed his backside. He'd been moaning when I got to him, and then a strangulated, gurgling sound came from deep in his throat. Todd, my hunting partner, didn't say anything more than "Damn wind," and there had been a terrible crosswind, but I had no business taking that shot and couldn't get the picture out of my mind of that creature dragging his hind legs like a busted wagon and trying to reach some kind of finish line that he thought would save him. I hadn't hunted since and that was six years ago.

Martin started barking when we came to a pile of brush with some wooden boards from a collapsed outbuilding. The deer, a big one close to three hundred pounds I figured, had its black-tipped tail drooped between its legs and had risen up from the thicket. His antlers were budding out and his coat had started to turn reddish brown from its winter gray; those big ears, were twitching independently of each other just like a mule's, trying to hear our movements upwind from him. He was considering whether it was worth bounding out of there, his flanks moving in and out like a bellows, exhausted, pained, and I saw too when he did bound up that his back leg was still barely attached to the bone. Calvert had shot him in the hip and about severed the leg. It was a horrible sight, worse than when I watched that bull elk crawl ahead like an amputee. This leg was swinging around as if it were a piece of the poor creature's intestine hanging out.

I squared my shoulders, calmed my shaking hands and squeezed my left eye shut to line up a shot that I prayed would go straight into his heart. It did, or close enough to drop him after a good two hundred feet before he flopped over. Martin ran up, sniffed warily and then backed off and lay down with his face on his front haunches whining and waiting for me. The buck's eyes bulged with hard pain in them. A mule deer ran different than a white tail, starting up from go and bounding eight feet and then coming down on all four feet at once like a landing craft, and I thought it was terrible to lose one of your legs when you got around like that, and that this buck had died without his due dignity.

I blew my whistle in short bursts. Before long Peck showed up. He'd already heard the shot, and we stood there silently looking over this big fellow and trying to decide what to do with him now. We could try to get one of our trucks up here and move him back to Peck's place and gut him there, but I didn't think that would be easy given the steep incline and loose shale down to this spot. If we were going to eat this meat, and I sure as hell wasn't going to let it go to waste, we needed to cut him up now and let him cool and then pack him out. The worst thing was to let him stay warm. He'd spoil for sure.

"Where's the kid?" Peck said to me.

"I don't know. Did you see him shoot it?"

Peck shook his head. "All I know is he's carrying around a pistol and shooting up things like he's in a saloon. I shouldn't have given them your number, Charlie. I should have checked with you first. We got no business letting strangers stay up here. This ain't no Woodstock."

"Can I have your knife?" I said.

Peck's knife was good and sharp, and I opened the chest cavity just below the sternum, cut around the diaphragm, and reached all the way up and felt for the trachea. If you did it right, cut from stem to stern, and you had the strength and a steady hand, you could pull the whole business down from the windpipe and avoid the mess of cutting out the gut sack by itself. I sliced the trachea across its diameter and started pulling. We each had a foot braced on one side of the buck and were yanking. I told Peck to hold up a moment while I sawed more through the center of the pelvis channel and then we started pulling again. It was the easiest way. I didn't want to cut out the organs one by one and risk piercing the gut sack and transferring the digestive juices to the meat and spoiling it. Somebody was going to eat this creature and do him the honor of a good death. It was ugly to think of his last hour or two with his leg twirling around like that. I stuck my hand back up past the lungs and grabbed inside the throat, and Peck pulled with me and we gave it one good heave and tore everything out. It was about then, just when I'd started to skin it and fold back the cape, that Calvert came up, panting. He took a good look at the buck's insides and bloody cavity and fainted.

Peck said, "This fella's one lame excuse for a human being." We stared at his sprawled out body and shook our heads. "If he don't come to in five, you'd better take him over to the hospital." I said I would and asked him what he thought I should do about the deer.

"Might as well enjoy it," he said.

"But should I report it?" Peck gave me a puzzled look. He'd bred horses all his life and knew them as well as anybody, but an animal was still an animal to him.

"Nobody's going to know any different if you don't."

"I'm not worried about somebody finding out. I just want to do what's right."

Peck opened his hands; he'd lost two of his left fingers in Vietnam. He was quiet about it except once to tell me he woke up every day and looked straight through that hole and saw the war. "If it was me? I'd get those people on their way and fill up your freezer with that meat. Case closed."

This made sense to me. You could say that an ignorant individual had made the mistake of thinking he could shoot his dinner and that it was more an accident than a crime. You could say, too, that they were young and naive. But what you couldn't say is that any of it was right, the way a crooked line down a highway wasn't right, and you had to fix it. I'd had a perfect record over the years of inspecting roads. I saw plenty of bulges and rough spots in the asphalt and places where the excavation had cut corners, and I had offers, some lucrative, if never put in so many words, to look the other way. Rosalyn once told me that cheating was so pervasive in the schools these days it was almost an anachronism to be honest, maybe even quaint. But I'd never been tempted.

When we got back to the cabin, Meredith was there staring dumbfounded at her groggy man coming through the door. She'd set up a little housekeeping in the cabin, a box of teabags and some water boiling in a pot on the stove, a couple toothbrushes and toothpaste on the one windowsill, and two sleeping bags rolled out on the bed next to a flashlight. This was no kind of place to be expecting a baby. I'd always planned to build on and shore up the foundation to get the drainage working right so there wasn't mold growing up the walls. The last owner had used the place for storage and that was about all it was good for now.

"What happened?" she asked, her eyes wide.

"I'll see you," said Peck—wisely making his exit. Up to my elbows in blood from reaching in for the deer's trachea, I'd washed my hands and arms in the stream, but you really never got out the stains unless you scrubbed at them with a brush. We had the deer and all its dismembered parts in the back of my truck after dragging up the whole mess—and Calvert too—on a tarp.

"He just needs to sit down," I said. "He fainted." I helped Calvert over to the bed and he lay down and held his head and moaned. He put his arms across his eyes and stayed that way. Meredith sat down next to him. "You have one?" she said to him. He made a clenching sound with his teeth and nodded. She turned to me. "He gets these terrible migraines. They make him vomit and faint." She got up and went over to a plastic jug of water. A towel and washcloth were laid out neatly on a corner of the bed and she picked up the washcloth and got it damp and then came back and folded it over Calvert's forehead. He was still gritting his teeth and his toes were pointed out the door, his fingers clenching the bare mattress.

"I'm going to report this in the morning."

Meredith turned her head toward me. "Report what?"

"The deer. You can't shoot a deer without a license and out of season too. Even on private property." I repeated what I'd told Calvert, it was illegal and despite having the animal all carved up in the back of my truck and my burying the carcass tomorrow, we'd broken the law of the land.

"I'm sorry. We should have asked permission first." She had changed from this morning and put on some stretchy pink sweatpants and washed her feet and combed her brown hair, her eyes a soft shade of jade. "Calvert didn't want to. He said we'd sell some of our stuff in town. But I can't wait. I need some meat now. My baby needs it. Calvert doesn't think so, but I know different. I'm hungry all the time."

"Where'd you shoot him?" She pointed down by the stream.

"I was *hungry*," she said again.

"You should have just asked. I could have brought you something."

"We're not beggars," she said.

Calvert moaned, "Your voices!"

"He can't stand noise when he gets like this," Meredith said. "Let's go outside and talk."

We stood there in the dark with the stars pulsing above and not an artificial light in sight. I had mixed feelings about running electricity over here and plundering the darkness. Peck's house was on the other side of the ridge and hidden from view. You could hear coyotes howling, and I'd seen the remnants of a mountain lion's kill, and what did it matter if another deer died on the property one way or another? I could hide the evidence, ignore the deed, and the taint to the land—the purest thing I had in my life at the moment—would disappear. But there's a thinner line between rigidity and tolerance than most people think. I'd always tried to stay on the latter side of that line, but I knew my position as of late had been corrupted by a foolish kind of anger that wanted everyone held accountable.

I went to my truck and got out my jacket and put it around her shoulders. She was standing there with her thin arms shivering and nowhere to go but back into that dark cabin with her partner sprawled out and his head exploding.

"I think about getting away." She looked back at the cabin.

"Are you afraid of him?"

"No." She pulled her arms tight around her chest. "Sometimes."

I wasn't surprised that Calvert who snapped his "Sir!" out at me might be the same fellow who could slap around this young woman not long out of her girlhood with her pretty pale face. For all that traveling she didn't have much color to her. She was more pallid than Rosalyn ever looked when she was pregnant and had three miscarriages, before we stopped trying. We had that river of disappointment under our feet, too.

"Come with me now," I said, and Martin trotted up behind me, as if to make his appeal too. He'd been guarding the tailgate of my pickup, with its deer payload.

She shook her head. "He'll find me. He'll—"

"You need to see a doctor. You need care. Nobody's going to harm you. I'll see to that. I know a lot of people here in town, folks who can help you legally." She winced at "legally."

"I don't want anything to happen to him," she said.

I had the idea that Calvert was no stranger to outstanding warrants, and that this had made my place more attractive to him than any so-called holiness. "I'll take you somewhere safe," I promised, and I had in mind the extra bedroom of my house, and if she wasn't comfortable with that—I had no untoward motives—I'd put her up in a motel and talk to the safe house people in Fort Collins where Rosalyn volunteered.

"I've got to go back in," she said.

"You need to eat. You need to take care of your baby."

"When he gets a migraine, he'll sleep forever afterward. I can meet you at the gate in the morning. I have to get my things out of the van and I want to make sure he's asleep because he has the keys in his pocket."

"I'll be here at dawn. Bring whatever you can carry and don't worry about the rest. We can fix you up later." The sleeves of my coat hung over her hands like sleepy puppets. I had all these thoughts I shouldn't have had, not the obvious ones that pertained to the wants of an older man in the presence of a young comely woman and how she might save his flesh and soul and that he might be so delirious he wouldn't know the difference between the two, but ideas about how the unexpected descended and snapped its fingers in your face and said "Awake!"

"You'll really come?"

I said I would. I'd be there at 5:45 when the sun cast its first light over the place.

I told her she could keep my coat, but she was already stripping it off saying no, Calvert would get suspicious. Before she ducked inside, she called back to me, "Bless you."

I woke with a start. I had left my wallet in my jacket pocket when I gave the coat to Meredith to put around her. I'd slept fitfully, if I did at all, on the surface of a plan that was simple in its execution and complicated in its reasons. Why was I getting involved? Peck had advised I chase them out of there as soon as I could. Rosalyn would have seconded that or told me to call social services and get the police involved if I suspected abuse. She would have told me I had some kind of hero complex to want to do this all myself, and maybe she'd be right.

I got up to check my jacket that I'd hung over the chair. My wallet was still there, all the money and credit cards inside, and I felt ashamed of myself for suspecting that Meredith had filched it while she was wearing the coat. I sat there a moment on the edge of the bed, flipping the wallet open and closed in my hands like a jackknife. I lay back down and must have fallen asleep because when the phone rang I jumped up again and didn't know where I was for a moment. The numbers on the clock said 4:50 a.m. and my first thought was that it was either Meredith or Calvert.

But it was Rosalyn. "I'm sorry," she said. "I...I feel terrible calling you."

"What's wrong?" I could hear her sniffling, then blowing her nose. "Where are you?"

"Home."

"From Atlanta?"

"I came home early."

I looked at the clock; it would take me twenty minutes to get from town to my land. Rosalyn never called at this hour. She was nothing if not independent and whatever motivated her to phone me up at five in the morning must have come at a price. "Speak to me, Rosalyn."

"I didn't know who else to call."

"Uh-huh," I said.

"I'm sitting here on the floor, it's dark, the house is cold, and I've got mascara running down my face. I didn't sleep on the plane—I took the red-eye back."

"What do you need, Roz?"

"Would you...would you bring Martin back today? I know it's earlier than I said, but I could really use his company. Is that all right, Charlie? Would you be okay with his coming here early?"

"I'll bring him over," I said. "I got to do something first, but I'll bring him back after."

"Thank you, I really appreciate it. I'm so sorry I woke you. I didn't know who else to call."

"You said that."

"You're mad at me."

"I'm not mad." I glanced at the clock again. Ten minutes had gone by, and I still had to throw my clothes on and scrub my face and teeth. I thought about that old saying, why buy the cow when you can get the milk for free? As far as I went with Rosalyn, she got the cow free and to hell with the milk.

"Why do men lie, Charlie?" She was slurring her words and I could picture the bottle next to her; Rosalyn always held the neck of a wine bottle like she was shaking your hand with a firm grip. "You never lied to me."

"I never lied to you," I agreed. I felt pain compress across my chest, as if someone were cinching a leather strap as hard as he could; if I hadn't been talking to Rosalyn, if I hadn't been witnessing her anguish over this man she loved the way she used to me, if I hadn't been thinking I could make it all better if she'd just give me another chance, I would have thought I was having a heart attack.

"Forgive me for waking you?"

"I was getting up anyway. I have an appointment." I heard her take a long gulp of whatever she was drinking.

"An appointment?"

"Somewhere I have to be."

"Oh," she said quietly.

"I'll bring Martin by afterward. Later this morning. I promise."

I went out the door, leaving Martin snoozing on the rug with his blanket smelling of me and Rosalyn both and drove up with one thought in mind, to get Meredith out of there. I should have had the sheriff come with me. I knew him a bit, and he was a calm, reasonable fellow, but I knew too Meredith would change her story out of guilt or fear if we both showed up.

She was waiting for me, just like she said, and she had a back-pack with her when I pulled up outside the gate. She looked just as forlorn as she had last night, but I shouldn't have been surprised when I got out of the truck and she gave me a wan, helpless smile, like she had no choice in the matter. Calvert stepped out from the clump of scrub oak where he'd been crouched down and pointed his pistol at my heart. The only thing I didn't know is whether or not they'd planned it from the beginning, whether Meredith had had any hesitation at all or just thought me another sad fool.

"You promised her money—if she'd fuck you." He jabbed the pistol toward me. "Right?" I looked at Meredith, that droopy mouth and pale hungered face and tried to find the truth in it.

"You told him that?"

"Shut up," said Calvert.

"What happened to 'sir'?"

"Fuck you. You were going to turn us in for shooting that deer."

"I still can."

He grinned at me, waving the gun around like he intended to lasso me with it. His fedora, with its dirty white feather, was pushed back on his head, and I saw he had a pretty good receding hairline. I should have been more afraid than I was; I don't know why I wasn't.

"You're a stupid old man, just like I thought."

"You going along with this?" I asked Meredith, who had her lips pressed tightly together.

"Hey, *you*," said Calvert. "Don't talk to *her*."

"You're not going to shoot me."

The dust splattered up at my feet. Nobody had ever shot at me before, and I stared at my feet. "Maybe I won't miss next time, old man. Maybe I'll get my deer."

"Let's just go," said Meredith. "Please."

"Throw your wallet over here!" Calvert commanded. "Get it," he told Meredith. And even this, the tone, I wondered if it was for my benefit alone. Would they have a good laugh down the road? Would she cry over what she'd done? Would they count my money and go for...whatever made them happy? Did he treat her so badly he owned her soul?

Calvert took out the cash and threw the wallet back at my feet. "Give me your keys," he said. I threw them to him. "Turn around and put your hands on that gate." He told Meredith to come over and tie my hands to the gate. She wouldn't look at me while she did. She smelled of wood smoke and oranges, and I told her so, and then I felt a whack on my head that turned my land dark.

"What happened to those people?" Rosalyn asked me later that day when I brought Martin over and she kneeled down for him to come running into her arms.

"They just left."

"Just like that?"

I snapped my fingers. "Just like it." She'd taken a shower and put on a black slip dress that had a scoop neck that showed off her freckled chest. Black for mourning or black for seduction; both were probably true. She wanted to see my eyes light up, to be appreciated by a man, even one cuckolded by thieves, a man who had decided he would stop punishing himself in all the obvious ways.

"Charlie," she said, "you look so tired. That's *my* fault." She seemed to have come out of her sorrow. I had a mean bump on my head and my vision wasn't back to normal, but I could see well enough to drive. The one thing Meredith had done for me was tie a slipknot, making it easy to get out.

"I've got to leave," I said.

"Another appointment?" Rosalyn said this teasingly. Then her face went soft as a bruised peach. "You want to come back tonight?" She never asked me over at night.

"I think I can do that," I told her.

Maybe fortune came with getting your head clonked.

She walked with me outside. "Whose is *that*?" she said when she saw the couple's blue van parked in the driveway.

"I'm borrowing it for a few days. From some acquaintances."

She stared at the bus with its bald tires and cracked windshield. "What's wrong with your truck?"

"Nothing. That I know of." I nodded at the van. "Makes me feel young again."

Rosalyn lifted her well-shaped eyebrows. "Oh yeah? You'll have to give me a ride in it sometime."

I smiled. "That I'll do."

I had one more job before I quit for the day. I drove the van back toward town. The seats smelled of cigarettes and the engine whined and lost what little power it had going up a small rise, but I had my arm out the window and it was beautiful spring afternoon, and I felt fitter than I should have when I pulled into the Division of Wildlife parking lot. You were supposed to leave them intact on the animal for state identification so the game warden could check your license to see that you'd shot the right sex, but I couldn't really bring the whole carcass in here and throw it across this gentleman's desk, could I?

"What you got there, mister?"

I untied the rose silk scarf that Meredith had left behind in the cabin, an awfully nice scarf for someone who had lived out of a robin's-egg blue van and had picked a bad seed of a man to father her child. "I take full responsibility," I said.

"What the hell..." The wildlife officer got one look at the buck's putty colored testicles and about gagged. But I was all about rules and doing right by them and making the best of what time I had left on this merciful earth.

Spin

The BLM auction took place at the county fair. In the corner of the world stood five sorry-ass enclosures with about twenty or thirty animals inside—mostly horses, but then a few burros, too, carted over from Yuma. It would be my horse, technically. I was just going to keep it at the Arizona School for Girls as part of an "enrichment program." They could call it anything they wanted for all I cared.

The website had featured two kinds of animals: sad little hopeful ones, waiting to be adopted, and robust thriving productive picture-book horses—the before and after of it all. I knew it had to be more complicated, but even so I wasn't prepared for what I saw. Behind those green bars the yearlings and the two-year-olds, mostly bays, were like wind, captured. They moved together. One heard a pin drop somewhere in Idaho, and they all skated to the other side of the enclosure, a whoosh and a rumble and then there they stood, in the new location. Side by side, facing the world as one, ready to go.

Still fenced in, however.

Let's just say it was hard to choose. They wanted blind bids, anything over a hundred and twenty-five dollars. I stared into each pen, mares on one side of the lot, geldings on the other, half ignoring and half catcalling to each other. I could be reasonable about this. I could check their legs, eyes, conformation. But I didn't want to be reasonable. I saw one who'd been in some kind of accident and had a scar running the length of her nose, I wanted her. I saw a beautiful dun who looked like he'd come from a herd far from the others, I wanted him. I saw two chestnut yearlings huddled nearly on top of one another, and I wanted them, too. I wanted every horse the BLM could sell me. I had to give up. I had to get away from there.

Then I saw him staring through the slats, looking at me, as if we'd made an agreement a long time ago and I was about to run off and forget all about it. He was a bay, probably just under two.

The tattoo under his mane looked like Chinese lettering. All the wild ones had these markings, white fur filling in the shapes of letters and numbers burned into their necks or haunches, a precaution against slaughter.

He looked away. I looked away. I looked back. He looked back.

The BLM cowboys were sitting in front of their trailer, shooting the shit and squinting at me, a horse gaper. I wrote down my offer. If you're not a gambler, you want to offer everything. If you find what you want, you're liable to offer it all. Not a hundred and twenty-six bucks, not two hundred. How about five hundred or a thousand? My horse, Number 433 from Elko, Nevada. I could see his ribs when he breathed out, short anxious huffs. He had a good coat, somewhere under the dirt and the burrs, and his legs were strong. He moved with the others, jammed together, but he kept one eye on me as I held on to the rail. Fifty thousand, a million? Still, he wouldn't come close to the fence. *It's all right,* I told him *telepathically, we'll talk later.*

I turned in the bid—just about what I had in savings, not quite as much as you'd hope for—and got a few *Thank you, ma'ams,* and *You'll get a call in forty-eight hours.*

The girls at the center weren't as attractive as they are on HBO: little jailbaits, the blonde troubled sexpot and her dark-haired, smart sister. These girls came stumbling out of the building and into the sunlight, eight lost souls in some kind of gym outfits. Jesus, they didn't need gym clothes for this—I'd told Jack Jones that. And couldn't he let them wear sunglasses? It was God fucking forsaken Arizona. They huddled together at first, the girls did, even in the heat. They had to stick together, form a large body to combat me: a new problem.

"Hi girls," I said, and waited. No response. "I'm Dr. Laura Benjamin, and I'm really glad to be here, glad to have this chance to be together."

"Glad someone's glad," said a girl with bangs in her eyes. I couldn't read her expression, but I can assure you it wasn't "winning," "happy," or "eager."

I launched in anyway. "As you know, the Bureau of Land Management culls the wild burro and horse herds in Arizona and across the United States, and these animals can be adopted. I've adopted a two-year-old, and today we're bringing him here. This is an opportunity for us to raise him together."

"Horses are dumb as hell," said someone.

"What makes you think horses are dumb?" I asked. Still fresh, still inquiring.

"I grew up on a ranch, Doc, and horses were just about the dumbest animal, just about as dumb as—"

"Dumb as dumb ass you?" said a compatriot.

"Shut the fuck up."

"You've got to be dumb as hell to end up here," said another girl. Her arms were crossed over her chest; she had long hiding hair.

"Look, ladies. I don't really care if you think horses are dumb or not. You signed up for this program—right? It's better than P.E. or whatever. It's better than watching, what, Oprah. So you're going to learn something about an animal. About taking care of the horse. You're going to help me train this beauty, and, over time, he's going to be a good companion for us. It's going to be something to see."

"So you like took this horse from the wild, out where he was free? You took him from the place he grew up and you're dropping him here? What's the point of that? What makes that so great?"

"What makes that so great? Well, for one thing, if they get thirsty out there and can't find water, that's it, they die a long gruesome dehydrated death. If they break their leg, they fall down and rot. If they get sick—it's a slow miserable road to horse hell. It's the end of the little pony story. That's what makes it so great. It's better here. All right? Better to be alive, don't you think?"

They looked blankly at me. Eight girls, mostly a little overweight, some too thin entirely. Most were brunettes; half were white, half Hispanic. All wore mesh shorts and teal T-shirts that read *A Better Day*.

"All right. Here's the trailer." Take a deep breath, doctor. "Now, listen. The horse is going to be pretty freaked out at first, all right? So you can watch us get him out of the trailer, but you've got to step back, back by the fence there, and don't make any sudden movements or noises, okay?"

"Now she's telling us what to do," a girl said.

"Stay away from the horse," someone else said slowly, replete with irony.

"He's going to need patience," I said, under the bluest sky imaginable. "But the first thing he needs will be a little space."

"What's his name, Mrs. Doctor?"

"He doesn't have a name yet," I said. The trailer was backing up to the gate.

"Call him fucking Lucky," I heard behind me.

"Fucking good idea," I said. I wasn't here to be a disciplinarian.

When I opened the trailer door there he was, sad as a creature can be, huddled up against the side of the stall. Once the light hit him, he started knocking at the trailer with his front hoof, as if he'd scramble up the aluminum if he could. Then he slammed the side with his body, and the whole trailer trembled and the din drove him crazy. He lurched back, pulled sideways, hit the end of the rope, swung toward the wall, lurched, knocked, swung, shook like a baby. It was a complete disaster, worse than when we got him from the BLM site to the clinic; worst I'd ever seen.

"What do you think?" said Jan, from the clinic—she'd driven him out for me. "Tranqs?"

"No. Jesus. I'm trying to show these girls a better way." Eight juvenile delinquents and I'm going to pull out the drugs immediately?

He was back to climbing the wall; he was quaking in the corner.

"I can take care of this."

"Don't get hurt now," said Jan.

"Man, that horse's totally mad!" said one girl.

"He hates it here!"

"Don't worry," I said—full of bravado, right? "It just takes a little time. Getting in and out of the trailer is the hard part. If he could get it through his head that my being here means his freedom, things will start going our way. I'm just going to open these windows, see? Open these windows on the side."

I was stalling, is what I was doing. Baffled completely. I wasn't a horse trainer by profession, just someone with my head filled with hay.

"C'mon, let's go over here," I said to the girls. "Sit."

I was met with a chorus of mumblings about sand and scorpions, but they all sat down. The horse stood stoically, ass to me, like we'd never met before, like he was in the process of getting sentenced for a crime against the country.

Finally he turned his head and looked toward us. Briefly curious—then he turned his head back. A couple more minutes passed. He looked again, a longer scrutiny. After he turned back to the wall, he stomped a foot: not fury this time, but impatience. I got up; I started back in. *Come on, come on, come on. Do me this favor, little one.*

I got a hold of the halter and unhooked him from the trailer. Leaned on him, leaned on him hard, and one step back, two steps back, I was in a storm. A rush of noise from all directions, hooves on metal, wooden slats groaning, and we were at the edge, down the plank, turned around.

I released his halter and he was gone. Pissed right off. Pissed at me and everything I stood for. He ran to the far end of the corral, jammed up against the fence, snorted, ran again—this time full-tilt to the other end. No luck there, either. He raised his head high as love. He was never going to look our way again.

"Okay," I said, brushing my hands together, pleased with myself.

I turned to the group of girls standing by the fence. A couple of them were comparing tattoos; one had lifted her shirt and was looking at her stomach. A girl with short red hair, red as in Bozo red, watched me with an unnaturally mild expression, like she was the best pickpocket in the world.

So the girls were right. So maybe the horse wasn't as happy as he might have been elsewhere. The BLM culls the healthiest, the "adoptable" horses. In other words, the good ones are taken from their home, away from the landscape they've memorized under their hooves, tracing and retracing their geography, their history. So what was I supposed to do, object to everything? Say no, fuck it, I'm going home?

The next day I sat for a couple of hours against the shade structure (to call it a barn would be going way too far). Lucky was walking. He walked and walked, staring down into himself, down into a dark and empty well. When I first ducked under the fence and slid down to sit, he'd swished his tail and trotted to the other end of the corral. Now he was mostly ignoring me, but every once in awhile I'd catch his eye—and then we'd both look away again, like we were back at the auction.

This technique, Magazine Reading in Vicinity of Corralled Animal, didn't look fancy, it wasn't in the books, but I didn't want to rush him.

"Is he lonely, do you think?"

"What?" I asked, turning around. It was the girl with clown hair. She had a tattoo around her neck, I noticed this time, like a black chain choker.

"He knows I'm here," I said. "You're in the class, right?"

"Yeah." She showed me her profile then: proud, lucky.

I should have asked if she had a pass or something—the place was replete with rules of every kind. I'd been sitting in the heat, not rushing the horse, for a long time by then.

"You want to come in?"

"So it's some sort of feel good program?" Jack Jones had said on the phone, when I'd first pitched him the idea. "The girls get in touch with themselves?" I explained that it was more than that. Better, even, than that. "As long as you keep the disruption down," he'd finally said, after a meandering rumination on the school's thirtieth anniversary, on extracurricular this and that, and on what the goddamned hoity-toity delinquents were doing up in Phoenix.

Girl-units. He used the term *girl-units* once.

This girl—her name was Kris—sat down next to me and pulled her knees up close to her chest. Her regulation khakis were blown out and frayed at the knee. Right away she started worrying the hole with her finger.

Lucky was standing by the westernmost fence, staring out past the school's property, a half dozen saguaros and some mesquites and scrub brush and some old equipment (torture devices, for when punishing the girls had more range?). *Go west, young pony!* And actually, yes, west was the way home—three hundred miles west and six hundred north and he'd be back where he began.

"He's nervous," she said.

"It's going to take awhile to get used to it here." I glanced at the girl. Her home was some kind of Stephen King nightmare building, nothing really wrong that you could immediately put your finger on.

"Yeah."

"Do you like animals?"

"Who doesn't like animals?"

"True," I said, too quickly. You want to ask, "So what are you in for?" But that question seems like a lie, and everything else is a mistake.

"I used to have a horse," she said after awhile. She was watching the pony watching us.

"Did you? Neat." Now I was a moron. "Neat" was an anaesthetized little word, like I was trying to cozy up to a Mouseketeer. "When was that?"

"At my first dad's. Long time back." She started twisting a hunk of her hair. "Of course, at this hellhole, no pets allowed."

"Yeah."

"But now we've got Lucky."

I smiled into the sun. "We do," I said. "That's right."

Every Tuesday and Thursday the lady administrator handed me a sheet of paper, eight names altogether, and on the other days I just came out at lunch or after work, whenever I could squeeze it in. Lucky and I stared across the corral making monkey faces at each other. Kris joined us maybe half the time. She'd see my truck, I guessed, though I never really asked. In a few minutes there she'd be, a red comet ducking under the fence.

"What was she *like?*" Kris said one Wednesday afternoon, responding to yet another of my grown-up drone questions. She laughed, threw a pebble. "Well, it depends."

"Yeah? On what?"

"Once she made me this amazing dollhouse. She found this bookcase on the street, you know? And fixed it all up with these little rooms and with lamps and curtains and all this? It took her like a whole week to do it."

"Nice."

Kris was staring at the horse, her eyebrows completely, as in Clint Eastwood, scrunched. It really was fucked up that they wouldn't give the girls sunglasses for Christ's sake.

I said, "So, that was awhile back?"

"Yup."

Somewhere a sun stroked dove was calling, as if it had forgotten the time of day.

"When you were just a kid," I said, half to myself, all pissed off.

"She got us back one time, for about six months. Then she lost custody again. It was mostly the drug thing."

I blamed Jack Jones. I didn't have anyone else to blame so I thought I'd blame him.

"She's out there somewhere, doing her own thing I guess," said Kris, dropping her head back to rest on the fence. A Roman warrior in repose, red hair, tattooed choker unaccountably moving, like she was holding something in or something down.

I hated talking, I really did. I've always hated talking. "How long have you been in here," I asked the ground.

"Since Christmas."

I drew a line in the sand with my finger, erased it again.

"I want to stay," she said.

"Stay here?"

"I saw this show on TV, where they trained a horse in like two hours. It's not like that really? It'll take longer?"

Lucky: the name was a way to trace him, to run your hand along his mane, his back, his black tail.

"Yeah, we're just going to take it easy with him. I want him to get to know us first, you know? Get to know his surroundings. We'll get him used to us, and then we'll teach him on the lunge line, and then try the saddle and bridle. It could take years—months, anyway."

"I want to stay for all that," she said, and then looked at me as if I'd just said something harsh—like it was going to rain or something might rip—but I hadn't said anything.

Sometimes the heat here becomes a shape, as if it's hauling itself into the form of an apparition of some kind, and then you sigh, or pass out, and everything is muted/normal/gone again.

A couple of days later Jack Jones called me into his office.

"The animal benefits from human interaction—that's the whole point," I tried to tell him. "And the girls, they benefit—"

With his hands, he made a little fascist church. Here's the steeple. "That's terrific, Doctor, but Kristine G. Wick and the others must, first and foremost, adhere to the rules of the Arizona Home for Girls. Then and only then does your animal therapy program come into play."

"The corral is, what, ten feet from the building? So, what? They're not allowed out of the building during the day? Did Kris miss a class or something?"

"She missed recess. She missed lunch."

"Recess, Jack? I mean, I can see the issue with lunch."

He kept his eyes leveled at me then, practicing his Intimidation Stare—good for the headmasters of girls' detention centers. I kept my mouth shut for a minute. I could do this, I thought.

"I'll talk to her," I said, just to get out of there. Jack swung his bright white sneakers up onto the desk and leaned back, head resting in his palms.

"You better do more than that."

"Well, but—I didn't actually miss lunch, I mean, I ate my food and everything?" she said to me. We were sitting by the fence in the corral.

"Really?" I said. "Figures. Okay, just keep an eye out for Jack, got it?"

"Right."

Bureaucratic bullshit.

Lucky had gotten pretty comfortable with us by then. He didn't balk and snort when we came in under the fence, a young one and an old one, dodging the splinters in the railing. Sometimes we'd both read magazines, sometimes we'd talk. After I'd dispensed with my message from Jack, I handed Kris *Veterinary Medicine*, and I had some newsletters to read. She was reading the drug ads at the back of the magazine when I suddenly had this feeling.

"Okay, Kris, you ready?"

"Ready for what, Dr. Benjamin?"

I'd already told her about the all-important "join-up," the moment I'd read about in some of the training materials, seen on a video that came to us at the clinic. I believed it could work. You had to believe in something. If you weren't going to truss up their legs and hobble them into submission, you had to have a backup plan.

"I don't know, I mean—you said he wasn't ready," she said, when I told her what I was thinking. "Aren't we supposed to wait for him to come to us or something?"

"We can't wait forever, right? May as well meet him halfway. Just go out there, go out a little ways."

"Well, okay," she said—seesawing up, awkward. I got up, too. She ran her hand through her hair. We were both pretty excited then.

"Go on," I said. "I'll stay back here, by the fence."

Standing, you become smaller in a corral in the middle of nowhere, save one monolithic building on your right and a tilted sign at the end of a long driveway—pockmarked, actually, with bullets. Arizona Home for Girls. What would the Road Runner do here? Probably side with the administration and clock the coyote with a piece of lead. You become small, under the sun. Weak, little, not much breath to speak of. But Lucky stood strong, magnificent.

Kris put one soft foot in front of the other. She stretched her arm out in the gentlest arc.

The horse stopped his phantom chewing and looked at her, his head still close to the ground. She moved a little closer, stopped again. Ten feet between them. She stood for the longest time. She wasn't looking at Lucky anymore, but at the ground.

The sun went up another mile, radiated outward, a nuclear pinprick. The horse sighed, swayed forward on his front legs and went back to center. Blinked. Kris was standing alone in the dirt corral, like the red bull's eye of the universe. Finally Lucky dislodged himself from his lonely place, his famous last stand, and took one, two steps, toward her outreached hand.

I drove home unbothered by the traffic on Oracle, on Ina. I was driving into the wind, my windows open, the radio loud. I didn't know what I'd do for dinner. Pizza, I thought. I didn't know who to call, what to do with the daylight left. Seemed only right to keep driving—to drive, and sing, until it was night.

Two weeks later things were still going great with the horse. After Kris got him to come up to her that first day, I joined the two of them. We stood on either side of him for a few minutes, touching his body like we were blind. I pulled a burr out of his mane. The next few days—okay, with a little reluctance, a little backtracking—we were able to lead him to the fence, lead him around the corral. The girls started grooming him with me on Tuesdays and Thursdays. You should have seen them with that horse. At first, they were like, "Ew, disgusting," but then it was as if I'd gotten them the biggest Barbie model in the store, and they brushed, and primped, and combed him to a shine.

Kris had forgotten that part where she wanted things to go slowly. She was greedy for the horse, wanted to get her hands all over him. She still couldn't quite get the hand over hand motion to trot him in circles with the lunge line, but she'd been walking him close, up and down the fence, and in some figure eights of her own. I told her I thought we'd be able to ride him by fall. "You up for some hard work?" I'd asked. She'd said, "Nothing's hard with Lucky."

We'd sort of started ignoring the whole missing-lunch thing. She didn't bring it up again, and neither did I—and pretty much I had been avoiding Jack Jones.

Then I got a call from him. Five in the morning, some girls had tripped an alarm sneaking back into the building. They'd been out with the horse; they'd given him some food. Now he was sick—lying down. *I thought I told you this had to be a no-problem situation? A see-no-evil, smell-no-ponyshit kind of deal?*

Manny the non-English-speaking maintenance man met me in the driveway. He gestured toward the *caballo.* "Muy mal, senora."

Muy mal, indeed.

Lucky was in the corral. Above the mountain, a tide of pink disappeared into the flat light of dawn. His neck was hot. His stomach was strained and bloated, his eyes rolled to the side. I threw open my bag and took his pulse and temperature. Cheese puff bits were everywhere, orange confetti. A domesticated horse would eat himself sick too, but a horse that's gone from meager roughage in the desert to this? How many bags of cheese puffs did they find in that goddamned kitchen? How many cheese puffs does it take to choke a horse?

"Can you help me?" I said to Manny—shouted, really.

I got the equipment from the truck and Manny held the horse's head while I forced the tube down. Behind me I heard Jack Jones shouting at the girls who'd come trotting out, shorebirds to the wave's edge. Later I'd remember seeing Kris there, in her Tweety Bird nightgown and big untied sneakers, her arms crossed tightly against her stomach.

They'd called me in time. Within an hour, he was standing back up. Drinking water, too, before I left for the clinic. When I came back a few hours later, it was as if nothing had ever happened. The crazy horse wanted food more than anything.

On the way out Thursday, I rehearsed a full-tilt speech on responsibility and horse care for the girls. Now, I *thought* I'd gone through this before, but I guess the message hadn't really sunk in. (Though the girls had looked terrified the other morning, horse down.) I'd go over the fact that Lucky was a wild animal, dependent on us now. I'd use Kris as an example. I'd say, *Look what she's done.*

The ground around the building was tamped down, dark and hardened by an early monsoon the night before. The rain had released a smell from the greasewoods and mesquites, bitter and strange.

"What does this mean?" I asked—two times. Luanne and Twila looked at each other. They weren't surprised by it, by anything. But I, the teacher, self-appointed horse angel, didn't get it at all.

Hall, Luann
Lauterio, Lisa
Rivera, Dorothy P.
Roan, Enriqueta
Smitt, Libby Rebecca
Torrez, Maria
Villareal, Twila

And instead of *Wick, Kristine G.*, there was a new girl at the bottom of the list.

There she was, *White-Eagle, Donna,* standing at a distance from the others, holding her arm with the opposite hand. Her elbow was bent in the wrong direction, double-jointed.

I turned and went inside to talk to Jack. He looked up from a phone call, gave some kind of glamour-actor smile and waved me to a chair until he finished talking.

"What can I do you for? How're all creatures great and small?"

He said she'd been reassigned.

"Re-fucking assigned?"

"You want to get reassigned too?"

"You can't reassign everything," I said, unknowing.

The girls were waiting for me when I got back outside, quiet, faces screwed up in the sun. I didn't go through with my speech.

They took turns grooming Lucky, first Twila and then Donna and then Luann. Each girl had her own scent. I knew this from standing near them, helping them figure out how to care for the horse. Each had her own personal blend of grief, Suave shampoo, and perfume. Each girl, too, had a little different way of holding the brush, holding her own hair so it didn't fall in the way. Lucky, the luckiest horse in the world, let himself be groomed. Then the forty-five minutes was over and all the girls went inside and I was alone.

He stood, brushed to velvet, believing that I had won.

I snapped on the lunge line, a twenty-four foot green tether, and we walked together to the wide part of the corral. His gait was smoother now; he didn't as often trip over invisible stones. *Your honor, I must disagree,* I would say. *Your honor, as a doctor of veterinary medicine and an instructor of young girls—*

The saguaros stood guard around us, wouldn't let us go. I began to let out the line, hand over fist, backing away from the pony. Tension animated the rope, drew it taut between us. He sighed, threw his head down for a moment, then stumbled into a trot. Two years old, fourteen point two hands, bay. Dog food.

I followed him with my eyes, and then my body. My arms and hands held the rope, and he began to whirl around me. I followed him, circling, circling, my footprints a hash in the sand.

Sunday Morning at the Marlin Cafe

1.

I knocked on the picture window of the Marlin Cafe, trying to get the bartender's attention, so I could get in and have a Sunday morning hangover drink. The Marlin was an old man's dive on Broadway near Cathedral Parkway, a street that everyone in the neighborhood called 110th Street. Technically, the bar was closed. But if the bartender knew you, he'd let you in. As I knocked on the window, I noticed one customer near the door. He appeared to be a local pizza-parlor waiter who often drank there, though sometimes I mistook him for the famous Russian poet, Joseph Brodsky, who I'd seen occasionally having a drink in the bar, too. The Marlin stood in the extreme southwest corner of what might be considered historical Harlem. Most people referred to the neighborhood as "Morningside Heights," though the comedian George Carlin, a former native—he of the seven words you can't say on television—called it "White Harlem," which is more funny than true. Morningside Heights danced with more cultural diversity than just about any neighborhood on the planet.

I had lived for many years down the block from the Marlin. This Sunday morning ritual of looking for a drink when the bars were closed was nothing new. Yet each time I swore I would never do it again because the wait for the bartender to open the door was eternal and humiliating. Now I knocked harder on the window, either to attract the bartender Don or one of his customers.

Finally Don stopped what he was doing and came to the door, unlatching the lock.

"Well, look what the cat dragged in. What do you want?"

"To come in," I said, shaking.

"For what?"

"A drink," I answered.

"What the fuck makes you think I want to serve you a drink?"

"Because I'm a nice guy and you love me, Don."

The bartender was well over six-feet tall, barrel-chested, big-limbed, and nasty. He kept a baseball bat behind the bar and would use it if provoked. He was not the good-listening-type barkeep, but one of those restless, irritated, opinionated New York bartenders who could care less about a customer's needs. Don served you not when you wanted to be served, but when he was good and ready.

"Listen, you homo, you start coming on to me, and I'll never let you in the joint."

After a little more banter, the bartender let me in, probably because he was getting thirsty.

When I sat down at my usual spot—maybe three or four stools from the entrance—I drank a few beers and got my bearings.

Don sat on a stool behind the bar. I made the mistake of thinking that this was an invitation to conversation. The bartender had been a combat veteran in the Korean War, and somehow we got on the subject of the Chosun peninsula.

"You'd be surprised how much Korea has changed," I said because at the time I frequently traveled to East Asia. I tried to tell Don how he could travel there for free under a government program that invited Korean War veterans back to see the land they fought for.

"Look, asshole," he said, "the last place on earth I want to hear about is that godforsaken hellhole where I lost my fuckn innocence. Do me a fuckn favor, shut up or drink up and get the fuck outta here."

Just then the man who had been sitting at a stool near the door came back from the men's room.

"Oh, Jesus, Khrushchev is back!"

It was then that I realized it was Joseph Brodsky, the Russian poet.

"Vodka," he said.

Although he was supposed to be setting up the bar for the day, the bartender was getting hammered, something he did every day he worked. After pouring more vodka for the great Russian poet, Don the bartender opened a beer, sat down in front of me, and watched the television set at the other end of the bar. The station was HBO, and it was Richard Pryor doing his shtick.

Joseph Brodsky watched the show, too.

"Abomination!" he screamed.

"Shaddup!" Don called back at him, and the poet fell silent. Then Brodsky got up and went to the men's room again.

"I don't like his Roosky ass," Don said.

"That's Joseph Brodsky," I whispered.

"I know who it is," the bartender answered. "He's a cheap son-of-a-bitch who makes too much noise when he gets drunk in here."

"Brodsky?" I asked, astonished. Somehow, I couldn't believe a word that Don was saying. Joseph Brodsky was one of the most patrician writers in the world, a person of impeccable tastes. He had been teaching at Columbia on and off for years. He was moments away from being awarded the Nobel Prize for Literature.

The Russian poet came back to his stool at the end of the bar, took a seat, drank his vodka, and stared intently at Richard Pryor on the television set.

Once again Brodsky appeared agitated. He pointed at the television set posted above the far end of the bar. Shaking his fist at the set, his whole body seemed to quake.

"This is what's wrong with America!" he yelled.

"What the fuck are you yappin' about?" Don asked.

"Profanity. Obscenity. The need to be so vulgar. Why do people have this need to be so vulgar?" He caught his breath. "Expletives. Horrible words. Unnecessary figures of speech. All of it from the street." He drank his vodka. "This need to expose every part of the body for laughter and ridicule!"

"Hey!" Don shouted, drawing a bead with his long arm and meaty fist in the Russian poet's direction. "One more word..."

"This is what's wrong with America," Brodsky repeated.

"Hey, you don't like it," Don shouted, then under his breath he added, "go back to the Soviet Union, ya son-of-a-bitch."

The bar got quiet again. Brodsky drank his vodka. Don set up the bar, taking occasional breaks to drink his own beer. My shakes had settled into a benign quiver. But finally Joseph Brodsky could take it no longer.

"Turn off this abomination!" he ordered the bartender.

"Keep your shirt on!" Don screamed back. "I'm watching the fuckn thing."

The Russian poet looked so upset that I thought he might have cardiac arrest right there at the bar.

"This man is terrible. How do you allow him on your media? To rant and rave in this obnoxious and vulgar manner. America has become a decadent country. You have no restraints. You allow this vulgarity—this profanity—to be spread throughout the world. It is like a virus. A contagion. It is an insult. It is..."

Don had not yet arrived at the handle of his baseball bat, but I could tell he was getting close to a meltdown. He banged his huge hand on the wooden bar in front of Brodsky. Then the bartender hunkered down the way Don did when he was going to make a point. He almost looked like Jackie Gleason's Joe the Bartender. Bits of his wild hair streamed over his eyebrows and across his eyes and he pushed it back with his other hand. His eyes grew big and he appeared to be a humongous pug or French bulldog. Something looked dangerous and potentially violent in Don's manner. It was an effect not unlike Marlon Brando's Don Corleone. He had the poet's attention.

"Look, asshole, one more word out of you, and you're out of here, you're history..."

Brodsky was about to speak, but Don slammed down his big fist on the bar again.

"I'm the boss here, you understand? I can lose my license serving youse before the legal hours."

"I understand," Brodsky said, quite formally. "I am sorry."

"Well, understand this: I'm going to set up my bar and not be bothered by you or anyone else. I'm going to listen to Richard Pryor on Sunset Strip or wherever the fuck he is. Why? Because he's funny. That's why. He's funny. And you're not. You ain't funny at all. You're a royal pain in the ass. That's what you are. Am I making myself clear?"

"This is not civilized!" Brodsky shouted.

After Don smashed his fist into the bar one more time, the poet stopped arguing with him. The bar got awfully quiet. But as soon as Don went into the back room for more cases of beer, Joseph Brodsky went back to his criticism of Richard Pryor's stand-up comedy routine. I pointed to Richard Pryor on the television.

"He's like Aristophanes," I said.

At first he ignored me. Then he said, "It is nothing like Aristophanes. Language is the domain of poets. The Greek dramatists were all poets first and playwrights second. Language was their domain. This fellow is not using language. He is speaking words—vulgar words from the street. No, no, you're wrong. This has nothing to do with Aristophanes."

The poet seemed to mumble to himself.

"The Greeks," he said, "are a different matter, since they rubbed shoulders with us quite a bit."

Then he said things that were not necessarily intelligible to me but perhaps were a shorthand to himself, maybe a way of making notes for a poem or an essay. I heard him use the word "Homer." He went on: "All we know are a dozen lines of Aeschylus, nothing more. Not much more than that with Euripides either. Passing references. Nomads don't deserve any better. We know Ovid. That's it. Virgil doesn't acknowledge us. Nor Catullus nor Propertius. And, now, behold this crumb from the table. Aristophanes, he says."

Joseph Brodsky, the future Nobel Laureate, paused to drink his vodka. He looked at me as if I were a hallucination in the delirium tremens. Not only was I unreal, I was beneath contempt, certainly not worth engaging in conversation. But the poet did respond.

"Aristophanes," he said, "was never vulgar simply for the sake of being vulgar, was he?"

But before I could answer him, he asked who I was.

I told him my name.

I wanted to tell him that Richard Pryor was in a long theatrical tradition that went back to ancient Greek comedy, as vulgar a tradition as you'd find anywhere. I wanted to say that Pryor went further back than that, maybe back to Sicily and even Atellan farce, with characters like Bucco, wearing their rabbit's foot for good luck and their leather phalluses to assure fertility—and maybe a few jokes. What I wanted to tell Joseph Brodsky was that drama itself was an obscenity, a collision of the sacred and the profane that was propelled by the rituals of a nearly religious fervor combined with vernacular stories.

"What do you know of Greek drama?" he shouted.

Then he answered his own question: "Nothing! That is what you know about Greek drama. Nothing!"

2.

Joseph Brodsky won the Nobel Prize for literature in 1987. A year later I got sober. Joel Oppenheimer, the Black Mountain poet whom I studied with at the Poetry Project on the Lower East Side of Manhattan in the 1960s, died a few months after I got out of rehab. Seymour Krim—my colleague at the Writing Program at Columbia University and my former prose-writing teacher from the St. Mark's in the Bowery days—committed suicide the year after Joel died. A year or two after that the Marlin Cafe went out of business. I see cause and effect with several of these events, namely the Marlin closing and my getting sober. One of the last times I saw that bartender Don, he stood outside the bar, beckoning me to come in. When I told him that I didn't drink anymore, he assured me I'd be back for more. "Oh, you'll be drinking again. Make no mistake about it. You'll be in here drinking like the rest of us." Then he angrily walked back into the bar. I thought that he would drop dead first—before I drank again. I was right about Don. But I was wrong about Joseph Brodsky.

I found his poetry too formal for my tastes, being someone who studied with Joel Oppenheimer and Seymour Krim at the Poetry Project in the East Village. But what brought me back to Brodsky's writing was his prose, not his poetry. Nonfiction had become my passion. I had moved to Boston and was teaching workshops in memoir and personal essay, and I had come across his piece on Marcus Aurelius in a paperback anthology. At first his prose struck me the way his poetry did. I found it too formal. But this superficial response was superseded by a deeper one. I remember taking the anthology and placing it in the bathroom of my studio apartment. The anthology lay there with other books, newspapers, and magazines, but I ignored it. I refused to get beyond my pat response to it—too formal, too academic, too patrician. But I read beyond the first long, heroic paragraph into the second elongated paragraph. I took the anthology from the bathroom to the bedroom. I read some more. The next thing I knew I had the anthology in a knapsack and I took it with me to a nearby cafe. I sat and read the essay from start to finish.

Marcus Aurelius did not interest me but Joseph Brodsky did. Put another way, the poet-turned-prose-writer made me want to know more about the Roman leader. Isn't that always the case with a good personal essay? It is the voice that seduces us, not the content; it is the rhythm of the prose that draws us in, not the thoughts necessarily. At least I am more often attracted to an essay by the prose style. It is only later that the content registers. This has been true for me reading Thoreau just as it has been reading Orwell. In fact, it is the rhythm of Emerson's essays that I most struggle with, not the thoughts themselves. Still, by the end of reading about the Roman leader Marcus Aurelius, I had learned quite a bit about the ancient Romans that I did not know.

I had vowed, upon graduating from high school, never to let myself be drawn into another Roman narrative as long as I lived. I had suffered through Latin in nine years of parochial school and in the liturgy of the Mass. My language in high school also had been Latin, and I remember struggling through Virgil and Ovid in my senior year. That's when I vowed never to revisit this material, though I can't remember ever reading about Marcus Aurelius in these Latin journeys when I was growing up. Perhaps that is why I was willing to read the essay, because Brodsky's prose rhythms were so good that they drew me into his orbit.

The prose of that first essay was sculpted and muscular, the paragraphs long and elegant, flowing well beyond the confines of a single page. I love a well-written paragraph. I am reminded of George Orwell's observation that as long as he remained healthy and well he would continue to take an interest in prose style. The best prose writers compose, and their measure is the paragraph, not the sentence. This is as true for Kafka as it is for Proust, for Melville as it is for Conrad; the paragraph is what drives their prose. With Emerson and Thoreau, the difference was how they composed.

Yet, for all my admiration for Joseph Brodsky's essay, I did not pursue his writing any further until I read *Watermark,* his prose incantation to the city of Venice. Here was nonfiction that was lyrical and quirky; it was driven by long paragraphs that rolled off the page. *Watermark* had no chapters per se, only bursts of prose, no more than a paragraph or two in length, the storyline not so much linear as like a collage. Venice is revealed not by narrative but by such poet's devices as images and metaphors, characterizations and the evoking of particular moods.

"In winter you wake up in this city, especially on Sundays, to the chiming of its innumerable bells," Brodsky writes, "as though behind your gauze curtains a gigantic china teaset were vibrating on a silver tray in the pearl-gray sky. You fling the window open and the room is instantly flooded with this outer, peal-laden haze, which is part damp oxygen, part coffee and prayers."

A prose writer sees a "pearl gray sky," but it is a poet who notices the "peal-laden haze" of both the sky and the tolling bells. Most poets write prose that is too dense; the prose lacks spokenness. It is the rare poet who writes prose that is as good as their poetry. Yeats, Coleridge, Valery, Shakespeare, Dante—all wrote impeccable prose. Joseph Brodsky's prose is in that rarefied company. When he referred to Venice as "part damp oxygen, part coffee and prayers," he employed common speech to evoke the city, and yet, like Dante in another era and city, it was the vernacular that rendered such prose into poetry. *Watermark* was another way for Joseph Brodsky to write poetry, but these poems were in prose—prose poems.

What makes Brodsky's Venice different from a shelf-full of other books on the city is the prose, but also the temperament. He chose to visit the eternal city at the dreariest time of year—during his winter breaks from an American university—when the city was wet and cold and inhospitable. He would return to Venice time and again, almost like a monastic figure making a pilgrimage.

3.

This perambulation that began with an essay on Marcus Aurelius and progressed through a short, lyrical paean to Venice seemed to prod me to read more of Brodsky's nonfiction. Finally, I read a copy of *Less Than One*, his first essay collection that had come out around the time I had my run-in with him at the Marlin Cafe. The archness, the cleverness, the imperiousness—all the things that irritated me about him in the bar—were apparent in the essays. Yet here I found myself admiring what was being said. Had I changed or did he? In an essay called "A Poet and Prose," Brodsky says that "a poet can get along without prose," but I kept thinking to myself that his prose had a voice, an accessibility, and even a brilliance that I had not experienced in reading his poetry. Brodsky had mastered the English language well enough that his prose in these essays was as good as the best prose written in English. What I especially admired about the essays was how Brodsky was both deeply formal and colloquial, the way all the great essay-ists were from Montaigne to E. B. White to Joan Didion to Annie Dillard to Tobias Wolff to Joseph Epstein. In many respects, the prose was as rich and intellectual as Walter Benjamin's, only more conversational, less angst-freighted. Brodsky's essays also remind-ed me of Susan Sontag's early essay collections that were intellec-tually revealing and stylistically elegant. His poetry, of course, is translated, and as Brodsky was a great admirer of Robert Frost, I am sure he would not disagree with the New Englander when Frost observed that poetry is that which is lost in translation. The prose entertained and moved me in ways that his poetry did not; finally it changed me, too, because I no longer could look at that Sunday morning in the Marlin Cafe quite the same way. The moral fervor of the essays was an attractive quality; the ranting moralist of the bar was not.

4.

It was in his Nobel lecture that Brodsky's objections to someone like Richard Pryor became utterly clear, even if I don't share his certitude about language and morality. I don't think his objec-tions to the profane utterances of Richard Pryor were driven by class or race. In the Nobel lecture he speaks of his distrust for the language of the street because it is "an attempt to subordinate art, in this case literature, to history." The poet did not believe that lit-erature must speak the language of the people—or the street—but rather "the people should speak the language of literature." I suppose that Joseph Brodsky did not hear Richard Pryor speaking the language of literature. Of course, he had not studied poetry with Joel Oppenheimer at the Poetry Project, in which case the language of the street would be the measure of all poetry.

Aristophanes was as vulgar as Rabelais who was as scatological as Swift who was as "dirty" as William Burroughs. Richard Pryor seemed to be a descendant of the classic Greek comedic riffs of Aristophanes through the comic exaggerations of Rabelais and later Jonathan Swift, right through to Mark Twain and William Burroughs. (I would not exclude Joel Oppenheimer from this parade of street-talking lyrical punters.) Pryor was no more obsessed with shit than Lemuel Gulliver, and Joel was as obsessed with shit as either Swift or Pryor was. Weren't all of them speaking the language of literature? Wasn't it Dante—the greatest poet of any era—who invented "the vulgar tongue," the vernacular? Dante decided to eschew Latin for the more colorful and energetic utterance of the street, the language of the people, what eventually became known as the Italian language, a beautiful language in all respects. Richard Pryor might not be Dante, but I put him among the literary voices, as I think of him as a storyteller, a fiction writer, even a poet at times. He was a stand-up comedian, more in a tradition of foul-mouthed vaudevillians, but his monologues also fit into a literature of the street.

This literary tradition that Richard Pryor belonged to also included a tradition of performance, and so he was likewise aligned with Redd Foxx and Lenny Bruce, two of the most tragically beautiful comedians to grace a stage or nightclub floor. I first heard Redd Foxx in fifth grade when I would go to a classmate's house and, in his basement, play a Foxx record in which he announced, like a sport's announcer, the outcome of a farting contest. Oops, he shit in his pants and is disqualified! I listened to Lenny Bruce obsessively in my late teens and early twenties, playing his records almost nightly. Yadda, yadda, Farda Flotsky! But how does this hook up with Aristophanes? By the seat of the pants. By the leather phallus. By the great unbroken comic tradition from then to now. Ask my old poetry teacher Joel Oppenheimer.

5.

I don't know if it was because Joseph Brodsky was drunk so early in the morning that his displeasure with Richard Pryor was so great or if he had a genuine revulsion for this kind of physical, vernacular humor. The word "motherfucker," for instance, is used so often in the Richard Pryor monologues that it loses any meaning, which I think is exactly the point that Pryor is trying to make. Language is a bunch of sounds; it works for or against you, Richard Pryor seemed to say. Motherfucker is a powerful word, to be sure. I have heard that as curses go, its origins are more African than European, and if that is linguistically true, then Richard Pryor was simply operating in the tradition of a great African storyteller. Does that make it less important than Aristophanes's Lysistrata screaming, "We need to get laid!"

What I find so interesting about the word motherfucker is how, after a while, it becomes pure sound value, losing all meaning, so that its purpose is to mark other words and syllables, creating a kind of emphasis in the same way that some African languages use *klik!* sounds to emphasize words and syllables. On the street where I used to live, 110th Street, I rarely if ever heard the word motherfucker used to mean a fornicator of mothers, but rather as a way to slow down the sentence being said, give it a longer rhythm.

I once heard this sentence in the Marlin Cafe.

"I said to John, John, I says, and the motherfucker is my good friend, John is, he's the kind of motherfucker you can count on in a pinch..."

Clearly John was not a motherfucker in any kind of evil sense of the word. John was the speaker's friend. He was someone who could be counted on. The Marlin Cafe was located at the southwest corner of Harlem. This fellow was a Harlem regular in the bar. He knew how to speak the language of the street, the language of the ghetto, and the language of the neighborhood, and in every one of these instances, he was speaking correctly.

6.

There is a comic routine in one of Aristophanes's plays in which two characters make fun of classical Greek playwrights. One of the characters shows that he can affix a meaningless phrase to nearly any line of Euripides without losing effect. I have always thought that if I were directing the play I would redo this scene using an adolescent game in which the phrase "in bed" is affixed to a fortune found in a Chinese almond cookie. "You will go on a long journey—in bed." "You are about to come into some money—in bed." "You are about to meet a beautiful stranger—in bed." This shows that language—a mere concatenation of sounds—can become meaningless or pure sound, poetry even, when driven to such extremes.

Brodsky, the co-opter of the English language, the man who adopted our language and then wished to excel in it, using it better than the natives, had almost no ear for the word motherfucker that offended him to the core. I would disagree with Joseph Brodsky then—at least that drunken Joseph Brodsky—who said that

Aristophanes was never vulgar simply for the sake of being vulgar. Being vulgar is what makes comedy go. Old Comedy was gross— but with dramatic purpose. That happy-go-lucky, purposeless, happy-ending-driven comedy we experience ad nauseam on television has a long tradition, to be sure. But it has nothing to do with the Old Comedy of the Greeks. The comedies about finding a pot of gold at the end of the rainbow and marrying the girl of your dreams—and living happily ever after—derive from Roman comedy, not the Greeks. Plautus, not Aristophanes, was their touchstone.

If Marcus Aurelius wasn't a spectator at gladiatorial matches or spectacles in which Christians were fed to lions, he most certainly observed Plautus's comedies of mistaken identities, the comedy of manners Romans loved, not the roiling, boiling, roistering satires of Aristophanes. Old Comedy, though, was not about destroying the past; it represented a nostalgia for it, the present situation being the intolerable one. Aristophanes, like Rabelais and Swift—and Richard Pryor—also longed for the past. At its root and stem Old Comedy makes fun of the new because of nostalgia for the old. In other words, Richard Pryor, like Aristophanes, was a conservative being, which nearly all satirists are. That includes Redd Foxx, Lenny Bruce, Eddie Murphy, or Bill Murray. Vulgarity is simply their smokescreen for what ails them at the root.

The connection I saw between Aristophanes and Richard Pryor went back to the origins of drama—in fertility songs and satyr dances, wine orgies to Dionysus, the old frenzies. This unwieldy energy was not domestic but spiritually renegade and irrational. Drama was dedicated to Dionysus—god of the theatre, but also god of wine, god of emotional excess, god of orgy. Aeschylus might explain the way of the gods to men; Sophocles explain the way of men to the gods. But Euripides was there to reveal human nature to all of us, and Aristophanes did not like that. Which is why he made fun of Euripides more than any other writer. Satirists are pagans, not blasphemers, and never are they heathen. That's what I don't think Joseph Brodsky understood about Richard Pryor. Sex and crotch humor and fart jokes and the gamut of bawdiness are not necessarily heathen, without tradition, unanchored and adrift culturally. They are rooted to the earth. That is what the word "humble" means—of the earth—and the satirist is a humble-voiced creature.

7.

In reading Joseph Brodsky's essays and his travel meditation on Venice, I had two reactions. One had to do with my admiration for his prose. The other was reflective, harking back to that bar-room incident with him. I cannot help but recall that look of condescension the poet gave me when I tried to engage him in conversation about classic Greek comedy. His look was Caesarian in its marble-like aloofness. Clearly I was a barbarian. Now I saw him like Marcus Aurelius when the poet asked: "How do you feel now, among barbarians?" Yet it is in that classically observed essay on Marcus Aurelius that I most see and admire Joseph Brodsky. For it is not the Roman emperor but the Soviet-exiled poet whom I see revealed. Brodsky writes of the emperor that "loneliness, of course, comes with the territory; but he was lonelier than most." Is he not speaking of the imperial urge to write poetry, to be a poet? And wasn't that a lonely poet I saw that Sunday morning in the empty city of New York on the Upper West Side of Manhattan in the Marlin Cafe?

I often wonder how much Brodsky really knew about drama. He might agree with Hegel that tragedy was about two rights colliding, but would he likewise accept that drama begins with the collision of the sacred and profane? Certainly he respected Dante in his musings on Italy, but is it possible to admire Dante without acknowledging his indebtedness to the vulgar tongue, the vernacular, the language of the street?

Who knows what brought Joseph Brodsky to the Marlin Cafe that Sunday morning? He was not your typical habitué of that sleazy, reeky, old man's dive on Broadway near Columbia University. I can reconcile that vodka-drinking, opinionated, patrician man with the style of his poetry and even the content of an essay like the one on Marcus Aurelius. But his prose has a rhythm, a spokenness to it, making it also a literature of the people and the street, and that is something both humble and beautiful, too. It was, I think, his American side coming through in a way it did not in his poetry. I am reminded of something William Carlos Williams said when asked where this American idiom came from.

"Out of the mouths of Polish mothers," he answered. In other words, the language of American literature *is* the language of the street, and that is where Richard Pryor and Joseph Brodsky meet, in a Marlin Cafe of the mind.

When Thou Art King

The summer school boys wore coats and ties, even in the heat. They were the irreverent children of suburban lawyers, of diplomats, of hopeful scientists working in the big federally funded labs outside of the city. When their parents dropped them off at the top of the school's long drive, the boys' required coats were stuffed into their backpacks, and their mandatory ties were knotted into headbands that cut face and forehead in two.

Ruth taught French to the boys in a school building partially staffed by elderly monks for whom there were no younger replacement monks, so the old monks hung on. They were eighty or ninety years old. The youngest was sixty. They mowed the lawn on riding mowers on Saturday, four or five of them on orange Husqvarnas making blocks and patterns out of the acres around the school buildings and monastery.

The monks would die off one by one, and the monastery building would be turned into classrooms, and there would be no more soft swish and tick of fabric and foot down the linoleum halls in the morning. They would end up with headstones in the graveyard on the school's grounds, with the other monks who had died at the school, and school boys would stand back by the graveyard smoking stolen cigarettes as boys had done there for years.

There was something improbable about the school: acres of land and trees and stone buildings in the middle of the city. The whole school, set in a corner of the city that had once been slated for gentrification but had been passed over, had the feel of something turning in on itself and giving over to a future of freewheeling decay.

So when Ruth took her class way off course, when she wandered off from the expected curriculum and into a ruleless terrain, she told herself it was okay, expected even.

"Don't tell your parents," Ruth told the boys when she passed out photocopied French tabloid articles instead of excerpts from Baudelaire.

"It's summer, no rules," she said to them, and they scratched their ears, half asleep, or looked to see if they could spot her breasts when she leaned over just a little to secure the latch on one of the windows. It was an old building, and Ruth knew it was full of lead dust and asbestos.

It was a class of seven boys, and they were all seventeen, and it was easy to drift, to talk to them as if they were her own age, and then remember that there was supposed to be some important line between them and her.

"French doesn't really matter," she said to the boys. "You should be studying a language that matters." Ruth always felt stupid about teaching what people called a romance language. She wished she'd learned something with pictures that meant words or something Cyrillic, an alphabet different from her own. So some days she talked to the summer school boys about music or movies. "You should do nothing else before you see *The 400 Blows*," she said to them and wrote it on the board in English and then crossed it out and wrote the words in French instead. "Or Hal Hartley. He's not French, but his movies seem French in a weird way. Watch all the Hal Hartley movies this weekend. And then listen to Nina Simone. She wasn't French, but the French loved her, and that should count for something. Watch *The Umbrellas of Cherbourg* and *Breathless*, back to back. That's your homework."

Ruth stopped translating fifteen minutes before the end of the hour and told the boys to put their heads on their desks. They were too old for it, she knew, but they looked relieved. She looked at their mussed hair and then watched the window. Birds formed small troupes outside the classroom window. They sat still and looked through the glass. Grass made an island all around the stone building.

Charles lifted his head up from his desk. "I have to DJ at the school dance on Saturday, and some of the CDs are seriously French," he said to Ruth. "So it's seriously appropriate to listen to them in class. At least that's what I think."

"Seriously," Ruth had said, and then she took a CD player out of the supply closet, moved to a chair in the back of the room and motioned to the desk. "It's all yours, Charles," she said.

Charles put on Stereolab, and Ruth made him stop and start every few seconds so they could translate. Adam stood at the board with a piece of pink chalk and wrote all the lyrics they could decipher onto the board.

"This is some real learning," Charles said, and then a grackle flew straight up against the window glass and crashlanded into cedar chips below the window.

"C'est la vie," Eugene said, and they all went to the window to look out and see the corpse.

None of them knew it yet, but the night of the school dance would be the night Tom Evans, one of the summer school boys, one of the boys enrolled in Ruth's class, would be hit by a speeding diplomat's fat Lincoln, arcing too fast around Logan Circle. They would find out the following week, when the school was populated by grievance counselors, when the monks were lurking and listening outside of every classroom door, that Tom Evans lived with his father at the upper entrance of Logan Circle, that he had been walking to the nearby market to buy ice cream that he and his father were going to eat together while watching a movie. At the moment of the crash, Ruth would be rounding the upper edge of the circle, only a few carlengths from the Lincoln, in the car with another teacher and three of the summer school boys packed across the back seat, post-school dance, all of them on their way to a bar to see an all-ages show the boys begged to be driven to. The other boys didn't like Tom Evans, but they didn't dislike him enough to tease him to his face. It was more of an indifference that meant he walked into and out of the school building by himself every day, and Ruth had found something tragic about the quiet space that made a pocket around him. During the week after the dance, the fact that he wasn't in the room when he should have been would make the boys feel antsy, not because they missed him but more because they didn't. They would go whole minutes laughing or talking, and then they would stop and see his desk and in that quiet you could see the surprise passing across their faces as they realized, some for the first time, how quickly a person could go.

The school dance was on a Saturday, and Ruth had agreed to meet Jason, who taught anthropology and had also agreed to chaperone, in front of the school building at seven. They would go in together, and they would go for a drink after, at least that was the plan Jason had proposed. Jason had been a student at the school, a scholarship boy who had returned after college to teach. "It's embarrassing, but apparently I can't keep myself away," he'd told Ruth when he'd led her to her classroom on the first day. A week later, she'd seen him a few blocks from her apartment, walking two tiny beribboned dogs with his mother. "I can't stand these things," he'd told Ruth when she stopped, and his mother scratched his arm with an acrylic nail and said, "Liar. These your dogs," and he'd started laughing and shrugged.

The night of the dance, Ruth waited for the bus and watched other people's dogs scratch circles in the dirt and bark themselves silly. It was that point in the summer at which people gave up. They wore almost nothing. They dropped popsicle wrappers on the sidewalk and kept moving. They punched each other without thought of consequence. The parks around Ruth's apartment were filling up with trash. Dogs shit in the grass, and people scraped as much as they could into plastic bags and threw the bags into overflowing trash cans. Dogs bit into each other in the heat and left one raw edge of fur leaning into another raw edge. Even though it was a weekend early evening, politicians still took the fast track down Connecticut from the embassies, surrounded by the brash roar and whistle of police escorts in formation around a trio of limos. Rats made tunnels in the garden. Someone had placed small golf flags next to each hole and had written on the flapping yellow, "rat hole number one," "rat hole number two," etc. Men slept without blankets on benches. They took their shoes off and used them as pillows. The bakery on the corner sold bad white cakes with gaudy plastic flowers on top and a sick sort of raspberry filling, and Ruth had seen homeless men back in the dumpsters, folding partial discarded cakes into pieces of newspaper. In the corner by the slide, a group of mothers held babies at their chests and slung small towels over their shoulders to keep their t-shirts protected from circles of drool.

Ruth—who was raised by her grandmother after her mother, overwhelmed by motherhood, simply moved away—had spent years withholding, pretending not to want anything too much. As part of that guise, she claimed she didn't want children: the frantic bird squawk in the middle of the night, all that need. But when she let herself really think of a future, sometimes she saw a baby, an apartment with radiators that crackled and popped while a baby was sleeping an arm's length away, and a husband sat with a book by a lamp in another room. But she always worried she wouldn't be able to do it: to stay and to stick. She was twenty-eight, and had never had a real relationship. She had done random jobs, worked as a tutor to embassy children, worked as a temp. Everyone she knew was in a similar holding pattern, stitching together a series of low-level decisions with all the meaningful ones pushed off for someday.

The day before, Ruth had been on the bus in the morning, and a boy, maybe sixteen, in a blue hat had smiled at her and then moved to the seat next to her. She'd turned away from him and looked out the window at the usual morning things: sparrows flying up to a birch branch right outside the bus window, a man taking t-shirts out of a box to set up for sale on a table in front of the Safeway. Then the boy in the blue hat had taken Ruth's hand, kissed it, and pushed the front door of the bus open and gone into an electronics store inside of which radios and hair dryers and clocks and microwaves were stacked up to the windows. It was the most meaningful touch she'd had in months, and that fact made her feel a sadness that she wore the entire day.

When she got off the bus close to the school Saturday evening, it was still light out, and the heat sat in the air like a solid thing. She saw Jason walking toward the main building. He was tall and heavy and wore a dark red brocade smoking jacket. "It's loud and improbable and maybe even a little pretentious, I know, but it's me," he said when he saw Ruth looking at the jacket. "Besides, it lends an air of festivity to any event," he said. And before she could respond, he launched in again, "You should really learn about brachiation," and started mock swinging from the low branches of a tree by the building's entrance.

"You're cracked. What are you doing?" She laughed a little and adjusted her skirt and wiped her forehead. A group of boys was congregating by the entrance. They yelled and imitated Jason, but Ruth knew they worshipped him.

"Apes and movement, tree swinging, means of transport, etc.," Jason said. "Brachiation, as I mentioned. It's what I'm teaching next week. Not that they'll listen. They'll ask me if I've ever seen LaDonna naked, which they ask me every day, it's like: she's black, I'm black, so I must have seen her naked, right? They never ask me if I've seen you naked."

Ruth paused. She hadn't thought of Jason like that. But then she let herself: the slight paunch above the belt line, the shaved line of rough hair on his chin. "They are all smartasses, hyper-ironic, too cynical for seventeen," Ruth said. "But then, you know. You were one of them."

"Well, I was one of them, but I wasn't really one of them. I was-n't the me I am now then, if that makes sense. I was quiet, and I didn't have a lot of friends."

What had Ruth been back then: a surly, introverted high school girl, a reader, prettier than most but not beautiful in a way that would take her anywhere important, a girl who drank too much but didn't let it show, a girl who slept with more people than she could count just so she could feel alive and needed in that moment of so much wanting.

"True. I can't really picture you like them," Ruth said, "like they are now: the coat and tie, the know-it-all-ness." When Ruth tried to think of Jason as a high school student, she saw someone smaller, walking the two dogs in the morning before boarding the bus and watching pigeons dive in a curve, wings out, coast into angles and glide and then mad flap up, up again, and over the side of a brownstone, over the side of a graffiti giraffe head. For a minute, she hated the school boys for their teenaged arrogance, for their inability to see beyond the small space of their own lives and into the future where different things would matter. But then what were those things? Ruth didn't know either.

Jason looked at her, about to say something, but then looked away. The face, Ruth thought, should have a cape, a wing, a covering.

"In, I say, let us go in," he said, and Ruth ducked under his raised arm and into the dimmed-down, fluorescent-lit school gym. One of the boys sidetracked Jason with a question about a test, and Ruth settled on the bleachers. The monks stood where any other school's wallflowers would, against the far dark wall by wide metal doors that were propped open with trash cans. Outside the doors, Ruth could see car lights popping on as the cars moved behind the row of trees that bordered the school's grounds. The lights moved fast and made hollows out of the branches and then swam past leaving gray spots in the coming night.

The boys had strung Halloween crepe paper from one wall hook to another: small bats and skulls on an orange wrinkled background, even though it was months from Halloween.

"Got it from my mom," Eugene told Ruth as he stood tapping his foot against the metal riser of the lowest bleacher step. "She's got a drawer full of holiday shit. I mean stuff. Holiday stuff, Miss Phillips."

Ruth shrugged and gave Eugene a half smile. She didn't think it would matter in ten years what teenager had said shit or fuck at his high school dance. In fact, she was almost certain that those who did would somehow be more interesting.

The dance was sparsely attended. Most of the students were at expensive camps or being dragged through Europe or China or Africa by their parents. Charles had set up speakers and his iPod, and music echoed in the large gym. A long table was covered with an orange cloth that wasn't quite large enough to drape over the whole thing, so on one end Ruth could see, "Get me out of here," carved into the wood and then painted over with what looked like white-out. Parents had sent food with their sons, so there were odd items spread over the orange cloth: chocolate-covered blackberries in a crystal bowl, a thick butcher's block slab with four imported cheeses surrounded by expensive crackers probably left over from some dinner party, liter-sized bottles of raspberry mineral water.

Some of the younger boys were carrying the bottles around and drinking straight from them, pretending to stagger as if drinking champagne instead. Eugene took a mangled toothbrush out of his pocket, apparently his prop for the evening, and walked over to stand by Kalev and kick a small ball back and forth. Kalev played air guitar while Charles' music rose and then dropped, and then he pulled his arms in in a stop-time moment of self-consciousness and kicked the wall lightly in a way meant to suggest that he never really cared about anything. Adam and Tristan sat in folding chairs and hit their heels into the metal in time with the music. Adam wore a t-shirt with a cartoon picture of an airplane on the front of it, and he had a stack of library books next to him.

A group of girls from their sister school walked in the open gym doors, past the trash cans, and then stopped to huddle on the dark side of the gym before deciding on their next move.

LaDonna, who taught middle school English, who often ate lunch with Ruth, sat down next to her. LaDonna took the straw out of her paper cup of 7Up, and chewed the end into shreds. Ruth watched her teeth working, white white and then the straw in tatters. "You know those movies where they have high school dances, and two teachers who have been secretly in love for about one point five hours start slow dancing or something, you know what I'm talking about? It's the last ten minutes of the movie, or something, and they're slow dancing, and all their students are smiling at them. That's Mars, man, that's not any high school I've ever been in."

They nodded and watched while a few other teachers ate chocolate-covered blackberries by the handful and talked about which students had gotten into which college.

"Not enough Ivies this year, our students have not been accepted to nearly enough Ivies," Ruth heard one of them say, and they all shook their heads in a way that, to the students, might have looked oddly in time with the music.

Ruth watched the girls on the other side of the gym, now in small packs around the boys. They were a generation of individualists, or at least they'd been convinced they had to dress as if they were: one girl in big-heeled black shoes and a tiny corduroy skirt and a ripped pink shirt decorated with ribbons. And another in yellow capri pants with tiny whales on them and white patent leather Mary Janes and a Clash t-shirt. They asked the boys to dance, and if the boys said no, they don't dance as a general principle, they all huddled together, boys and girls, wondering what to do next. Ruth liked the immediacy of being close to their static energy, the long moments in which something really had to happen but then didn't.

Jason stood at the door watching before walking over to the table of food next to which Ruth was sitting. One of the monks went up to Jason and asked him something. Ruth watched the way the huge floor fan blew air from the corner to stir at the hem of the monk's robe. "The dress men," Kalev called them. "The dress men are coming," he might say, and they would know that meant it was time to put away the *Paris Match* article about Janet Jackson's breast and take out their textbooks.

LaDonna went to the bathroom, and Ruth sat by herself and listened as somewhere beyond the school's grounds, a car peeled out, and the tire squeal and fast rubber sound filtered in through the open gym doors. Tristan and Adam started clapping, and the other boys joined in. When they stopped, the room felt quiet. Charles turned the music up louder, and the speakers shorted out, actually sparked out into the air in front of them. Ruth stood still, waiting for something more dramatic to happen, a fire that would take the velvet stage curtains in flames up to the ceiling. But nothing more followed. Charles' face reddened, as if the quiet that quickly filled the gym were his fault. "Okay talk, people, keep it moving," Charles said, and then ran for the door to the bathroom. Ruth wanted to lean into the summer school boys and all their striving and say, "High school doesn't really matter," but then that was too simple. It mattered, just in different ways and not as much as they thought it would.

"We should leave. Jailbreak, you know," Jason said as he walked up in front of her. "I've got my car here, so no bus or metro." There was nowhere to park in Jason and Ruth's neighborhood, so Jason often left his car at the school, sometimes for weeks.

"Okay, I'm in," Ruth said. It was 10:30, and some of the sister school girls had left. The monks had gone back to the monastery, and most of the teachers were leaning against the bleachers looking at their watches. She and Jason went for the door, not looking back to see if anyone was watching. They were supposed to stay until eleven, but there was something appealing about the dark outside of the gym windows. As they walked out, she listened for the crackle of the fluorescent lights that circled the parking lot but instead heard some of the boys, slouched over on one of the stone walls that made the lot's perimeter, scraping tennis shoes into gravel and laughing about something she couldn't quite make out.

"Take us to the Black Cat, will you?" Eugene asked. "It's an all-ages show. It's not like there's anything wrong with us going. We just don't want to walk." The bar was miles from the school, and Ruth knew walking wasn't even an option, knew they would have taken a cab or Metro had Jason said no, but she told them yes anyway.

"We'll take you," Ruth said before even looking at Jason. People should do things without thinking, she thought. I'm teaching them a good lesson, she convinced herself, and opened the passenger door and let Eugene, Kalev and Charles into the back seat.

"Alright, way to not be a Prufrock," Eugene said as he slid over behind the driver's side. They'd just finished studying Eliot, and suddenly everyone who was stuck or immobile was called J. or J. Alfred or Prufrock.

Jason's car had the back seat ripped out and seat cushions from a sofa strapped in with duct tape and secured with a two-by-four across the cushion's midsection.

"Dude, you should seriously get a better job and then a better car, in that order," Eugene said. He and Charles started laughing. Ruth noticed that Kalev's forehead looked green from the reflection of the streetlight on the glass.

"I love this car," Jason said, and he drove faster, down past the tiled dome of Catholic University and over across New York Avenue. An alarm was going off somewhere, and Ruth looked back at the boys, their wide expectant faces.

"So this car doesn't even have a CD player, is that right?" Eugene asked while he drummed his thumbs against Ruth's head rest.

"Tape deck, circa 1987," Jason said and hit the car's dashboard. The boys laughed, and Jason turned on the radio. It was half static because the antenna had been ripped off, but she could hear through the static what sounded like polka.

"Great musical choice, my friend," Eugene said, and then the boys started talking quietly about something Ruth couldn't quite hear.

Ruth saw that Jason had a scar that looked like a shoe on his forearm. The trees were dark out the window, and Ruth saw two men in big clothes run down an alley. A couple stood on the sidewalk in front of a video store, and their daughter lay flat on the sidewalk, hitting her fists into the cement and crying. The streetlights were a wash on the windows. Men sat at the park in the circle, their possessions socked into bags and carts in small cities around them. They were a few feet of personal space, they were what they said in darkness to no one. The arched windows of brownstones made patchwork out of buildings. She could almost imagine what it would feel like to roll out from the moving car, to let go of age and move into a moment of accumulation of motion, not time.

And then she heard the noise of a car somewhere in front of them and the lumpy response of the body that then went airborne for Ruth didn't know how long, but for what felt like full minutes. It was a movie moment, not something she ever imagined seeing, and she registered the look on the boy's face as he flew from in front of the car, the stungun expression that meant it was only a body and whatever had made it more was already gone. "That looks a little like Tom Evans," she thought in that moment, but then thought it couldn't be, too much of a coincidence, and so she didn't say anything.

The car that hit the boy rolled up onto the circle and stopped only when its front rested against a tree, and the driver, seemingly drunk, stumbling, bent onto the pavement and started throwing up and crying into his hands. Jason kept moving, pulled his car around the far lane that skated the circle and went onto a side street. "They shouldn't see all this," he said, and nodded back to the boys who were mute and staring. "Plenty of witnesses, anyway," Jason said, and they saw more than twenty cars stopped around the circle, frozen, and they heard sirens.

Maybe if they had circled back around in Jason's big car, Ruth thought, the flying boy would have rolled over, brushed grass off his pants, and gotten into the back seat with the rest of them, and it would have been another summer night. Later, when they found out it was Tom Evans, one of the summer school boys, Ruth thought: I was a Tom Evans, quiet and withholding. Almost no one has ever known me, she thought during the next whole week as she stood in front of her classroom, and wondered how she had fooled herself into thinking there was something tough and strong about hiding everything important for years.

Instead of taking the boys to the bar, Jason drove them up Connecticut to the Cleveland Park Metro stop, a safe and almost suburban stop from which he knew they could all easily find their way home. "Enough drama for tonight," he told them, "no Black Cat. That was a bad idea from the beginning. You should all just go home." Ruth knew they wouldn't go straight there and wondered if she and Jason ought to drop each boy right at his doorstep. Let them get into trouble, she decided, let them drink too much and throw up in the alley and walk all the way home to the green square lots of the suburbs.

It was the wrong decision, all of it—leaving the dance early, the car ride, not stopping at the accident, the Metro drop-off—and they both knew it. Later, the boys' parents would call them. The Headmaster would reprimand them and tell them they'd come close to losing their jobs.

She and Jason circled Adams Morgan until they found a parking place on 15th. They got out and turned onto U Street and passed the check cashing place, the Brazilian restaurants, the shoe store that had pink knee-high boots in the window next to five or six pairs of multi-striped tennis shoes.

"I go there with my mom every Sunday night," Jason said pointing at a bar with the silhouettes of musicians stenciled on the building's side. Ruth thought of the woman with the acrylic nails sitting at the bar with Jason, drinking through a tiny straw and shaking ice around in her glass while Jason talked about apes and movement.

As she often did, Ruth wondered about her own mother, whom she had only seen in photos. She was also the kind of woman to sit in a bar on a Sunday night, Ruth believed. She would be one of the regulars at some divey coastal Oregon bar, in the small town where Ruth knew she lived but where she'd never tried to contact her.

When Jason and Ruth got to 18th, they wound through the maze of people waiting to get into bars. Girls stood in front of The Diner talking on jeweled cell phones. Inside, people ate pancakes, and the waitresses bobbed their heads to the music as they walked. A rat dragged a pizza crust from a paper plate someone had dropped on the sidewalk.

"That thing as big as a kitten," Ruth heard a homeless man say.

"Rats can chew through concrete and swim up to three miles from shore," Jason said. He put his arm at her back as they moved toward her building.

"In Paris, there is supposedly one rat for every person," Ruth said. In the basement of her building, she'd seen rats nesting in a bag of winter clothes she had left in her storage space and had since then left the entire storage space alone. Ruth bobbed around a drunk frat boy who grabbed at Jason's smoking jacket and said "Nice threads, bro."

"This street is a nightmare on the weekend," Jason said as they reached the block's peak and crossed over toward the gas station that bordered Ruth's building.

"It really is. I usually walk blocks out of my way just to avoid it," Ruth said. For some reason, Ruth felt frozen, her voice and her face. She couldn't say more than a few words, and so she kept walking and looking and hoped the chaos of the street would distract from her quiet.

An extended SUV rolled around the corner, stopped, and let out a trio of tall blond girls in metallic tank tops. "I am going to get totally, totally smashed," one of them said to the other two, and they clicked down the sidewalk, past a woman in a stained vinyl jacket trying to sell a half-eaten bag of sunflower seeds to bargoers.

During the week, the block was different: Dominican women loading groceries onto rolling carts and shuffling up Columbia and men from the embassies wearing bright robes and eating falafel out on the decks of restaurants.

Jason and Ruth went to Ruth's apartment even though she wasn't sure what she was doing. Her place was a mess, and she left the light in the bedroom off so he wouldn't see anything. For a second she thought about school on Monday, about how she would be calm in the halls and how she was capable, if it came to that, if she needed to, of pretending like nothing had happened. Jason seemed earnest, but she thought maybe it would be better for this not to matter. It was hard for her to believe that someone could love her or that she could sustain feeling for someone for days, for years. So instead of looking at his arms or his face, she looked at the floor and closed her eyes.

Ruth tried not to wonder about the boy in Logan Circle, thrown against the night in a single shock of metal. Instead, she thought about driving home in the dark country air of her late adolescence, driving back to her grandmother's small house in the middle of hundreds of acres of unused farmland in western Maryland, the cool swoop of coming up over a hill and charging back down into a valley of asphalt and summer night, Elvis Costello or the Ramones coming loud out of the car windows and nothing but grass and the postcard light of high barn windows announcing that yes, somebody was out there.

She imagined Eugene and Kalev walking drunk along some suburban stone wall, yelling into the dark and hearing only the response of crickets or outdoor dogs in pens and the black of night and possibility. In the morning, if she wanted to, she could walk out the door with nothing, get on a plane and fly to another country. It was a time in her life when she had no entanglements, and she guessed that in two years or five years, that would all be different. Maybe she would have a husband or a baby, and her nights would be spent in a sort of quiet canceling out of self, tiptoeing across wood floors, careful, careful not to make a sound. With that in mind, she kissed Jason. There was something sad and needy about the way his stomach pooled over his boxer shorts, and that made her want to hang on to him. Maybe this is real, maybe this is something, she let herself think, as she felt the heat from Jason's palm slightly dampen a circle of her hair. She watched his closed eyes and saw the reflection of the changing stop light outside of her building making patterns on the white wall of her bedroom: yellow to red to green.

On Monday, she would tell the summer school boys everything. She would move past the tabloid articles and get to what life really was, what they should expect, what they would want, what they wouldn't get. She would let it all out.

Old Sins

It was only because he liked to sketch that he noticed it at all. Spring was late and there were still large patches of snow; as he rode along he noted the contrast, light and dark, the shapes and mounds, the texture. That's all he was thinking when his horse snorted once, the air from its nostrils visible, another pattern. At the same instant he realized that there was something odd about the dark patch up ahead. He'd thought it shadow but suddenly something in his vision shifted and it assumed depth, dimension. A dark mound looking, now that he thought about it, like a bundle of old rags. Though why anyone would dump a bundle of rags in the far corner of Webster's fenced lot, he couldn't imagine.

By then he was off his horse, leaving the reins dangling. He made his way along the fence where the snow had drifted deeper, cold to his knees, and that may have been what made his breath come faster, or perhaps he was close to running. As he drew nearer he noticed that he was clapping his hands together, the sound ringing up to the empty blue sky, spreading out to the trees, rattling off the boards of the fence. As if the dark shape was some slumbering beast he hoped to rouse, as if he hoped to see it push to its knees, shaking a massive head, as if he hoped to see it run from him. But as he came closer the tricks of light and shadow withdrew, the thing now looking clearly like what it was. A body, a woman's body, sprawled as if it had tripped most clumsily. One hand reaching out and up to rest against the rough boards of the fence.

It was a small hand, the fingers mottled and discoloured but showing clearly, reaching out of the dark half-mitten. Dark hair too, loose and matted, and he walked slowly around until he could see the face, certain, suddenly, that it would be someone he knew.

It wasn't. A woman he'd never seen before, lying dead in the field. Snow melting from the boards of the fence splashed onto her upturned cheek, the only sound. With a sigh he turned back to his waiting horse and rode, not too fast, to find Thompson.

She didn't think about it often but sometimes someone would ask a question and she would realize that it wasn't like a story, that there were so many things she didn't remember. As if she suddenly woke up and found herself standing in a street or moving a shuttle, raising a tumbler to her lips, and everything started from that moment. Although that moment, that starting moment, happened again and again. What came before something like a lantern show, flashes in the darkness that she couldn't string together, especially not when someone was waiting for an answer to a question. But not really like a lantern show because the flashes were more than a picture, had movement and sensation. One had sunlight pouring through a small window, warming the surface of a table that was worn so smooth that even the gouges were soft, the sunlight showing the depth of them. There was a blue bowl with a chip on the rim that was rough to fingertip or lip, milk and a bit of bread to dip in it, and a voice singing at the edge of things. She didn't think it was from her own life, maybe something her mother had described so well, or a story her sister Abby told when the grim ship pitched and rocked and they thought they would surely die.

It was not a pleasant thing to move the body. There were four of them and they lifted it on to the cart and trundled it across the rutted field to the shed at the back of the old Webster house. Her legs were bare and McKenna cursed when a bit of skin came off under his hand. Then he made a joke about cold flesh, and they all laughed a little.

They wheeled the cart into the middle of the shed and the dust they had disturbed danced in the light coming through the low window. It was suddenly different being shut in with her and there was a musty, mouldy smell rising from her clothing, or her person. McKenna moved to prop the door open. Their breath filled the place but noone spoke until Coroner Thompson said, "She'll be one of yours then, Isaac."

Isaac Carne was the keeper of the county poor house down the road. He shook his head and spoke in that way he had, his voice strangely high and brittle, coming out of the tangle of dun-coloured beard. "Not her," he said. "I've not seen this one before. No I haven't."

They heard the sound of horses approaching as the jurymen Thompson had called on began to arrive. He sent Charles away, since he had found the body, and he told Isaac that he could go too, although he didn't say why.

Late that night Charles sat by his fire, seeing shapes and faces from so long ago. When he was a boy it was monsters he'd see in the flames, giants and one-eyed ogres. His grandfather telling stories from his old chair, Charles and his sisters sitting shoulder to shoulder, whispering beneath the cracked sentences. "There's his eye—oh glory, do you see? And his wicked claws right there." Until a popping log made them jump and scream and their mother appeared, shooing them off to bed.

Another place entirely, Charles thought, and one he had no right to even think about. He rubbed his hand over his face, leaving a smear of ink across his nose and cheek. The floor around his chair was littered with paper, another sheet on the smooth board on his knees. He reached to dip the pen again and it scratched along with the crackling fire. Black lines on a white page, the curve of fingers on a rough board fence.

All the next day men were in and out of the shed, and the stories went around. It was thought that the body was that of the English girl from the Corners, the one who'd been making life difficult for Barrie, the shopkeeper. By all accounts that girl was fair-haired, but who knew what might happen, months under the snow. Then there were the wives and daughters from the isolated farms, who hadn't been seen for some time. Cooler heads observed that they never were seen, that they'd be hauling wood and water, cooking and sewing like always, but that didn't stop the talk and riders went around to check, and to spread the word. Carne's boy went by the shed with some friends after school and met up with his father outside; someone saw him get a good clout about the ears. The jurymen were supposed to keep quiet but word got around that her underclothing was all on properly, that there were no marks on her, so it wasn't like that other one a few years before.

From the place where he was chopping wood in his shirt sleeves Charles watched the steady parade of horses and wagons, and wondered about the hearts of men. What did they need to see, there in the cold, murky shed? Did any of them really think they might know her, and what kind of possibilities did that raise? Or did they all, like him, have something dark and buried; did they all assume, going through their lives, that it would one day rise up and face them.

She'd been so many places, places miles and miles from each other, and that was not even thinking of the ship that must have come from another world, the slate-coloured sea and the empty sky. There'd been places that were bad and places not so, and once an old woman who tied a ribbon in her hair and taught her hymns, singing in a quavery voice with her eyes looking up to a dim corner of the room. Maybe that could have been a good place but she was sent away; she didn't know why. Only that the old woman had wept but she herself did not.

She'd been many places but that was just the way it happened. She was a fighter, she knew that because Jimmy had told her, although up to that moment she hadn't even thought that there might be one word, any word, that fit her. He was a fighter too, she knew that the first time she saw him in the steamy, lint-filled room, not any taller than she was but everything solid, his shirt tight over his arms. There were scars on her body but she wasn't sure where they came from. Jimmy kissed each one in their room near the factory and whispered things she could not quite hear over the clanging and call-ing from the street.

The inquest was set for the following day, giving the doctor time to make his examination. By nightfall most were saying that she'd be from the Poor House, no matter what Carne said. It was thought that several had run from there over the winter and not been heard of since, and, although that was not unusual, people wondered why he had denied her.

Later the moon came up, bathing the fields and the dark, hud-dled houses, and Charles went walking, unable to sleep. It was cold enough that he could still see his breath but there was a smell of the river from far off, of the soggy ground at the water's edge. He was thinking that already he'd stayed too long, let himself get close to comfortable. Now there would be an inquest, questions asked and testimony and his name would appear; even though it was not his own name, the thought made him uneasy.

He had hidden himself in the city at first, found work and cheap lodgings, saved his money. Relaxed into thinking that maybe he was the person he claimed to be. His sane mind knew that he had nothing to fear from the census takers, but it couldn't contain the panic that bubbled up at the thought of them knocking on doors in the winter night, writing down names, asking their questions. He started again, took up a grant of land and built his cabin, raised enough to live his quiet life. But the town had grown much faster than he'd expected, each new face a possible danger, or so he told himself. He knew he could cram his pack and just walk away, head farther north, deeper into the bush. Wiser though to sell to someone like McKenna, to take time to find just the right place, to have money enough to keep to himself for a good long time.

He heard some kind of scuffling sound from across the eerie fields, the jingle of a harness, but he paid no attention. Something had ambushed him and he was back home in another country, one hand on the latch, ducking his head to come in through the doorway. His sisters sat by the fire, an empty space between them, their hair gleaming in the light as they turned their heads. His mother sitting in his grandfather's chair, raising her eyes slowly from the sewing in her lap. The dawning on their faces when they saw that it was him, really him.

His foot struck a frozen clump of something and he cursed and stumbled, dragged back to the desolate moonlight. He saw that he had come in a straight line to the shed, the empty stone house looming out of the dark before him. He ducked his head through the low doorway, his eyes getting used to the deeper shadows within, and it took some time for him to understand what he was seeing. The body was gone, she was gone. Just a blotchy dark stain on the rough surface of the cart and a cracked leather boot lying on its side on the dirt floor, as if kicked off in a mighty struggle. His heart beat faster and faster and then he was running for his life again, his chest aching, stumbling and running until he slammed shut his own front door.

"Trouble alive and trouble dead, that one," Carne's wife said, brushing out her hair. "And you, great fool that you are—why didn't you say? What were you thinking of, even Robby recognized her, and he only saw her the once."

Carne sat on the edge of the bed, taking off his boots.

"Now there'll be talk," his wife went on, "and you'll have to explain. Well, I suppose you could just say you weren't sure, noone could call you a liar for that. And she must have looked—tell me, had the animals been at her at all?"

She turned to face him and something about the set of his shoulders, the look of his eyes, staring at the boot in his hand, made her fold her lips over whatever she'd been going to say next.

Jimmy could always make her laugh and she couldn't stay angry with him, even when he stumbled home singing, his pockets empty. He had lost two fingers to the carding machine and when he stroked her cheek with the shiny, puckered skin, her knees went loose, and something similar happened when she watched him rocking the baby in his arms, singing with his face close to hers. Her body remembered something the first time she held the baby but it also remembered an emptiness that she didn't want to think about. All she knew for certain was that nothing lasted, that there was no point in dreaming or running away, that it was always better to stand and fight, even if it made no difference. Nothing lasted and noone stayed, not even Abby, who had said they would run together. Not even Jimmy, who could make her laugh, who could make her knees go weak. She said No when he said he was so going to fight Mulvaney, but of course he didn't listen. When they came to tell her she didn't go with them but she could picture him lying on the cold stones, his beautiful head all broken.

The moon was high and cold and even wrapped in all his blankets Charles shivered, and things swirled around in his head. Had he known her after all, as a woman or a ghost, had he already known what he would find, when he saddled the horse that morning? He had no memory of ever meeting her, ever seeing her, but there was no comfort in that; he knew he was capable of things he had no wish to remember. A time he ran down an empty road in the dawn and the white mist rose like a living thing, come to divide his life in two.

People said someone had something to hide, and Aiken said it in the newspaper, and wondered why the coroner had not put a watch on the body, out there alone in the middle of the fields. Thompson made a sound of disgust and threw the paper down.

"Why would I?" he said to his wife, who was stirring something in an enormous pot. "How could I ever have guessed? Oh, it makes no sense. She was one of those wretches that ran from the Poor House, I'm as sure of that as I am that I'm sitting here. No stockings, no coat, no shawl—she froze to death, there wasn't a fresh mark on her, except for her arms, we would have seen."

His wife said that she'd heard of certain slow and subtle poisons that killed without a trace, that made it look as if a heart had just stopped beating. Thompson snorted. "You know as well as I do," he said, "that round here they tend to just bash them over the head and have done with it."

She said No all her life but it never made any difference. No to the long-nosed woman with her hymns and her prayers, and no to a new life in a new country. No in the green field and the cow barn and no against the rough wall in the stinking alley. She forgot, those few years with Jimmy, but she said No when he drank from the bottle and walked out the door. No to the greasy-faced man at the factory, but she'd already sold the few things they had. The only people willing to help her did it by taking her child away. Just for a little while, they said, just until things are better, and she couldn't say it then but her bones did, seeing the sharp-ringed fingers resting on her daughter's soft hair.

Searches were made along the riverbanks, and courting couples made jokes but were wary, pushing aside branches. The inquest was adjourned, week after week. They sat in the evenings in the schoolhouse, windows open and the room slowly filling with the scent of wild grass, of blossoms at dusk. That cold, wet lump in the field seemed to have little to do with it. Witnesses appeared, letters were read, nothing surprised. It seemed to the men drowsing in their chairs that they were there, not to discover anything but to hear, week by week, the chapters of a story that had long been written.

And so they heard that her name was Millie Sears, that she'd been some months in hospital in the larger town nearby, that she'd been committed to the Poor House just before Christmas, almost cured but unable to support herself. In hospital she cried with pain, but rarely spoke. Twice she threw herself to the floor, apparently in some kind of fit, and banged her fists and said *No no no*, although no question had been asked. When told she would be discharged to the Poor House she locked herself in the water closet, causing great inconvenience to the other patients, and only Miss McKay's constant whispering through the crack in the door brought her out at last. She said that she came from the city, that she had friends there and a child who was being looked after, but no-one came to see her the months she was in hospital, and she received no letters. She showed no gratitude for the care she received, nor for the clothing supplied her. She was given a soothing drink before she left, as Mr Brodie was afraid he'd have trouble on the journey.

A man with a high collar and a wobbly eye wrote a name on a piece of paper, a town some hours away with a mill that was always looking for women. He said it was all arranged, the fare to be held back from her wages; he said it would be a better place, a healthier place, and at the time she thought him kind. The mill itself was as noisy as any with clankings and raspings and shouting voices, but the town was indeed almost peaceful and she thought it a good place to live with the child when she had paid off the fare, had enough money to keep them both. Things happened like anywhere, fights in the taverns and thefts and ranters on the street, but when she walked on a Sunday it didn't take more than minutes to be alone with the trees and the birds and the soft green fields. Once a lantern flash of a leafy lane, an old brown cow, and rounded hills in the distance that she was certain was real, although she didn't know who had seen it.

But in the new town the pain came again, and she couldn't do her work because she couldn't stand up straight. She said No, but they took her off to the hospital anyway and people poked and prodded and fingered her body, like the strangers who'd gone through the last, shabby things she'd had to sell. She kept on saying it any way she could but the man with the thick, white side-whiskers said there was no choice, and then the Poor House reared up, square and grim, out of the snowy fields. The man with the high voice clicked handcuffs on her wrists and gave her arm a vicious tug. In the cold room she

saw herself in the spotted, wavering mirror, saw someone looking
back that must have been herself, and she felt so very tired.

Carne testified that he'd been warned she was a bad one, that's
why he'd put the handcuffs on, but she threw herself to the floor,
drumming her heels and using foul language and he took them
off as soon as Brodie's sleigh was out of sight. She said she'd never
stay and he told her she'd have to request her discharge properly,
and that quieted her for a time. No, they never forced her to come
down to her meat; the second day she said she was not well and
they took food to her room. No, he didn't know what she could
have meant, complaining to anyone of harsh treatment. That first
day she'd refused to go into the bath house and he'd had to lift her
by her rigid arms, perhaps that had marked her. But she was calm
enough coming out, and his wife said there'd been no trouble
with the bathing. Of course he'd looked everywhere the night she
ran off, and sent his boy to check the station, and his hired man to
check the farms nearby. No, he didn't know why noone recalled it.
No, he didn't remember saying, *Let her go.*

Mrs. Carne testified that she couldn't describe Millie Sears at
all; she'd been there such a short time that she hadn't left an
impression. The women who'd shared her room remembered
more. Her thick, dark hair and smooth complexion, her small
hands and feet. She had a purple lustre jacket and yes, it was quite
faded and could look gray, like the one on the missing body. Yes,
she had red flannel drawers, although they couldn't say if there
was a worn spot at the thigh.

Grace Lemon thought she recognized the stockings and hand-
kerchief found in the snow. Yes, she was sure about the handker-
chief, now that she looked again, for her own poor baby used to
play with it. That was how she knew about Millie Sears's chipped
front tooth, from seeing her smile and talk to the baby. Maybe
noone else had seen her smile, she couldn't say. Mary O'Donnell
said she recognized the boot shown to her as belonging to Millie
Sears. She said she had handled her boots many times, although
she couldn't say why. It was just getting dark when she left that
night, not snowing yet but the wind was picking up and it was
drifting. They'd first thought she was going to the outhouse and
no, they couldn't say why they'd decided that she must have run

off. No, it wasn't such a long time, twenty minutes maybe, less than an hour. Yes, they'd told Mrs. Carne, and she went to find her husband.

They brought her food but she couldn't stomach it, one day, two days, three. She stayed in the bed when the others rose and dressed; they came and went but most of the day she was alone, voices and sounds far away in the rest of the house, and so many things flashing in her head. If this was what was left when the fighting stopped then there seemed no point, but she couldn't summon the energy to change it. She thought she might be waiting for something, thought maybe a part of her had always been waiting.

It was difficult to distinguish the other women from each other, difficult to care enough to do that. One of them was named Grace, a thing that would have made her laugh if she'd been in any kind of mood for it. A sour-faced, sparse-haired woman, always with an ache or a pain, a sickly baby she was usually too tired to tend to. She knew it was a good thing she had nothing left worth stealing, for it was clear they were a light-fingered bunch. A fat one had tried to make off with her boots more than once.

Maybe it was the work she did, coaxing from the baby a loose, toothless smile. Something made her hungry and she dipped the spoon in the watery soup, wiped the chipped bowl with the heel of bread. The wind rattled the window and she stood on shaky legs, looked out at a swirl of white. Into her mind came the ship full of children, and a picture of Abby so sick in her berth, her sweat-soaked hair and her eyes big in her face. How frightening it was to see Abby like that, to know that she could be without her. Above on the deck it was hazy but the air was clean and there was nothing but empty sea and sky all around. She had never seen so much space, and somehow it calmed her. There was a sad woman who sat beside her and stroked her hair and she leaned against her, felt something begin to ease, flow away. A moment, just a moment, and then someone yanked her up and along with a swish of stiff skirts. She tried to look back, but the place where she'd been was empty.

The Carne boy didn't seem to spend much time in school and Charles often saw him about the town, loading supplies into the old wagon or perched on the back of a bench, watching the train chuff out of the station. Sometimes he followed the McKenna brothers down the main street, his heels hard on the new boardwalk as he tried to copy their strut. Once he saw Charles watching; his cheeks flushed, even as he shot a wad of spit into the street, and Charles remembered exactly what it was like. A boy trying things on, looking for his life. So far from him now, that time, that it didn't seem real, as much a phantasm as the picture of the fireside, the love shining out from his mother's face.

Like others, Charles was drawn to the schoolhouse and the testimony. He sat on a hard bench beside a pile of primers and looked at the pinned up maps, the shapes and faces; at times his fingers ached for a pencil. McKenna had offered more than he'd expected for the cabin, his plot of land, but that shouldn't have surprised him. It was a cruel irony, how he was made for this country, how he succeeded at everything he tried. He knew that this would be the pattern of his life, packing up the few things he needed to start again, feeding his sketches to the fire, one by one, and watching until there was nothing but ash before he rode away, the pencils and inks buckled deep in his saddle bag.

When he was certain that the roads would be good enough he travelled north to look at some available land, stood on a bluff surrounded by the crazed sky, waves rolling and crashing below. He had stood like this in the stern of the ship that had carried him across the ocean, the few bits of silver he had left weighing him down. The only thing that kept him from throwing himself over was the thought that he would be lost under another name, that his family would never know. He knew that it made no sense, but somehow he felt that as long as he was alive in the world, he would not have destroyed them completely.

But he had, he knew that he had, and Annie too. He had left them alone in a place that was not kind to women without a strong-armed provider. Left them to face the shame and the scandal, and perhaps some part of the punishment that should have been his. He knew that he had often been a dreamy, useless sort of boy, but he had been there, at least he had been there. Until the evening that he met Annie in the high field, her tears and her small hands clutching the shawl over her stomach. He had soothed her, promised that he would do right by her, felt her bird's heart fluttering against his chest. But when she had walked away with a lighter step, his head began to swirl. Until that moment he hadn't realized that he expected something more, but suddenly he saw the years ahead, saw Annie's smooth cheek weathered and scored, a life that was nothing but work and worry, no time to wander the hills with his sketchpad tucked under his arm. He sank to the ground and stared at his life while the night fell down around him.

It was the chill that made him get up and move, under the high, cold stars. His way home took him by Daley's cottage and he thought of the story that everyone knew, the fat bag of silver old Daley tucked under his pillow at night. No thought in his head but how a little would help, and then he was inside with the old man's smell and whistling breath, the red glowing light from the dying fire. Holding his own breath and then a strong, bony hand on his wrist and he had hit out with something, whatever he had in his hand, and someone was grunting as he hit again and again. He was startled, that was all, he was frightened; he hadn't meant to hurt anyone. But he ran through the dawn and the white mist rose and one hand pressed a hide bag of coins to his heart.

Thompson's wife said she thought it was like being caught in a storm, how you could see nothing else, hear nothing else, there in the swirling centre. Or like being ill, like being so ill that you can't even imagine that you will ever feel well again, can't remember that you had ever felt well before, what that was like. The body was found and then lost in those blank, muddy days when spring was just thinking of coming, and for weeks people talked of nothing else. Fear and theories and new possibilities for old grudges.

The coroner was thinking of that as he walked along the main street, his lips twitching a little, although he wasn't exactly talking to himself. Thinking too about the work at the new mill not going on as it should, about the pain in his wife's back that was getting worse. Thinking that maybe he'd let the whole thing go on too long, as caught up in it as everyone else.

There were things that maybe he should have done. Made more enquiries in the city, he could have done that. Tried to find the child, if there really was one. There had been a photograph in the jacket pocket, though it had been so cracked and stained that it was difficult to make out what it was. A face, a pale section that could have been a dress, could have been a white or a light coloured dress. Could have been a child. Could have been the dead woman herself. Could have been the dead woman when she was a child—

He titched his tongue in annoyance. He'd done enough, more than earned his fee. He'd wondered at first about Bailey, who had found the body. A man who had appeared from nowhere, although to be fair that was not so unusual. But no friends, no family, a man who kept to himself, with a manner that didn't invite any probing. There was a question in his mind about Bailey, but no reason to connect him with this business. There was no doubt now that the body was that of Millie Sears, that she'd run from the Poor House on a stormy Christmas Eve, that she'd not made it far before she'd frozen to death. The things that nagged at him still, that had so engrossed him at the beginning—he decided that he'd have to let them go. Why she was not found that night, if Carne had made the search he said he had, and what made her run so wildly in the first place. Why were her stockings and hand-kerchief so far from the body, why were her legs bare, her boots unlaced. There was something odd about it all, so there was, but it didn't matter as it once had. Perhaps he'd write a letter to the Inspector, let him decide if more questions should be asked. Though people were saying that Carne's wife was planning to go back to her people, taking the boy with her, so they'd need to find a new couple anyway.

As for the body's disappearance, by now he was fairly sure he knew the way of that. Others were wondering out loud but he kept his thoughts to himself, for once he opened his mouth it would have to be official. Confrontation, investigation, more time and trouble. And she was dead, poor wretch, and noone had come looking for her, so what did it matter where her bones ended up?

The other women sniggered and told her she'd have to see Carne, that he had to approve her when she applied to be discharged. "He lo-oves to do it," they called after her, as she made her way down the creaking stairs. She found him in the shed at the back of the house, shifting sacks of potatoes with his boy. He sent the boy away and he had that look when he said, in his horrid high voice, that he had to make an Inspection before he could recommend her. It was what she had expected, but when she reached to lift her skirt he told her to remove everything, all her clothes, so he could Inspect her properly. She unbuttoned her jacket, peeled off her stockings and looked for a place to put them that wasn't the muddy floor. And then something like fire whooshed through her head and she was running, just running, her feet crammed back into her boots, the laces slapping and the shed door banging behind her. The world she ran into was nothing but white, and after the first moment, not even cold, and she ran like a person would run in a dream, not even feeling her feet on the ground; she had no idea she could run so fast, so far. She ran until she wasn't running anymore, and although she didn't remember noise, it was so quiet where she lay on the ground, so soft. There was wood beneath her fingers and she thought it might be a sun-warmed table, and everything was white all around. She thought again of that time looking out at the empty sea, remembered leaning into someone, letting go.

Robby Carne lived to be a very old man, and he carried a bit of a finger bone in his trouser pocket until the day he died. For luck, he said, but there's noone left alive who remembers that, or anything else about him. He'd heard the McKennas talking about a doctor they knew of who would pay good money for a skeleton; they thought it was funny when they found him waiting outside the stable in the dark. Tam reached down a hand and pulled him up behind him on the horse. They passed a whisky bottle back and forth and they were all stinking of it when they rode past the big stone house in the moonlight.

They'd planned to deliver the body that same night but stuffing her into the sack was worse than they'd imagined, and then one of the horses went lame. Instead, they buried it deep in the dung heap at the back of the livery stable, and told Robby they'd do for him if he breathed a word. There was much more fuss than they'd expected too, and it was weeks before they dared to go back with a pitchfork and shovel. They threw the sack into the river, where it ran deepest, and never told a living soul.

Alex, the Barista

Café You was more than a coffee house, more than the campus hangout. More than a dungeonesque door, a sunken room, and sofas leaking white stuffing, as if mice tunneled in the cushions while customers chatted overhead. It was more than a refuge when winter made life miserable. It was magnetic. Each roasted coffee bean, shiny, black, bifurcated, was a lodestone, pulling people towards the brick façade, the decorative iron railings, the giant panda tilted in a chair.

Alex Buckner, on the eighth floor of a Gothic dorm, stood before his drafty window, sniffed at a black Café You shirt, and flung it back on his bed, satisfied. Clean. Clean, for her. But wrinkled too, showing off his new indifferent look. Alex was short, and small for a university sophomore. Several years' growth, and more muscle mass and confidence were still due him. Though he tried hard to be taken seriously, it didn't help that he rode a moped around campus, since the law required an orange safety flag, and it bent behind him on its plastic mast as he towed it through the air.

He had a short neck, and ears set far from his head like Prince Charles. He came from careful, quiet folk. His ancestors had stayed ahead of the carnage that tore Europe to pieces after the Enlightenment by fleeing military drafts, enlisting as musicians, and volunteering for the monotonous duties of clerking and accounting. The innumerable forces of history added and subtracted their bits and pieces to the making of him, and he was their inescapable sum.

On the quad below, students bent against the wind, aiming for the shelter of the stone buildings. It wasn't snowing yet. He'd have to bundle up and hurry if he wanted to run before work. He pulled on a sweatshirt, a jacket, then a knit hat embossed with the school mascot, the unicorn, which he had bought at the campus bookstore, despite the exorbitant markup, in a surge of university pride and loyalty.

"Ready to go jogging, Tony?" he asked his roommate. "I need a break from this scholarship application. It's driving me crazy."

Tony, broad-shouldered and sociable, closed his marketing textbook, grinned, and dug his large, smelly running shoes from under his bed. "Breaks are good. I'll study later at the café, before I go out," he said, with characteristic self-assurance. "Or maybe I'll just come bug you while you work."

In the English building, Ms. Jennifer Carter, thirty years old, a graduate Teaching Assistant, checked her e-mail. She had one more class, in a cold room without any windows. Her cat was sick, and her Ph.D. thesis, which she would defend in six months, was only a one-page outline. And now this—some man from the online dating service had misunderstood her polite refusal, and announced he would be waiting for her at Café You. How humiliating.

Her mother, a trembling Sunday voice on the phone, demanded weekly justification of her disappointing single status. Her eggs, after all, were not getting any younger. Eggs didn't care how educated she was. They would mercilessly hurl themselves, one after another, lemming-like, down her reproductive tract, shrivel slowly, and let their chromosomes fray like dragged ropes.

She studied the picture. Not a bad looking man. If she cancelled now, he might not get the message in time. In the end she went through with it for her mother, to prove she was trying, like going to job interviews to stay eligible for unemployment benefits. What was a half-hour of her time? Why were all the other grad students she knew female, or married? She nervously picked up her purple book bag, with its unicorn appliqué wearing off.

In class, she accidentally made the chalk squeak, so that her students shifted and moaned, and grabbed their ears; she misspelled *Austen,* dropped the chalk, and chased the rolling pieces across the floor, nearly tripping, so that students, as in all her classes, wondered if she was really qualified to teach them, because she was always teetering on the edge of some apparent breakdown, and they whispered among themselves that perhaps her mental lapses would affect their grades, and debated whether they really ought to go, *en masse,* to the dean.

Dr. Kevin Hawkins, across campus, was in clear command of his math lecture. Thirty students sat with open notebooks, trying to keep up. No one dared ask him a question. He filled the wall-length whiteboard with esoteric calculations, deftly changing markers when the ink ran dry. He was a serious man. He had been teased as a child, mocked for his meticulous attention to detail, his affinity for his teachers, and the clumsy way he hurled a baseball. When the opportunity for academic mastery came, he seized it, finishing his Ph.D. at nineteen. Now, he lived aware of a deeper reality, similar to that of the Platonic forms. In class, he sometimes pretended he was Newton, fully at ease with the language of mathematics, swimming in intergalactic space, where minds communicated without the constraints of time, where Euclid, Tycho Brahe or Einstein might drift from behind a star, and wave congenially to him. If only other people understood.

He completed an equation forty steps long, ignoring his students' bewildered expressions. He had left the board only for an instant—to stand over one dozing boy, and repeatedly clear his throat, and clasp his hands, until a poke from a sympathetic classmate roused the sleeper and the totality of his domain was restored.

Lodestones, pulling, pulling, pulling. Each polished bean, inside a sealed coffee bag, or poised in the plastic cone of the espresso grinder, exerted its irresistible force.

"When's the snow supposed to start?" Alex asked, on the dorm steps, zipping his jacket. The wind came through the bare trees without mercy. His breath clouded behind his hand.

"Midnight," Tony said, coughing into his glove.

They stretched, pretending to ignore girls in thick coats who glanced at them with admiration. They had started running freshman year, partly to drown out hangovers, partly to explore campus, familiarizing themselves with the institution to which they had somehow, despite atrocious grades, gained admission. Alex had gradually come to realize, as he stopped to stretch and spit in the grass, and incidentally read the tarnished plaques and mower-bent signs, that he was on a campus built by the East Coast layering of American history, the European settlers and African slaves, survivors of the moods of the sea, which allowed the arbitrary passage of this ship or that, these people or those. The land itself came through grants to a Lord Proprietor, by patchwork acquisitions from Native Americans, by the upheavals of the Revolutionary and Civil Wars. It seemed to Alex, however, as his heart pumped young blood through his elastic veins, that this university had been rightfully in development for over two hundred years solely for his edification.

"Let's go," Alex said. "It's getting late."

The gloomy dorms on the quad, sporting gargoyles with open, devilish mouths, mercifully blocked the wind. Without leaves on the trees, the stolid buildings were clearly visible, and reminded Alex of literature's famous prep schools. They were a charming place to study, or to go mad. His first girlfriend had dropped out; she cracked, she said, under the lingering weight of the patriarchy. Other desperate females, kids from suburbs who had naively majored in philosophy and collided with Sartre, or in literature, dragging their desks into circles and debating Humbert Humbert's desire—girls like these suffered, she claimed, from education's distillation of history into a litany of human dysfunction. The deeper they looked, the more madness they saw. She and her friends pierced their faces, wore Army boots, and drank and drugged themselves into such stupors they had to be bumped out on ambulance gurneys, which were not built for the narrow, dark, intricately-carved mahogany stairwells.

Alex slapped his hands as he ran. Two miles, then two and a half. A bit of sleet fell, hissing through dried leaves on the oaks. Alex kept pushing himself, trying to beat Tony, who jogged easily, knees high, as if humoring him. The bell tower said four o'clock. Alex pulled his hat close to his eyes, pumped his arms faster, whooped, and put on a burst of speed.

A few science buildings sat, as boxy afterthoughts, on the campus fringes. When they reached them, they turned back towards the center of campus. The university showpiece was a soaring cathedral where Sunday attendance, in sterner days, had been mandatory. Now, only freshmen and seniors went to services. At the cathedral, Alex sprinted the eleven steps, and despite his avowed agnosticism, had a look through a window flanking the locked doors. He cupped his hands, smudging the pane. A candle flickered in a red globe above the altar, cradled like a glass heart, suspended by gold chains thirty feet long, the veritable center, he believed, of campus. As if there really were something at the core of it all. Human hope, perhaps? He pulled away, blinking.

The tiny lodestones were doing their jobs. The grinder whirred, the cash register dinged, the espresso printer spat out orders: lattes, macchiatos, hot cocoa. Alex, in his rumpled shirt, worked the register. His supervisor, Keith, a tall senior, sunglasses on his head year-round, stayed cool and aloof.

Alex watched the door. On Thursdays, she came in around seven. He'd look up and there she'd be, enigmatically smiling, in a gauzy poet blouse, with drilled conch earrings twirling idly beneath her lobes. And that scuffed book bag. She had been so nervous in class. It wasn't mocha she needed, it was to sit nearby and overhear his brilliant comments, remarks that showed he was listening to her lectures, and cared, and would, if necessary, prevent other students from reporting her mental lapses, her confusion, to the administration.

The line stretched to the door, and everyone seemed impatient, as if to finish studying and then beat the snow home. It was hard to keep up with the barrage of orders. A short man came forward and Alex pushed the cash drawer closed, too hard, and smiled, warily. "Dr. Hawkins! How are you?"

Dr. Hawkins had a goatee, a bulbous, shiny head, and eyebrows slashing out from his nose. His forehead leaned in while his small chin remained behind, as if he were paying attention but nevertheless withholding approval. His tie pin was a silver right triangle, Pythagoras' proposition I-47, Euclid's cornerstone of geometry.

"Alex. I didn't know you worked here too. A busy young man. When does the math job start up?"

"The math job? I didn't take it. What can I get you?"

"You didn't? Really? I'm surprised." He made a petulant face.

"What kind of coffee do you want, sir?"

"The strongest bean you have."

"To go?"

"No, for here. I'm meeting someone." Dr. Hawkins pulled off yellow deerskin gloves by the fingertips. "You didn't take that job? Why? And you dropped my differential equations class."

"I'm sorry, I know we talked about it. Room for cream, sir?"

"Was my class at an inconvenient time?" Dr. Hawkins waved two dollars by their corners. Alex rang up the sale and dumped coins in his outstretched palm.

"I changed my major," Alex said.

Dr. Hawkins looked surprised, then impressed. "Oh! On to the applied sciences! Engineering, astronomy?"

"No, English, actually," Alex said. He picked dried whipped cream from his Café You shirt.

Dr. Hawkins turned red. He folded a napkin into fourths and daubed a drop of milk off his shoe. His disdain was obvious. Alex's working at a coffee shop—instead of accepting the math research position—was a waste of talent, and his desertion for such unreliable company as English must have been caused, not by whim, but by spite. Spite which deserved spite.

"You know," Dr. Hawkins said, straightening up and shaking an empty half-and-half pitcher in the air, "some theorists have argued that the field of English literature, *per se,* as opposed to world literature, which harks back to the ancients—the field of *English* was created in the 1800s to cement a British national unity between the classes."

"Interesting," Alex said. "I still like it."

Dr. Hawkins pulled out his leather coin purse, brown with a gold unicorn stamped on it, dropped in a quarter and a penny, and let its star-like mouth snap shut. Fourier series and identities of transforms! Other students would kill for that job. A waste of time that had been, lobbying for the boy on the slim evidence of one semester as a student aide. That was the trouble. Young people were not willing to buckle down as he himself had done, factoring out almost-prime numbers for fun, and, by coincidence, preserving his virginity until late in his twenties.

"Do you intend to teach?" Dr. Hawkins said. "When you graduate with your—your English degree?"

"Maybe," Alex said. "But then I need to get in grad school."

"Well, good luck with that," Dr. Hawkins said. He shook his head. Frowning, his goatee trembling, he made his way through the crowd. He nodded at two shamefaced colleagues—eating tiramisu—in a career-destroying affair everyone in the department was tired of whispering about. A student he had advised last

semester fiddled with her earphones, looked down, and pretended not to see him. He felt relieved; he had forgotten her name. He
always forgot their names, except this Alex, who for some reason
had touched him and now stuck in his craw.

He took out a stack of papers. He looked at the first hopeless
one, and marked it up with red ink. When his date arrived, he
would talk about Alex. Students were always a safe topic. Shame,
shame! The boy was deluding himself: he was not a wunderkind,
with unlimited time and energy to recover from professional mis-
steps. He wouldn't understand until he needed a mortgage, a car,
children, life's animal trappings with which lesser minds must
content themselves, what a solid career path he had recklessly
flung to the winds.

He planned the conversation as if it were a proof. After he
impressed dates with his high position, associate professor and
former undergraduate department chair, he tended to fall into a
hasty, overly-familiar frankness, as if he had been confiding in the
same woman his entire life, floating in space like Euclid, Brahe
and Einstein, eternal, but with various names and faces.

"Alex, let's clean up fast and get out by midnight," Keith said,
pushing up his sunglasses, once the line of customers was served.
"And we're almost out of whipped cream. Someone on another
shift stripped the threads on one of the empty canisters, so don't
use it. No, the left one. Your other left. The manager was really
mad because those things are expensive," Keith said, cracking
open a roll of quarters. "Did I hear right? How come you changed
your major anyway? Math grads make good money."

Alex filled the espresso hopper. The beans sounded like a rain-
storm, running in. There were a hundred other things to do, like
put away inventory in the stock room, but he lingered to defend
himself against this lunacy charge.

"I know math grads make more money," Alex said, keeping his
voice low so he couldn't be overheard. He swept coffee grounds in
a pile. They were damp like sand; he pinched them into shapes,
and then swept them into the trash. "Math was too intense. I felt
like I was—getting warped."

"I guess everything warps you, one way or another," Keith said,
slamming the milk fridge door.

"Only if you let it," Alex said. He washed his grubby forearms, getting off the various coffee and milk blotches and sticky spots.

"Think so?" Keith said. He knocked the tight puck of coffee grounds from the portafilter: bang, bang, bang, the blows in the knock box echoed from the ceiling, and then he wiped the oily silver basket with a rag.

"That thing's like a gavel," Alex said. "Are you condemning me, man? I got out of math once I realized it wasn't for me. I'm not saying anything bad about you being in finance. Don't get me wrong."

Keith said, "It's your life. You know, you should get that guy to write that third scholarship recommendation you've been moaning about all semester. Why not go ask him? He seemed to think you're smart."

"Him?" Alex asked. "It's English. He's mad because I didn't take that math job."

"People change their majors," Keith said. "It's not against the law. When is it due?"

"Next week."

Keith whistled. "Better hurry up. No one's gonna do it for ya, kid."

Alex sat on the counter. He had to think. When Keith looked at him contemptuously, he jumped off. His face lit up with certainty. He pounded his fist into his palm. "Well, you're right. If I got the scholarship, and studied for a summer in England, I'd be a shoo-in for a good grad program."

"What's the worst he can do, say no?" Keith asked.

Dr. Hawkins was frustrated by his table lamp. He made an impatient gesture, jerking a phantom chain. Alex took him a new light bulb, and the man unscrewed the old one, making the threads scratch noisily. Alex looked at his shiny head, regarding every familiar furrow and crooked wisp of hair with mild trepidation.

"English is kind of mathematical," Alex said, abruptly, too loud, still trying to justify himself. "Someone makes a point in class and you rebut it with evidence from the text. Really, math was good training for English."

Dr. Hawkins raised a spear-like eyebrow. He held out the cold bulb, and Alex accepted it. Alex felt a flicker of regret when he saw the tests on the table, with their equations and formulas. It was like seeing an old girlfriend. A world of possibilities was gone. For the first time in his life, something, by his own choice, was forever lost to him. When he dropped the bulb in the trash, it shattered.

"I'm going on break," he told Keith. "Now that we got the line served. You can handle it, right? Call me if it gets busy." He took his sandwich with him.

In the office, Alex propped his feet on the desk. Even Austen was good company after the drudgery and humiliation of manual labor. Books were his refuge. On weekends, before work, he would put on jeans and a ragged sweater, and read until time to clock in at Café You, sustaining himself in his dorm room on saltines and flat orange soda that hissed evilly when he opened it. In this way, he followed Proust through Paris, Dickens through London, and Melville across the South Seas. He spent weekday mornings in the library, afternoons in class, and evenings in used book stores or the library, magically transported from the East Coast to the streets of Calcutta, the brothels of Dublin, the trattorias of Rome.

Now he opened *Pride and Prejudice* and immersed himself in the romantic entanglements of the Bennet girls. The stilted language bothered him. Repeatedly, he had asked Ms. Carter what made this novel great. She had developed multiple arguments about money and power, and her face reddened with excitement, but he just didn't understand. He chewed his peanut butter sandwich and thought of England.

"Hey," Keith said, intruding, his black canvas apron wet from a spill. "It's getting busy." He rapped with unnecessary authority on the desk.

Alex put the book down. At the espresso machine, he jumped back into the workflow. He made a game of it, the way he made a game of jogging home when he started to tire. He imagined he was a Navy cook, feeding his crew. He made drink after drink, grabbing milk pitchers, flinging empty jugs into the trash. A group came in and everyone ordered cocoa. He jerked the whipped cream canister, slick and damp, from the fridge. He sculpted dramatic floating whorls on the brown cocoa surfaces.

When Jennifer Carter came in, he fumbled the canister, and nearly dropped it. She looked anxious, her head tilted over her delicate shoulder. Alex had changed his major after one day in her literature class, a general distribution requirement he'd been forced to take. A Shakespearean sonnet, something about a summer day, had done the trick.

Alex jerked his head upward, acknowledging Ms. Carter through the kaleidoscopic bakery case reflections, the upside-down ghostly orbs of cinnamon rolls and grainy tops of muffins. She didn't order a drink, but instead looked around with uncertainty. Alex felt hospitable; he was the happy cook, she, the captain's daughter. Alex noticed, as always, her intense excitement, as if she were a nerve laid bare. She was a poet, as well as a scholar, author of a chapbook of surprisingly hostile poems, dedicated to her ex-boyfriend, entitled *You are Salt: I am Slug.*

He set down the pitcher. He waved, redundantly; she waved back as if distracted, then he tried to look as busy as possible. Another group came in. When the rush was over, he headed out on the pretext of emptying a bus tub. He looked for her in the sea of people. There she was, but not alone. His hands shook. He took short, confused breaths, turned, and then retraced his steps. He made himself keep going to that problematic bus tub as if nothing were wrong.

Ms. Carter, her purple book bag against her shin like a Greek shield, sat at Dr. Hawkins' table, with its stack of ungraded exams. Dr. Hawkins and Ms. Carter. It was shocking, out of place, and rather frightening, like a poodle stuck in a tree. She clutched a pen, her knuckles pale. She smiled as if glad to see him. "Alex, how's your paper going?" she said.

He whispered, "Great. It's just great."

"I noticed most of the Austen books are checked out of the library," she said.

"That's me," he said, "I love Austen."

"I'm writing my dissertation on her," she told Dr. Hawkins.

Alex said, "My paper is on her perception of Victorian lawn tennis. I can't find any mention of it yet."

"Really?" She smiled, encouragingly. "I think I know why. Talk to me after class."

Dr. Hawkins cleared his throat, trying to regain control. "Alex is an excellent student," he said categorically, "possessing a fine mathematical mind."

"I was a math major," Alex said, "but I fell in love with literature." Ms. Carter smiled. Dr. Hawkins patted her sleeve. His hairy paw covered hers, and she did not move it away. Alex jerked up the bus tub. All the dishes trembled. *In love with literature,* he kicked himself.

He retreated to the kitchen and yanked open the dishwasher. The latte bowls, slick with sanitizer, steamed in his face. He didn't like old men chasing younger women. It wasn't fair. He started loudly philosophizing. Wasn't that why she came in, and sat nearby? To listen to him? He'd be in full form!

"Hey, Keith," he said. "Do you ever step back and think about the big picture here?"

"What do you mean?" Keith said, suspiciously.

"Mugs, cups, plates, forks, all dripping and steaming, all going to their separate places," Alex said. "What a silly routine. All these people come and study, and leave after a few years. Forks and knives used until they're too scratched. Mugs served till they're chipped or broken, or hairline cracks form in the handles and they have to be thrown away, so they don't fall apart while somebody's drinking. It's all intellectual consumerism. Is that any different from material consumption?"

"I don't know," Keith said. "Frankly, I could care less. We have a lot to do. That big rush put us behind in cleaning."

Alex persisted. "Is any poetry to be written after Homer, any drama after Shakespeare? Are we just keeping ourselves busy, killing time? Perhaps it's all illusory; we're fooling ourselves into thinking we're superior because we've chosen one life's work over another."

Keith shrugged. He brushed his apron. "Then quit," he said. "Go live with your parents. I could use your hours."

Alex slammed the dishwasher door. Someone threw a tightly-wadded napkin at him and he turned, annoyed. His roommate leaned on the register.

"Hey!" Tony said, teasing. "Can I get some service?"

Alex threw the napkin back, hitting him. They both laughed because it was only a napkin. "Tony! Do me a favor. Remember that application I'm working on? I'm asking those professors, well, one's just a TA, for recommendations. Those two over there. Listen to what they're talking about. I want to know what's going on."

"You're crazy!"

"He doesn't know you," Alex said. "Hurry up."

Tony walked over, and made a show of noticing, as if by chance and surprise, a table next to the odd couple. He hadn't come to the café to study after all, but to bug Alex and bother girls, and so he had no books. He sat down and stared at his cuticles.

Don't be so obvious, Alex thought. Dr. Hawkins was in his late forties. Didn't she care that he was going bald? After twenty minutes of torturing Alex with various faces of surprise, Tony returned to the counter with exaggerated nonchalance. "Come outside," Alex said, pulling his arm. "You talk too loud." They shivered, without jackets, in the alley.

"He's trying to impress her with the creativity of geometry," Tony reported.

"Is she buying it?"

"I can't tell."

"Geometry? How is that creative? It's already figured out. I'm going to write great literature myself someday. I'll toss *The New Yorker* on her table and quip 'page 169, mine.'"

Tony looked thoughtful. "I bet he has tenure. Girls like a guy with tenure. Relax, turn into a baby factory. What, you disagree?"

"She wouldn't sell out like that."

"Really? They were also talking about you."

"Me!"

"How you bailed on him after he got you that research job. They were sort of patronizing."

Alex grabbed his head. He swayed back and forth. "I'm losing my mind."

"Are you sure that's the guy who was going to write your recommendation?"

"Yes. Her too. Well, neither of them now, I guess. Why does she have to waste herself on him?"

"You're asking the wrong man." Tony said, "How much did that math job pay?"

"You can't have it," Alex said, shaking his head. "You just can't."

"Only a thought. Maybe I'll work here. Are you partying with me and my friends tonight?"

"If we close early. We've got almost everything done."

"Well," said Tony, "see ya if I see ya." They punched each other's arms, as hard as they could stand.

Alex rolled up the rubber floor mats under the espresso machine. The stainless steel showed his mournful face, his short neck, his big ears. He swept and mopped. He imagined his teachers talking about him, pitying him. He restocked the paper coffee cups. All the conical cups were nested together in a flexible plastic sleeve. Dr. Hawkins would know the useless equation for describing that.

Jennifer Carter wished her mother knew how hard she was trying. Dr. Kevin Hawkins didn't look at all like his profile picture— a trim youth leaning on a castle parapet, his hair thick and black, under brooding clouds. If he hadn't worn a tie, like he'd mentioned in his e-mail, she'd have assumed he stood her up. Was he doing something suggestive with his fingers? That creepy lacing, lacing, lacing, and unlacing? Had he had seen her car, and could he follow her? Fortunately, people nearby could be coerced into providing assistance if necessary. Not only was there that pesky Alex, there was that married professor who'd once propositioned her, forking tiramisu with a woman who was not his wife.

Now he sketched equations on her napkin. Didn't he know the quickest way to make a woman mad was to make her feel stupid? Yes, she had gone on too many blind dates. Each academic department was a separate exhibit in the university zoo. Sociologists wanted to police her politics, and chemists—she didn't even want to start on them. The English types were already spoken for. Athletes were childishly inaccessible in their world of bouncing basketballs and echoing gyms. Geneticists slyly pried into her family tree. Perhaps she should try the men from the toothbrush factory south of town.

So here she was: living in a third-floor walk-up, unable to afford to take her vomiting cat to the vet, dating this stranger nearly her father's age, with his giant forehead, trying to impose his boring agenda. She smiled until her face hurt. Her napkin was completely covered with formulas. What the hell was he trying to do? She barely remembered long division. He was blathering on about transformations, Alex, and what a fine mind he was allowing to rot.

She leaned forward to find an opening for Alex' defense. He was saying something about almost-prime numbers. All those lonely numbers out there waiting to be discovered. He didn't look Scottish. Perhaps she could mention the picture, find out when it was taken, and why he was wearing a kilt.

Dr. Hawkins realized he was failing. Jennifer Carter kept trying to make illogical connections between math and literary theory. He was getting nowhere. He would always live alone, like his parents warned him, and when he eventually died of a heart attack, his Nobel Prize on a high dusty shelf, his corpse would be nibbled to an unrecognizable state by his Schnauzer.

Fueled by despair, he plunged deeper toward the intellectual side of things. He tapped his pen on her napkin for emphasis. It was good for her to be forced to think critically. He had a long-running agenda to make humanities people more practical, so they would eventually demand a smaller, more reasonable share of the university budget. She was being too careful, obviously thinking too much before she spoke. She had already decided against him. He changed tactics. Instead of her body, he could impregnate her mind.

He explained his research, his frantic race against Zimansky in Russia. Soon she looked peaked, as if her glucose were low. She started to talk about her cat. Women always had cats. He made his big move. Excusing himself, he ordered hot cocoas and returned to the table. "I hope you like whipped cream," he said.

Alex, glancing with annoyance at their order ticket on the counter, steamed cocoa, lifting his pitcher, lowering it, making an obnoxious squeal and then a low gurgle, as if something large, Dr. Hawkins perhaps, were drowning beneath the foam. Louder, louder! Students, books open, looked over in helpless disbelief. Alex didn't care. He ended with a flourish, a high sopranic screech of the frothing wand. Two latte bowls waited side by side, shiny white husband and wife with their ceramic lips touching. When he tried to garnish them, the empty whipped cream canister sputtered, blew gas, and spat flecks of cream onto his black shirt.

He grabbed an empty canister from the shelf. He spooned in sugar, poured in a quart of liquid whipping cream, seated the rubber gasket, and screwed on the top. It wouldn't go straight. He forced it. A little voice in the back of his head bothered him. Dr. Hawkins, waiting, cleared his throat.

"What's the hold-up, son?" he said. He straightened his tie. The Pythagorean theorem had gotten out of whack.

"I need to make whipped cream," Alex said, "but I'm not sure this one works."

"Looks fine to me," Dr. Hawkins said. "Or maybe, everything just looks fine to me tonight. Please hurry," he said. He glanced over at Jennifer Carter. "I take full responsibility for this monumental career decision."

"Dr. Hawkins, I know you're busy," Alex said. He was nervous. Now was the moment to get that promise, when the man was distracted. Alex screwed on a small silver charger, full of compressed gas. He started twisting it, hard, showing off his biceps. "But I'm applying for a scholarship to London—and I was going to ask you for a recommenda—"

Whipped cream blew upward, outward, spraying everywhere. The aluminum top hit the ceiling. Falling, it hit Alex on the shoulder. "Shit!" he said. He dropped the canister. He kicked it, set it spinning. It rolled to the garbage can, turned circles, and came to rest by the wall. White liquid, like paint, leaked from its mouth.

"My God," Dr. Hawkins said. His shirt was soaked. He had whipped cream on his face, in his goatee, and in his hair.

"Sorry," Alex said. "I'm sorry."

Keith ran in. "I heard an explosion," he said. "What the hell was that?"

"That would be me," Alex said. It was very quiet. It had sounded like a bomb; everyone looked around with big eyes. "Go back to studying, please," he said. "It was just the whipped cream. You learn something new every day."

A man clapped. Applause filled the room. Had he not been behind the counter, Alex would have taken a bow. Instead, he smiled sheepishly. It was a terrible, terrible mess. The floor was white. Whipped cream was everywhere—the floor, the walls, the ceiling, even spattered on the panda by the door.

"Wow," Keith said. He dropped the canister in the sink. "This is going to take forever to clean up. I don't even know where to start."

Dr. Hawkins took the rag Keith gave him and stormed away. He daubed Ms. Carter's gauzy sleeve quite vigorously. She held still, letting him, like a child. Her expression softened; she seemed hypnotized by his touch. Adversity and human contact were overcoming her defenses. Alex handed out more rags. A young woman wiped her laptop screen with a dry napkin. He took her some paper towels and glass cleaner. More rags, and profuse apologies. Soon everyone, everywhere, was finding spots around them to wipe.

"Well, so much for closing early," Keith said, setting a stack of clean rags on the counter. He walked carefully. Milk fat had slickened the tiles like ice.

"Look! I'm skating!" Alex said. He slid around the kitchen without lifting his feet. Then he did it faster, pushing off from the counter. He almost fell.

"You're going to have to throw those shoes away," Keith said, wiping whipped cream off the framed unicorn looming over the sink. "And probably that shirt too."

"Maybe it will come out in the wash," Alex said, plucking the sopping cloth off his belly.

"I'll let you do the floor," Keith said. "How about it, then?"

Alex poured detergent in a bucket, added hot water, and mopped again and again. His world became the mess under the counter, the long-lost spoon he pulled out, the milk caps that had rolled underneath. Keith, forgoing his break, took furtive bites of cold pizza. He wiped the walls, the fridge, the coffee canisters.

Alex changed the string mop heads several times. Customers, repulsed by the detergent smell, began to leave. Someone announced that it was sleeting. Alex watched them go, one by one, out the carved doors. He leaned on his mop handle, as if on a staff, or a lance. Then he got back to work, in a state of disbelief. He bent down to clean the shelves. He'd ruined two instructors at once: a record!

"You were asking me something," Dr. Hawkins said in a hushed tone. He had evidently been at the counter a long time, watching him. He seemed amused, even kind. Jennifer Carter was getting through to him. Alex glanced at her; she gave him a cold stare. It hurt. He looked again to make sure. She was gathering her things. Then he understood. They were about to leave together, probably to a movie, or some other baby step. And it was none of his business.

Alex grabbed his math teacher's nervous hands and gave them a firm, brave waggle, part handshake, mostly concession. He felt mature, taking the high road, swallowing a disappointment. "I don't remember what I was asking you," Alex said. "I'm sure it wasn't important."

"No, it's okay," Dr. Hawkins said. "About some scholarship. Continue. The probability of such an accident, given two such containers, was fifty percent."

"Okay. That's a good way to put it. You're right. I'll—come to your office hours. Tomorrow, if you don't mind. Are you still in there all day long?"

"Come before noon, or after one. No, after two," Dr. Hawkins said. He grinned. "I have a lunch appointment."

Ms. Carter gave Alex a wry wave on her way out. He raised his hand to his eyebrow. "See you in class," he called, then dropped his salute. It was, after all, a changing of the guard. Her book bag looked heavy from the way she carried it.

He finished the shelves. Soon, he felt let down. Her warm regard—of him, and her passionate love of literature—had been an orienting sun on an open plain. She had opened the door; now he was on his own. He had seen the brief crimp of disapproval in her eyes.

His shoes were wet and greasy. Keith alternated between being mad at him and making jokes to lighten the mood. He didn't stop him from opening the alley door and chucking the canister in the dumpster. Alex dumped the horrible mop heads, slimy and cold, in the washing machine. He left a prominent note, in neat handwriting, to remind the morning shift to put them in the dryer. He tried not to forget anything, but rather to improve his standing, because he would probably be working there the rest of his life.

"We did it," Keith said, when they finally finished. It had taken an extra hour and a half. The chairs were inverted on the tables, seats up, airing their chewing gum. The coffee beans, missions accomplished, rested together in bags and the grinder cone, like grains of sand in an hourglass. Alex turned off the lights. Keith set the alarm.

"So next time, listen to what I tell you, right?"

"Okay, boss," Alex said.

Outside, they went their separate ways. The cars, bushes, and buildings wore lacy shawls of snow and sleet. Freed from the wage-slavery that he believed both enlightened and oppressed him, Alex pulled on his knit cap and tucked his ears underneath. It was too late to meet Tony and his friends.

A taxi skidded under a red signal light, left snaky tracks, stopped, then ventured on. It was calm in the deserted downtown—with only the distant noise of the bars behind him. All he needed now was to wreck his bike. He'd walk. His moped was hard to push, but the exercise kept him warm. Gloveless, he kept one hand in his jacket behind *Pride and Prejudice.*

Next year he would be a junior. Eventually he would graduate, and then what? Maybe grad school. Perhaps clerking or accounting, the family professions. Unemployed afternoons dozing in the public library. His same job at Café You, until his golden years.

He didn't care. There were so many books left to read. He had only started. There were thousands, millions. Yes, he would have made a good mathematician. Or a good teacher. He was becoming a good reader. Perhaps that was all he could hope for, in a world without answers, or with a duplicity of them. As he passed the dark cathedral, toward the inviting dorms, he was certain that for such a reason alone, he was one of history's more fortunate men.

A Profile

James Alan McPherson mocks the Horatio Alger aspect of his background via the young writer-narrator of his first published story, "Gold Coast" (an *Atlantic Monthly* First in 1968), in a passage where Robert dreams that "there would be capsule biographies of my life on dust jackets of many books, all proclaiming: '...He knew life on many levels. From shoeshine boy, free-lance waiter, 3rd cook, janitor, he rose to...'" This self-mockery aside, McPherson's own life and career embody what he calls in his essay "On Becoming an American Writer": "a synthesis of high and low, black and white, city and country, provincial and universal."

McPherson was born in 1943, in Savannah, Georgia. Later, as he writes in "Going Up To Atlanta," he worked at odd jobs to help support his mother, brother, and sisters while attending a Catholic school where all the nuns were white and the children black, then the public schools, "where all the mean people went." As a boy he loved comic books but soon discovered the Colored Branch of the Carnegie Public Library, where he learned that words without pictures "gave up their secret meanings, spoke of other worlds, made me know that pain was a part of other people's lives." All the while, surrounded by aunts, uncles, cousins, and friends of his father's, he was struggling with the enigmatic figure of his father. McPherson senior had become the first black master electrician in the state, but only after the racist suppression of his repeated applications to get a license had caused him "irrevocable pain" and led to a drinking problem and a period in jail. At the time, McPherson did not understand the forces that had broken his father. "I had...been working every kind of job to help support the family I thought he had abandoned," McPherson writes. "During all my years in Savannah, I had never had peace or comfort or any chance to rely on anyone else. I blamed him for it. I was very bitter towards him." When his father died in 1961, he felt that "my father had died many years before." Only twenty years later would he come to appreciate his father "as an intelligent and creative man" and forgive him.

McPherson's progress as a young man was a movement away from Savannah and into the world. He worked as a dining-car waiter for the Great Northern Railroad in 1962 (an experience that contributed to two early stories and to his nonfiction book *Railroad*), attended Morgan State University in Baltimore from 1963-64, and then, having gotten a National Defense Student Loan, finished at Morris Brown College in Atlanta, graduating in 1965.

In 1967, he attended Harvard Law School, where he studied fiction writing with Alan Lebowitz. The publication of "Gold Coast" in *The Atlantic Monthly* initiated a close relationship with the editor Edward Weeks and led to McPherson's promotion to contributing editor in 1969. He went on to take his M.F.A. at the University of Iowa (where he worked briefly with Richard Yates) and published his first collection *Hue and Cry* in 1969, as well as a cover interview with Ralph Ellison in *The Atlantic Monthly* in 1970 (Ellison soon became his primary friend and mentor, along with Albert Murray, author of *The Omni-Americans*).

In 1972, McPherson received a Guggenheim Fellowship, married, and moved to San Francisco. He taught at the University of California Santa Cruz in 1974 and was hired by the University of Virginia in 1976. While at Virginia, he published his second collection, *Elbow Room*, and, in 1978, became the first African-American writer to win the Pulitzer Prize; however, his sense of being exploited at Virginia was so extreme that he felt exposed by the awards. "I was brought in to be in the window," he commented in a 2001 interview with Trent Masiki. "I was really frightened of that environment. That's why when I got the Pulitzer, I didn't respond to calls. I stayed at home and hid out. You should be allowed to take joy in what happens to you. But I was scared of the backlash....For them to see me doing well wasn't what they expected....Some whites get resentful when someone from the lowest levels of society starts winning 'their' stuff. So I've been very careful about protecting my privacy ever since those years."

McPherson's daughter Rachel was born in 1979. Not long after, his marriage began to unravel and he found himself involved in a divorce which he was later to describe in "Disneyland" as both

Lan Samantha Chang

bitter and complicated. At this point two forms of "kindly inter-ference" occurred. Jack Leggett offered him a job at the Iowa Workshop, and he was notified that he had won one of the first MacArthur Foundation "genius" grants. He told a caller from National Public Radio, "The gods are playful."

In the years that followed, McPherson bought a house on auction in Baltimore, which he then rented at nominal rates to needy tenants; he also bought a house in Iowa City and settled into a life that was largely reclusive, other than for his teaching. He continued to fight unsuccessfully in Charlottesville courts for the custody of his daughter. In the early eighties, McPherson felt that he had to choose between his writing and the fathering of his daughter. During her regular visits from her mother's in Charlottesville, he took Rachel for special trips to Disneyland, and sought to introduce her to rooms around the "big house" of the United States: "My bedroom was in Iowa City. Rachel's bedroom was in Charlottesville. Friends had guest rooms, for Rachel and for me, in Richmond, in Washington, D.C., in Stamford, and in New

Haven, in New York, in Boston, in Cambridge, in Chicago, in Oakland and in Los Angeles. All Rachel and I had to do...was to move from room to room in this huge house, bonding as we went with each other and with our friends" ("Disneyland").

But gradually he began to connect with his Iowa City neighbors, with colleagues, and with students, and to see in Iowa City the basis of a spiritually centered democracy. "I have many friends here," he wrote, "black and white and other. ... I am confident that here I am first of all a person, a human being. I have been accepted into the life of the community. I have open and free access to what in this community has meaning and value" ("A Region Not Home").

In Iowa City, McPherson also befriended Japanese author Kiyohiro Miura, developing an interest in Japanese culture that led to his lecturing in Japan. He also immersed himself in Greek and Roman classics. He studied the racist right. He studied American popular culture, including the films of John Ford. He became a master teacher, mentoring Eileen Pollack (see her tribute below), Kathryn Harrison, Gish Jen, Adam Schwartz, Samantha Chang, Z. Z. Packer, and many others. He developed courses ranging from the Bible to American Humor and Mark Twain. He also vested himself in "working on the industry from the inside" (as he puts it in his interview with Masiki), serving emerging talents that promised "new stories" and a new American perspective. He co-edited two issues of *Ploughshares* (1985, 1990), served as a *Ploughshares* trustee (1989-2005) and a panelist for the Whiting Foundation (1985-present). He became a contributing editor to Robert Coles's magazine *Doubletake* (1995-2007) and was inducted into the American Academy of Arts and Sciences in 1995; following Frank Conroy's death, he served as acting director of the Iowa Workshop (2005-2007).

Once his daughter was in college, McPherson felt "free to get back to my work." He published *Crabcakes* (1996), followed by a collection of essays called *A Region Not Home: Reflections from Exile* (2000). In addition, his significant, uncollected pieces include his two articles on "Chicago's Black Stone Rangers," the Ellison interview, articles on exile from the South, "Going Up To Atlanta," and "A Region Not Home: The View From Exile," a meditation on the film *Mississippi Burning*, "Burning Memories, Mississippi 1964," an essay "To Blacks and Jews: Hab Rachmones," and an excerpt from a novel-in-progress, *Deep River*.

In his fiction and nonfiction alike, McPherson penetrates to the soul of different perspectives, traditions, and values with his extraordinary mind and heart. His writing is remarkable for its humor, its tireless Socratic intelligence, stylistic invention and variety, and meta-fictional urgency. In terms of his observant conscience, he is as subtle and rigorous as George Orwell and James Baldwin, whom he professes wryly never to have read. Above all McPherson is writing the uncreated conscience of democracy itself, appealing to both personal and social justice, and "an enlarging of our humanity." —*DeWitt Henry*

A Tribute to James Alan McPherson

I was a member of Jim McPherson's first class at Iowa, and, like generations of students to follow, I was relieved to discover that Jim was the teacher I had been looking for all my life. The literature courses Jim taught—I studied "Literature and the Law" and "The American Vernacular"—were brilliant and original. And though Jim tended to be Zen in workshop, I soon figured out that a person could learn everything she needed to learn by meditating on the koans he whispered in class, by listening to his asides as he watched John Wayne hunt down Natalie Wood in *The Searchers* for the fiftieth time, and by hanging out at Hamburg Inn and witnessing the ways a genius transforms the stuff of everyday life into the stuff of art.

Once, in the early eighties, Jim and I were walking through Harvard Square when we passed a very upscale furniture store. A very upscale black couple—the man wore a stylish three-piece suit and carried a walking stick and leather case—stood inside the window, considering the purchase of a very fashionable living-room set. The woman sat primly and tried the sofa. The man sat stiffly and tried the chair.

"Dress that window, brother," Jim muttered, laughing to himself (*heh heh heh*), unable to resist the dig not at the couple but rather at the practice by which a corporation or university hired a solitary black person (often an attractive, well-dressed black person), installed him or her in a highly visible position, and considered its obligation to minorities to be fulfilled.

Jim waved at the man and smiled. Then—full professor, Pulitzer Prize winner, Guggenheim and MacArthur Fellow that he was—he scuffed off down the sidewalk in his well-worn moccasins, corduroy trousers, flannel shirt, and flat straw cap.

Rather than confine himself to administering lessons on point of view, Jim tries to convey a vision of what it means to be a writer, an American, a human being. He impresses on his students the dangers of losing or distorting what is most authentic about who they are and becoming "moral dandies." He celebrates the role of the imagination, not only in creating characters on a page, but in empathizing with people whose inner worlds are far different from your own and improvising new ways of behaving that might transcend the old. Instead of subject-and-verb agreement, Jim tutors his students in the grammar of love.

If one is not too strict in his conjugation of the verb to be, *he might wind up with a sense of living in the present. I believe now that love exists at just that point when the first person singular moves into its plural estate: I am, you are, he is, she is, we are. ... The saying of it requires a going out of oneself, of breath as well as confidence. Its image is of expansiveness, a taking roundly into and a putting roundly out of oneself. Or perhaps another word should be used, one invented or one transported from another context: I am, you are, he is, she is, we be.* ("Just Enough for the City")

Jim believes in family. You can't know who you are if you don't know where you came from. But as Jim often says, each of us is entitled to create our own family from any kindred souls we meet. The guiding metaphor in *Crabcakes* is the pilgrimage the author makes to Baltimore to bring home the perfect meal to share at a communal supper with his friends in Iowa City. For those of us who had moved so far from the families into which we'd been born, sharing such meals with Jim was the way we restored our souls.

Once, in my second year at the workshop, I needed emergency surgery, and since there were no free beds in the general wing of Mercy Hospital, I ended up in Obstetrics, where a sign warned visitors that only a patient's family would be admitted. My class-mate Gish Jen showed up first and claimed to be my sister. Katie Estill, who is part Native American and looks it, showed up with a similar claim, after which David Nicholson, who is black, claimed to be my brother. Finally, Jim appeared and said he was "the father."

The diversity of my visitors confused the nurses, one of whom came in to say that the staff couldn't figure out which baby was mine since all the children in the incubators seemed "completely white." Then she leaned closer and asked me what it was like to be married to a black man. I bristled—what concern was that of hers?

"Well," she said, looking around to see if anyone was listening, "I'm dating a black man, and we want to get married, but I don't know what to expect. How people will treat us and all? And I've never found anyone in Iowa I could ask."

Like the black male narrator of "Why I Like Country Music," who prefers square-dance music to blues and bebop, Jim is always on the look-out for Americans who defy or contradict the dictates of their histories. Once, when I took him on a field trip to the Henry Ford Museum, which is housed in a former auto plant in Dearborn, Michigan, the museum turned out to be celebrating Motown music. After buying some Marvin Gaye in the gift shop, Jim and I wandered into a room in which a video of The Tempta-tions was playing on the wall, with the musicians offering lessons on how to emulate their dance steps. Business was slow, and five or six white-haired, white docents had gathered in the room and were performing The Temptations' moves with a rhythm and grace that would have done a group of back-up singers proud.

If not for Jim, I would have spent a few minutes appreciating the refrain to "Heard It through the Grapevine" before moving on to the next exhibit. But Jim started dancing behind the women, smiling and applauding. Later, he explained that it made him cry to think that music invented by African-Americans laboring to build cars on an assembly line owned by Henry Ford should now be celebrated in a museum in that same factory, danced to and enjoyed by middle-class white women who once might have shunned it as vulgar, low-class, and black.

To which I now add the irony that a racist and anti-Semite like Henry Ford would roll over in his grave to know that a Jewish woman and a black man should have been standing in his auto plant in the middle of the day, appreciating the triumph of his workers' music over the kind of dancing he decreed must be played in the ballroom he ordered built adjacent to his factory because he wanted to combat the improvisation that was encouraged by newfangled dances such as the Charleston and jazz.

Many of Jim's lessons apply to everyone. But he also seems to sense what kind of lesson an individual student needs to learn. Once, at an after-reading party, Jim asked me to dance. As we stumbled around the room, he cried: "Ha, ha! I fooled you! A colored boy who can't dance!" This stunned me into silence. Wasn't this a racist thing to say? Didn't my being white preclude me from offering a similarly irreverent reply? But no, Jim loved contradictions and complexities, especially those involving gender, race, and class.

Suddenly, words popped in my head. I got into the calculus of the thing. I improvised. "Ha! I fooled *you*—a Jew with no money!" It was the first funny thing I'd ever said. At least, the first funny thing that had an edge. At which I realized that Jim had tricked me into finding my voice—not only as a writer but as a person.

Sometimes, if you took what Jim taught, you took a part of Jim along with it. Yet he never seemed to mind. As Jim says, the best writers are the ones who know from whom to steal. First, you steal from someone you resemble, an elder in your own community—in Jim's case, Ralph Ellison. But a clever thief also steals from less obvious targets, as Jim stole from Isaac Babel, who, like Jim, had gone to live among the enemy (the fox among the hounds, the Jew among the Cossacks, the black Southern man living among aristocratic Southern whites or Northern intellectuals). Under Jim's tutelage, I learned to steal from Grace Paley, Bernard Malamud, and Philip Roth. Then I moved on and learned to steal from Jim.

Jim was the person who first suggested that I write about my family's hotel in the Borscht Belt, of which I'd always been ashamed. I didn't want to write about being Jewish—my world was larger than that. And I was starting to suspect that making too big a deal about one's ethnic identity—whether as a writer or an American—was to indulge in nostalgia and kitsch. But the longer I argued with Jim's suggestion in my head, the clearer it became that such questions were what my novel would be about.

According to Jim, even within seemingly monolithic groups there live and work immigrants, blacks, and Jews who help to shape that culture. Certainly, plenty of blacks and Christians worked at the predominantly Jewish hotels where I grew up. And so my book acquired a self-educated, reclusive handyman named Thomas Jefferson, to whom I gave the same vision of America that Jim had given me.

When I finished the manuscript and showed it to Jim, I held my breath for fear he would chastise me for plagiarism. Instead, he offered me his blessing. He had only this one complaint: I had made the character I'd based on him too perfect. "Rough him up," Jim advised. "Give the man some flaws. Give him more facility with the vernacular." I followed Jim's advice and allowed Mr. Jefferson—whom I originally had envisioned as one of the thirty-six righteous men and women for whose sake God refrains from destroying the world—to be seduced by the hotel's female guests. I made his very prissiness and intellectualism seem like flaws. Sad to say, Mr. Jefferson retained so much of Jim's influence that he remained a magic Negro (you know, the part that Morgan Freeman plays in so many movies). And, sadder for me, the best line in the novel, the one readers most often cite, is a line I stole from Jim: "The only real refuge for a person in pain is in another person's heart."

The danger in thanking your teacher for everything he's given you is that you end up talking too much about yourself. But how can I fail to note that I also have Jim to thank for my one nonfiction book? As I was graduating from the workshop, he told me about a white woman artist who had moved in with Sitting Bull in the last years of his life and acted as his translator, friend, and lobbyist in his battle to save his people's culture and their land. "Someone ought to write a book about that woman," Jim hinted. He didn't remember her name or the title of the book in which he'd read those few paragraphs about her life, but he knew that to figure out who I was, I needed to figure out who she was.

I spent fifteen years studying everything I could find about Sitting Bull and Catherine Weldon. What I learned was that despite every betrayal and indignity Sitting Bull had suffered, he managed to judge each person on his or her own merits. He invited Catherine Weldon and her son to live in his cabin and become part of his family. He accepted everything she had to give and taught her all he could convey about how his people lived. In her turn, Catherine Weldon gave Sitting Bull her money, her political advice, her friendship, her heart, her son.

Sometimes, what one person teaches another is how much she has to give. And that, I am proud to say, is a lesson Jim taught me.

Although Hollywood only recently discovered the role of the magic Negro, the character has long been central to American literature. Think of Queequeg in *Moby Dick*, Jim in *Huck Finn*, King Dahfu in *Henderson the Rain King*, and all those black hipsters who guide Sal Paradise along his journey in *On the Road*. The cliché has been rightly criticized. The magic Negro seems so perfect he isn't real; his oppression and suffering are given short shrift compared to his white protégé's struggles to figure out his identity; he seems to exist only for the sake of teaching what he knows to the white protagonist, as when Will Smith materializes from the mist, teaches Matt Damon to play the perfect game of golf and win the perfect white girl (whom Bagger Vance would have gotten lynched for so much as looking at), then tips his hat and wanders back into the mist on a segregated golf course in Depression-era Savannah, where, as it happens, Jim McPherson was born in the terrible days of the Jim Crow South.

The trope of the magic Negro may be too problematic to redeem. Yet Jim taught me to see the value in even the most problematic artifacts of our shared American culture. (My bootleg copy of *Song of the South*, which Disney refuses to re-release because of the portrayal of Uncle Remus as a happy plantation darkie, I acquired as a gift from Jim.) Young black protagonists who set out on their quests don't usually need older, wiser white men as their spiritual guides since black people always have known white culture from the inside, if only as servants, and, if they did need such guides, were unable to find them. But sheltered, naïve white people who set out on quests to understand America usually need guides to those communities their parents have forbidden them to enter. A desire to transcend the categories into which a person has been born isn't racist; rather, as Jim often points out, such a journey is a prerequisite for understanding what it means to be human.

Once, when I was helping Jim check out of the hospital in Iowa City where he had been convalescing after a bout with pneumonia, the clerk assumed that Jim wouldn't be able to understand the medical bill and began explaining the math to me.

Another time, in Boston, I accompanied Jim and his daughter on an attempt to find Rachel a pair of comfortable shoes to replace the fashionable plastic sandals that were cutting her feet. We went from store to store, but none of the clerks seemed willing to wait on us. I grew so enraged I nearly shouted: "What's the matter? Don't you serve black people in this store?" Jim sensed my anger and steered me to a smaller store nearby, empty except for the Jewish owner, who waited on Rachel as if she were a queen. I was proud of my coreligionist, although even he, when making small talk with Jim, assumed that the only topic a black man would care to discuss was sports.

A few years after that, I flew to Charlottesville to testify on Jim's behalf in a court of law and was literally struck dumb by the blatant racism of the questions the judge asked me on the stand.

Recently, when I invited Jim to read in Ann Arbor, my partner and I escorted him to the check-in desk at the hotel adjacent to the university, at which the registration clerk (a beautiful young black woman, stylishly coiffed and polished) addressed my partner as "Professor McPherson," assuming, I suppose, that the black man by our side was our servant or our driver.

As one of the first African Americans to gain entry to Harvard Law (a period of his life that Jim describes with humor and restraint in his debut story "Gold Coast"), Jim is evidence that affirmative action benefits not only this or that minority but a geometrically expanding pyramid of people of all backgrounds. In the past quarter of a century, Jim has taught and nurtured writers as diverse as Breece D'J Pancake, Gish Jen, Daniel Woodrell, David Nicholson, Susan Power, Cynthia Kadohata, Lan Samantha Chang, Adam Schwartz, Julie Orringer, Ryan Harty, Alexander Chee, and me. Many of us have tried to pass along Jim's gifts to our own students, thereby creating a family whose members now number in the hundreds, if not the thousands, a family that takes this opportunity to gather around the table, pass the plate of crabcakes from hand to hand, and offer its thanks to Jim. —*Eileen Pollack*

Eileen Pollack's latest collection is reviewed in this issue. She directs the M.F.A. program at the University of Michigan.

Like Eileen Pollack, I was a member of Jim's first class at Iowa; and like her and others, felt him my dream teacher. He could, it was true, be gnomic in class. As we might have expected from the author of "Elbow Room," whose narrator "declares himself the open enemy of conventional narrative categories... [insisting] that 'borders,' 'structures.' 'frames,' 'order,' and even 'form' itself are regarded by him with the highest suspicion," Jim was not a fount of writing tips. Often he said nothing, and when he did say something, he spoke with extreme softness, as if to be sure that his inability to control his impulse to tell us something did not result in our—horrors!—being told something. Neither was he "supportive" in a conventional way, although he did share, from time to time, maxims such as "Never look to others for ego support." I'm not sure this was always what we would have chosen, but in retrospect I can see how very right he was to raise us, not as artistes, but warriors: His bracing support has proved a true gift over the years, as has his important tacit insistence that we find not only our own voices, but our own forms.

Our own visions, too; though, impressionable creatures that we were, some of us "found" visions that, well, bore a resemblance to his. Eileen will perhaps recall giving me, as a birthday present, a poster with the words "American Vision" emblazoned across the bottom—terms so embedded in our outlook that I only see them as worthy of remark now. As for how we came to be so imprinted, I must mostly credit osmosis, though it is true that in the one recollection I have of Jim commenting on something I was reading ("It's good to get that under your belt," he said), the book in question was William Carlos Williams' *In the American Grain*. So perhaps there was some facilitating of the osmosis.

Americanness, in any case, preoccupied Jim, as did—and this too strikes in retrospect—the related notion of citizenship. That was a strange idea to writers then; and indeed, "good citizenship," as conventionally defined, will always clash with literary values. But Jim was nothing if not a magpie, and viewing fiction, as he did, as kind of magpie's nest, he characteristically took a preoccupation of the law and ported it into fiction, forging en route a vision in which citizenship and literature were not opposed, but deeply related. In his beautiful memoir, he writes movingly of his early experiences with books, as DeWitt has noted. I quote here the same passage at slightly greater length:

At first the words, without pictures, were a mystery. But then, suddenly, they all began to march across the page. They gave up their secret meanings, spoke of other worlds, made me know that pain was a part of other peoples' lives. After a while, I could read faster and faster and faster. After a while, I no longer believed in the world in which I lived.

I loved the Colored Branch of the Carnegie Public Library.

Books were liberation and subversion; they alienated but also connected; they inspired one to choose new allegiances. They were in no way about "representation"; the mind boggles at the idea of Jim screening books for those about his "group." Rather, they were about fluidity. They were about imagining others and re-imagining oneself. "Imagining community," as we might say today, too—imagining family, as Eileen has described, as well as a citizenship that is not about the suppression of the self, but its expression. Jim went on to write wryly but insistently about the small interactions through which one claimed one's whole humanity, including its public face. In his story, "I am an American" (first published in *Ploughshares*), for example, he gives us a narrator in London who asserts his Americanness to a Japanese tourist in attempted Chinese—a delicious exchange:

"You are African?" the man asked, smiling pleasantly as we shook. "Nigerian, yes?"

"Woo sh Meei-gworen," I said.

He looked perplexed. "I do not know this tribe," he confessed.

As things happen, the Japanese tourist is eventually recognized as Japanese and the narrator as American, but in quintessentially McPhersonesque style, the recognition comes as part of a larger recognition of both characters' humanity. It is a lovely, luminous, blooming development: hurt, healing, identity, and possibility all coming together in an unsentimental, even matter-of-fact way.

Who could forget it? I note in homage that my entire career, such as it is, can probably be traced to the passage above, and to

Jim's magpie example; without him, I am inconceivable to myself. It is therefore with the deepest gratitude that I here join DeWitt, Eileen and others in raising a heartfelt crabcake: To you, Jim! May you ever chuckle to think how many writers trace their ancestry to the Colored Branch of the Carnegie Public Library—a most American story. —*Gish Jen*

Gish Jen is the author of four books, most recently The Love Wife.

During my first term at Iowa in 1982, I enrolled in Jim McPherson's fiction writing workshop. Jim began the semester by reading an Isaac Babel story titled "My First Fee," in which a twenty-year old proofreader and would-be writer goes to an older prostitute named Vera for his first sexual encounter. But when they get to Vera's room, the young man becomes despondent when Vera removes her clothes and he sees she's not nearly as beautiful as he had imagined. Vera senses that the young man has lost interest and he responds by inventing a story about having been a boy prostitute. Vera is visibly moved by the story, and pays him a high compliment: "So you're a whore. A whore like us bitches." The young man bows his head and, accepting Vera's praise for his story, replies, "Yes. A whore like you." At some point during Jim's reading of the story, I looked under the table and noticed that he didn't have laces in his shoes. He hadn't bothered to put on socks, either. The next week I looked under the table again. Still no laces or socks. Jim was certainly eccentric—in the more than twenty-five years I've known him, I've never seen him without his mangled jockey cap—but I wondered if he would find some socks and shoelaces before the weather turned cold. By the third week of the term, Jim was still without socks or shoelaces and the rituals of workshop had become well established: after class ended at six, all of us, except for Jim, would congregate at the Green Mill for dinner and drinks. Of course we would have loved for Jim to join us, but he seemed too inaccessible—too brilliant for us, too much in pain to bear company. Just as class was drawing to a close during the fourth week of the term, Jim looked anxiously around the table and then asked me if I wanted to go get a drink with him. It was like being asked out on a date in front of fifteen other people. Of course I said yes.

Jim walked splayfooted to his car at a rapid pace, as if he were trying to get away from me despite the fact that he asked me to join him. At one point, he paused to catch his breath and light a cigarette. "I'm a failure to the race, Adam," he said, "a failure to the race." He laughed, then so did I, and then watched with alarm as his laugh turned into a coughing fit. His comment was an acknowledgment of the poor way he cared for his physical health, but an also effort to put me at ease, to let me know that we could be open about about race without letting it define us. We drank and talked for many hours that night. Jim spoke mainly about the pain of being apart from his daughter. My own parents had divorced when I was very young—did he know that? was that why he asked me to join him for a drink?—and, drawing upon my own painful memories, I tried to share with him my experience of being a young child caught in the middle of a bitter divorce. That night was the beginning of my friendship with Jim and my true education as a writer and a human being—Jim, of course, would see both types of education as one and the same. Perhaps the central lesson I learned from Jim is that the imagination is the medium through which we develop a moral self. When he read "My First Fee" in that first class, I had no idea of what the story was about, but rereading the story years later, rereading it through the lens of everything I had learned from Jim, I understood that he was trying to teach us that imagination springs from empathy. The would-be writer in the story finally gets it right when his own pain inspires him to emotionally inhabit the reality of a prostitute. I'm still not sure why Jim reached out to me that semester. Certainly he sensed something sympathetic about me. Like all my classmates, though, I regarded him as a genius, and spent every class waiting expectantly for him to come down from Sinai and reveal The Word about our purple mimeographed manuscripts. But perhaps he knew that I was also looking under the table, looking to see if my teacher, my friend, had remembered to keep his feet warm. —*Adam Schwartz*

Adam Schwartz's stories have appeared in The New Yorker *and elsewhere. He teaches at Wellesley College.*

COHEN AWARDS Each year, we honor the best poem and short story published in *Ploughshares* with the Cohen Awards, which are wholly sponsored by our longtime patrons Denise and Mel Cohen. Finalists are nominated by staff editors, and the winners—each of whom receives a cash prize of $600—are selected by our advisory editors. The 2008 Cohen Awards for work published in *Ploughshares* in 2007, Volume 33, go to Jennifer Grotz and Bret Anthony Johnston. (All of the works mentioned here are accessible on our website at www.pshares.org.)

 **JENNIFER GROTZ** *for her poem "The Life and Times of George Van den Heuvel" in Winter 2007–08, edited by Philip Levine.*

Jennifer Grotz was born in Canyon, Texas (a small town just south of Amarillo) in 1971. Although her family moved around often, in part because of her father's job as an insurance salesman, she spent the first eighteen years of her life in Texas, and still considers the state her home. "I can't remember not writing," she says. "There weren't many books in our household, but my family was very religious and even before I could read, I had a children's illustrated version of the Bible. Some of my earliest memories are of adding my own lines and illustrations with a pencil to that copy of the Bible. A religious upbringing provided me with a strong connection to a key text—including memorization of many verses and passages—as well as an interest in close reading and a reverence for language—be it musical, poetic, or prayer-like."

Grotz graduated from Lubbock High School—the same school attended by Buddy Holly—and received a scholarship to attend Tulane University. At Tulane, she majored in English, French, and Art History and spent her junior year in France, studying literature and art history at the Sorbonne. "Utterly penniless, it was nonetheless one of the richest years of my life," she says. She began her study of poetry at Tulane, working with the poet Peter Cooley, then went on to receive her M.F.A. from Indiana University. After graduate school, Grotz spent several years working a variety of jobs, from arts administration to waitressing, before going back to obtain her Ph.D. from the University of Houston. There, she apprenticed with the poets Adam Zagajewski and Edward Hirsch, and at their invitation organized the Krakow Poetry Seminar, a weeklong celebration and exploration of the cross-pollination between American and Polish poetry.

Grotz's first book, *Cusp*, was chosen by Yusef Komunyakaa for the Bakeless Prize, and was published by Houghton Mifflin in 2003. Individual poems and translations from the French and Polish have appeared widely, and her work has been the recipient of awards and fellowships from the Texas Institute of Letters and the Fellowship of Southern Writers. She currently serves as the assistant director of the Bread Loaf Writers Conference, in addition to teaching in the M.F.A. Program at the University of North Carolina at Greensboro. This spring semester, thanks to grants from the Rona Jaffe and Camargo Foundations, Grotz was able to return to France, where she's been working on her second book of poems, as well as a book of translations of the "psalms" and other poems of Patrice de La Tour du Pin.

About "The Life and Times of George Van den Heuvel," Jennifer Grotz writes: "Like many of the poems in my book-in-progress, this poem is preoccupied with the past—both how time acts as an editor and how a poem might act as a vessel to contain and query memory. But mostly, 'The Life and Times of George Van den Heuvel' arose from an urge I had to write a poem that included humor of some kind, something my poems seem impoverished of by and large. Although I conflated a couple of the minimum wage jobs I worked in high school to save money for college, the content of the poem is unusually unadulterated autobiography."

BRET ANTHONY JOHNSTON *for his story "Republican" in Fall 2007, edited by Andrea Barrett.*

Born in 1971, Bret Anthony Johnston was raised in Corpus

Christi, Texas. His father was a supervisor at the Corpus Christi Army Depot and his mother worked as an accountant. He began writing seriously in high school, focusing more on poetry than fiction, but, he says, "After attending a reading by the novelist Robert Stone, I devoted himself exclusively to the prose forms."

He attended Del Mar Community College before transferring to Texas A&M—Corpus Christi, where he earned a B.A. in English with Highest Honors. Two days after graduating, he began the graduate program at Miami University in Oxford, Ohio. After taking the M.A. in English at Miami, he was accepted to the Writers' Workshop at the University of Iowa, where he studied with Frank Conroy, Ethan Canin, Marilynne Robinson, James Alan McPherson and Chris Offutt. He received an M.F.A. in fiction in 2002.

Johnston is the editor of *Naming the World: And Other Exercises for the Creative Writer,* and the author of the internationally acclaimed *Corpus Christi: Stories,* both from Random House. His fiction has received numerous awards, including a fellowship from the National Endowment for the Arts and a National Book Award honor for writers under thirty-five. He is currently finishing a novel, which will also be published by Random House, and he is the Director of Creative Writing at Harvard University.

In addition to the Cohen Award, "Republican" was selected for inclusion in *New Stories from the South: The Year's Best 2008.* About the story, Johnston writes: "The story was ten years in the making, literally. I wrote a first draft in 1998, and although the draft failed in every conceivable way, I couldn't make myself throw out the (floppy) disk on which it was saved. Some years I thought about Carlos, some years I didn't, but I was always comforted by the fact that he was still with me. Writing is, I believe, an act of faith.

"Then, last year, I was frustrated by a difficult chapter in my novel, so I decided to take a break and work on something else. In the ten years since I'd started 'Republican' (which my friends and I call 'The Carlos Story'), I'd secreted away other ideas—a father shredding a ragtop, an expensive guitar, a mother who calls her son in the middle of the night—and, though I didn't anticipate them all fitting in the same story, I'm delighted that they seem to fit well enough here."

Water: Nine Stories, *stories by Alyce Miller* (Sarabande): By its title, Miller's collection offers a fitting symbol for the multiple forms of desire that take shape within her characters. Filled with beautiful phrasings and descriptions of longing, the book sometimes shows desire's fluidity as a result of age; other times, as in the story "Ice," old regrets can harden from the substance of childhood. Whether related to love, loss, a desire to belong, or a need to reconnect, the various states of longing all seem to struggle for some level of equilibrium. Miller's characters, often backwards-looking, are in search of a bridge between their past and present, hoping it might lead them to a better understanding of how to conduct their current lives.

In "Swimming," water becomes a "way of forgetting" for a remarried art history professor who's suffered multiple miscarriages. The story, typical of Miller, begins as a quiet reflection, although it takes a surprise turn that transforms it into a thrilling encounter, one with bizarre and dangerous overtones. In this and other stories, the author provides no easy resolution to the plot, nor indeed to the question of desire itself. Such is also the case in "Cleaning House," which looks at the ups and downs of an intermittent love affair, or in "Aftershock," a story that unfolds through a series of letters to an ex-lover. In the latter, the narrative changes from innocent ruminations on the nature of disaster to more fatalistic, even threatening scenarios involving the ex. In one letter, "J" asks: "I...wonder, D, if you ever imagine that moment when the earth cracks open...and sends you...shimmying off the edge into those gray, choppy waters below." Seemingly spiteful, "J" is in fact more earnest in her confusions about moving on. For herself as much as for the one who spurned her, her questions about whether "speed will alter fate," or what it means "to elude destiny," all point to more general fears about loss of control and the impending dangers that may result.

Perhaps the most imaginative story in the collection is "Dimitry Gurov's Dowdy Wife," in which Miller reprises a Chekhovian tale from the point of view of the otherwise unnamed female character. In what might be a typical male-centric story of infidelity, Gurov's wife not only claims the narrative voice, but she reclaims her own honor and identity. In other stories, like "Getting to Know the World" and "My Summer of Love," Miller's characters come of age in a crosscurrent of changing values and generational differences. The former tells of a black girl in a small Ohio town during the Civil Rights movement, trying to understand the meaning of tolerance. In the latter, a teenage boy moves halfway across country to his aunt's and uncle's while his parents try to work out their marital problems. Through his observation of both couples, Oscar learns an early, valuable lesson about what he calls the "relative uncertainty of adult relationships."

This notion of uncertainty as being "relative" seems not only wise but far-reaching. It suggests a dependency on both other characters as well as on external, often unpredictable, conditions, while it also provides a fitting return to the book's title. The narrator in "Aftershock," as if speaking for the collection as a whole, describes her search for a "sense of well-being and definition that [make] up the contours" of her life. In *Water*, we see those contours constantly shifting, constantly being refashioned by outside forces. Just as water itself doesn't determine its own shape, so are the boundaries of our well-being rarely, if ever, determined by ourselves. —*Jonathan Liebson*

Jonathan Liebson's fiction has appeared in Chelsea, Meridian, South Dakota Review, *and has been honored by* The Atlantic Monthly *and the William Faulkner Society. He teaches at The New School and has finished a first novel,* A Body At Rest.

Above the Houses, *short stories by Susan Engberg* (Delphinium): In her fourth collection of stories, Susan Engberg explores the tentative, testing movements of people recently unmoored by change. Spouses die; marriages end or begin; there are new towns, new houses, new bodies to navigate. The landscape can feel hostile. A baby wanders alone down a sidewalk, holding a bottle marked by a "small handprint of blood." A deranged woman haunts a funeral, demanding coats from a dead woman's closet.

Yet in these nine stories, the gray, unforgiving territory we expect is surprisingly transformed; even a tired mill town offers the redemptive pause one character seeks, "the row of old experienced houses" creating "a surprising paradise, like a town of untouchable gold hidden all this time inside the other."

The pulse here is in Engberg's deliberate and curious rejection of the brutality she could inflict on her characters. Opening the collection with a bruised eye, Engberg lets us know immediately that cruelty is possible: "Your fingers test from the smoldering, plum-colored center of impact down to the eyebrow, the swollen lid." Violence and the potential for abuse feel comfortable, worn, like television violence; the image of the abused woman is hideously bland. There's even a mirror recording the image: "shiner, spiky new haircut, the shocked face of upheaval—in short, a sight." But this is Engberg's point—we know this story, we could settle into trauma easily. Instead, Engberg jars the character, and the reader, with a swift, authoritative movement away from the mirrored bruise, and away from what feels like glutinous and wasteful voyeurism. The bruise is not what we think, and we won't linger there. As Engberg informs us, "You decide not to dwell on the damage." There are other mysteries here: a compost pile, a friendship with a chubby child, the poetry of a hanging curtain: "The fine white material falls into a knuckle of itself, loops back into hiding and spills out again like the end of a sash girded around a waist."

Using the second person in the title story, Engberg teaches us how to read the stories that follow, how to look not at the mystery of pain and regret ("Your litany of losses is a useless scrap of grocery list on a table somewhere else") but, reminiscent of Grace Paley, at the mystery of resilience. How do we survive, rebuild, remain tethered here, to others? Paley's characters joined protests, saved parks, and reveled in city neighborhoods and talk. Engberg's often achieve a similar but less political romping appreciation for everyday life, alongside a heightened sense of mortality. Skinny-dipping is charged with an eerie joy, "Neither of them hesitates at the verge; there isn't time, they wade quickly through the cold shallows and then plunge forward, outward into shocking, bracing, primal liquid, dark and darker in its depths"; yet, in the same story, so is peeing: "In the bathroom, urinating, she feels the downwardness of life, of its fleshly, earthbound quarter."

Throughout the collection, objects (toys, houses, clothing, paintings, sculptures), like bodies, take on a life at once sensual and spiritual, luring characters back to intimacy and solidity, back to the "durable mystery," as Laura in "Beginning" calls it. Laura, building a new relationship late in life, weights herself to the work, to seeing this new person, his skin, his hands, his history, with stones. She fills her pockets as the two walk the beach, arranges her collection across his deck, and, finally, fills her bag with stones and carries it onto the plane home, achieving the kind of grounded weightlessness we feel throughout this collection, a soaring that is full of flesh and ordinariness. —*Sage Marsters*

Sage Marsters's story "Bear Story" was reprinted in Pushcart XXXII: Best of the Small Presses. *She is currently finishing a collection of stories.*

In the Mouth, *stories and novellas by Eileen Pollack* (Four Way): How's this for brave? One narrator, a son, is obsessed with fulfilling his dying father's request for a belated circumcision, even at the son's own hands. How's this for unflinching? Another narrator, a mother, is troubled by something as normal but taboo as a kind of lust for her newborn son's attentions. In the six stories and novellas that make up her latest collection, Eileen Pollack exhibits the fearless gift of taking the "un" out of unspeakable.

Best of all: she does it with precision. A nursing mother admits "vague irritation" at her newborn's insistence at her nipple "as if a street-corner beggar kept pulling at her arm." A young doctor reluctantly asking intimate questions of a woman patient is "shy as a boy whose mother has asked him to unhook her brassiere."

Widening her lens, Ms. Pollack stares unblinking at the larger groups to which these all-too-human behaviors obtain. She scores Christians for being "stingy, not only with their money but with their love," as well as a bunch of Hasidic Jews for channeling money for a camp for retarded teens into a getaway for themselves. (If anti-Semitism can ever be said to be funny, she tests its outside limit.) Even a well-meaning married couple, subset of a group we all recognize if can't necessarily name, doesn't escape the marksmanship of her pen: "They signed petitions. They volunteered. They were just a little too earnest. It wasn't that their lives were untroubled... They saw heartbreak every day. But these troubles didn't seem to trouble them. It was as if they were standing in the rain, talking about how wet they were getting, but you could see the water rolling right off their Gore-Tex shells."

One senses that it's anger as well as affection—and often a blend of the two, with grief for the human comedy tossed somewhere in the mix—that fuels her remarkable specificity. The shaggy head of an old man smells of "urine, sardines, and Vitalis." Another who keeps the trunk of his car "cleaner than most people kept their mouths," replaces a divot during a golf game with "the care a plastic surgeon might bestow upon repairing a young girl's face." In between forking bites of beef macaroni into his maw, yet another old-timer delivers a hug so monumental that it leaves him "as shaken as a soldier who has darted across a field to grab a fallen comrade." Gentleness shares space in the heart with brutality.

Perhaps inevitably, nowhere is Ms. Pollack more fraught than in describing the act of making love between middle-aged people with parent troubles. In the final story, "Beached in Boca," the woman is someone who prefers her beach water choppy. The man is a toy importer, someone whose father has scandalized his Florida retirement community with a particularly unseemly murder and who is endeavoring to care as little as possible about anything anymore. Nevertheless there's this: "He pressed one hand against her breast while sliding the other hand up her thigh. For some reason, she was reminded of the flat wood box in which a person could slip a coin and make it disappear. All those years importing novelties seemed to have given Adam Haber the sleight-of-hand required to remove a woman's underwear without taking off her shorts. He could palm her hand and make it vanish, and then, with a sideways smile, lay it back inside her ribs. It was a trick, but not a bad trick." —*Daniel Asa Rose*

Daniel Asa Rose edits The Reading Room, *a literary journal, and is the author of three books: the story collection* Small Family with Rooster, *the novel* Flipping for It, *and* Hiding Places, *a memoir.*

Fire Ants, *stories by Gerald Duff* (New South Books): Most of the fifteen stories in Gerald Duff's strong collection are filled with characters who are down on their luck. A mother's mentally handicapped son is in jail because he didn't understand that showing a gun to the cashier at the Sac'n Pac might be interpreted as robbery, and now she has to come up with bail. A Baptist preacher must make his way out of the woods, naked, after a run-in with a group of surly Native Americans. Two children meet a madman on their way to get milk. But what makes the characters in *Fire Ants* compelling isn't their problems, it's how they solve them. They typically lack the financial, emotional or intellectual wherewithal to do it easily, so they must make do what they have: wit, will and blind faith.

As you expect from a southern writer, Duff's characters are *characters*—the kind of people who might draw attention to themselves at the Piggly-Wiggly by talking too loudly, or because they still have a pink foam curler wrapped in their hair. They are best revealed through their explanations of their complicated and painful relationships with themselves, their families and God. It's in these moments where they assert themselves that Duff shows his talent with language and characterization. In "Texas Wherever You Look," a woman who is about to go into labor reminds herself that "All that is is *now,* a little word and a narrow place where you must stand and one which crumbles off beneath your feet on both sides, of what was and what will be. You cannot reach either place from here." In "Believing in Memphis," a failed musician picks up two female hitchhikers hoping to make it big in the music business. After many attempts at conversation, he dismisses them with the thought, "Most people I run into, I have learned over the years, don't like to be accused of having been influenced by anybody or anything outside of themselves in their acquiring of an outlook on the world. They like to believe they are one of a kind, you understand." Duff's characters are most vulnerable, and compelling, when they try to convince you they are not, that they possess wisdom no one else does.

What's particularly impressive about the collection is its wide range of voices and settings, and Duff's ability to infuse wry humor into awkward moments, or into entire stories. "Charm City," for example, is just plain funny. Though many stories inhabit similar locations, each character speaks with a nuanced cadence that is as different as they are—a little boy who has it out for his kid sister, a forlorn woman with a serious drinking problem. Duff manages light writing in his more modern settings, like "The Angler's Paradise Fish-Cabin Dance of Love," where the narrator "...hated to think of girls that looked the way they did, their hair all washed and shining and springy and their skin like brand new, freshly extruded latex just out of the machine, standing around in their costumes calling their boyfriends rimjobbing cool dudes...." He's equally effective when he slows down and creates a haunted atmosphere with stilted language and winding passages. "Redemption," "The Way a Blind Man Tracks Light" and "Texas Wherever You Look" pay homage to Faulkner as they tell the story of the Hoyt family at different time periods, sometimes from the perspectives of different family members. The diversity does work against him a bit, as Duff is stronger when he's dealing with the traditional southern fare, but even the weaker stories have plenty of merits. *Fire Ants* is a good addition to the Southern cannon, and will be enjoyed by anyone looking for an unexpected and satisfying read. —*Anya Yurchyshyn*

Anya Yurchyshyn works in the fiction department of Esquire, *and is a candidate for her M.F.A. in fiction from Columbia.*

CONTRIBUTORS' NOTES

Fall 2008

RYAN BERG, a graduate of The New School, received an M.F.A. in Creative Non-fiction from Hunter College in 2008. He received a 2008 artist residency at the MacDowell Colony, and is currently working on a memoir about the two years he spent working with gay, lesbian, bisexual, and transgender youth living in foster care in New York City.

MARK BRAZAITIS's latest book is *An American Affair: Stories*, which won the 2004 George Garrett Fiction Prize from Texas Review Press. A former Peace Corps Volunteer, he is an associate professor of English and director of the Creative Writing Program at West Virginia University.

ALLEN GEE teaches graduate and undergraduate fiction workshops at Georgia College, where he is the faculty fiction editor for the journal *Arts & Letters*. He is at work on a short story collection titled *Twelve Questions I've Asked Myself Late At Night*.

DAVID GULLETTE, one of the original editors of *Ploughshares*, has written two books about revolutionary poetry in Nicaragua. He performs with The Actors' Shakespeare Project, and teaches at Simmons College.

KIRSTEN MENGER-ANDERSON's first book, a collection of linked stories entitled *Doctor Olaf van Schuler's Brain*, arrives October 21, 2008 from Algonquin. She lives in San Francisco with her husband and daughter.

ALEX ROSE is a founding editor of Hotel St. George Press in Brooklyn. He has written for *The New York Times, Fantasy Magazine, The Reading Room, North American Review, The Forward*, and *DIAGRAM*. His debut story collection, *The Musical Illusionist*, was published in October of 2007 to critical acclaim.

STEVEN SCHWARTZ is the author of four books, including the novels *Therapy* and *A Good Doctor's Son*. He teaches creative writing at Colorado State University and in the Warren Wilson M.F.A. Program.

AURELIE SHEEHAN is the author of two novels, *History Lesson for Girls* and *The Anxiety of Everyday Objects*, as well as a short story collection, *Jack Kerouac Is Pregnant*. She teaches fiction and directs the M.F.A. Program in Creative Writing at the University of Arizona in Tucson.

M. G. STEPHENS's essay comes from a recently completed manuscript about the East Village in the 1960's and beyond. He is the author of eighteen books, including the memoirs *Lost in Seoul* and *Where the Sky Ends*, and the novels *Season at Coole* and *The Brooklyn Book of the Dead*. He lives in London.

AMY STUBER's short fiction has been published in numerous national literary journals, including *The Antioch Review*, *The Santa Monica Review*, and *Other Voices*. She lives with her family in Lawrence, Kansas.

MARY SWAN's stories have appeared in a number of Canadian and American literary publications. She is the winner of the 2001 O'Henry Award for short fiction, and the author of the collection *The Deep and Other Stories*, published by Random House. Her novel, *The Boys in the Trees*, was published by Henry Holt in 2008. She lives in Guelph, Ontario, with her husband and daughter.

JOYCE E. TURNER attends the Writers' Workshop at the University of Iowa, where she teaches literature and creative writing. She is revising her comic novel, tentatively entitled *The Dollar Zoo*.

~

GUEST EDITOR POLICY *Ploughshares* is published three times a year: mixed issues of poetry and fiction in the Spring and Winter and a fiction issue in the Fall, with each guest-edited by a different writer of prominence, usually one whose early work was published in the journal. Guest editors are invited to solicit up to half of their issues, with the other half selected from unsolicited manuscripts screened for them by staff editors. This guest editor policy is designed to introduce readers to different literary circles and tastes, and to offer a fuller representation of the range and diversity of contemporary letters than would be possible with a single editorship. Yet, at the same time, we expect every issue to reflect our overall standards of literary excellence. We liken *Ploughshares* to a theater company: each issue might have a different guest editor and different writers—just as a play will have a different director, playwright, and cast—but subscribers can count on a governing aesthetic, a consistency in literary values and quality, that is uniquely our own.

~

SUBMISSION POLICIES We welcome unsolicited manuscripts from August 1 to March 31 (postmark dates). All submissions sent from April to July are returned unread. In the past, guest editors often announced specific themes for issues, but we have revised our editorial policies and no longer restrict submissions to thematic topics. Submit your work at any time during our reading period; if a manuscript is not timely for one issue, it will be considered for another. We do not recommend trying to target specific guest editors. Our backlog is unpredictable, and staff editors ultimately have the responsibility of determining for which editor a work is most appropriate. Mail one prose piece or one to three poems. We do not accept e-mail submissions, but we plan to introduce an online submissions system this fall. Check for updates and guidelines on our website (www.pshares.org). Poems should be individually typed either single- or double-spaced on one side of the page. Prose should be typed double-spaced on one side and be no longer than thirty pages. Although we look primarily for short stories, we occasionally publish personal essays/memoirs. Novel excerpts are acceptable if self-contained. Unsolicited book reviews and criticism are not considered. Please do not send multiple submissions of the same genre, and do not send another manuscript until you hear about the first. *No more than a total of two submissions per reading period.* Additional submissions will be returned unread. Mail your manuscript in a page-size manila envelope, your full name and address written on the outside. In general, address submissions to the "Fiction Editor," "Poetry Editor," or "Nonfiction Editor," not to the guest or staff editors by name, unless you have a legitimate association with them or have been previously published in the magazine. Unsolicited work sent directly to a guest editor's home or office will be ignored and discarded; guest editors are formally instructed not to read such work. *All manuscripts and correspondence regarding submissions should be accompanied by a business-size, self-addressed, stamped envelope (S.A.S.E.) for a response only. Manuscript copies will be recycled, not returned.* No replies will be given by postcard or e-mail (exceptions are made for international submissions). Expect three to five months for a decision. We now receive well over a thousand manuscripts a month. Do not query us until five months have passed, and if you do, please write to us, including an S.A.S.E. and indicating the postmark date of submission, instead of calling or e-mailing. Simultaneous submissions are amenable as long as they are indicated as such and we are notified immediately upon acceptance elsewhere. We cannot accommodate revisions, changes of return address, or forgotten S.A.S.E.'s after the fact. We do not reprint previously published work. Translations are welcome if permission has been granted. We cannot be responsible for delay, loss, or damage. Payment is upon publication: $25/printed page, $50 minimum and $250 maximum per author, with two copies of the issue and a one-year subscription.

NATIONAL
ENDOWMENT
FOR THE ARTS

massculturalcouncil.org

"There is only one school of literature—that of talent."

Vladimir Nabokov

Michener Center for Writers

MFA in WRITING

FICTION   POETRY   SCREENWRITING   PLAYWRITING

A top ranked program. Dedicated and diverse resident faculty. Inspiring and distinguished visiting writers. $25,000 annual fellowships. Three years in Austin, Texas.

www.utexas.edu/academic/mcw
512-471-1601

THE UNIVERSITY OF TEXAS AT AUSTIN

Boston University Graduate School of Arts & Sciences
MFA in Creative Writing

OUR PROGRAM, ONE OF THE OLDEST, MOST PRESTIGIOUS, and selective in the country, was recently placed among the top ten by *The Atlantic Monthly*, which went on to rank our faculty and our alumni among the top five. The magazine might have been impressed by our two most celebrated workshops— one, in poetry, was led by Robert Lowell, who had scattered around him Sylvia Plath, Anne Sexton, and George Starbuck; the other, much more recent, was led by Leslie Epstein, whose students included Ha Jin, Jhumpa Lahiri, and Peter Ho Davies. Our classes still meet in the same small room, which allows through its dusty windows a glimpse of the Charles. These days, the poetry workshops are led by our regular faculty, Robert Pinsky, Louise Glück, and Rosanna Warren; those in fiction are led by Leslie Epstein, Ha Jin himself, and Allegra Goodman. Our famed playwriting classes are taught by Kate Snodgrass, Ronan Noone, and Melinda Lopez.

It is difficult to know how best to measure a student's success or the worth of a program to a writer. Our graduates have won every major award in each of their genres, including, in playwriting, the Charles MacArthur Award and six national playwriting awards from the American College Theater Festival; in poetry, The Whiting Award, the Norma Farber First Book Award, along with three winners of the Discovery/The Nation Award and two winners of the National Poetry Series; in fiction our graduates have won the Pulitzer Prize, the PEN/Faulkner, the PEN/Hemingway, and the National Book Award. Every month one of our graduates brings out a book of poetry or fiction with a major publisher; and some, like Sue Miller and Arthur Golden, have spent a good deal of time on bestseller lists. Over the last decade we have placed more than a score of our graduates in tenure-track positions at important universities (Peter Ho Davies and Carl Phillips direct the creative writing programs at Michigan and Washington University in St. Louis).

We make, of course, no such assurances. Our only promise to those who join us is of a fair amount of time in that river-view room, time shared with other writers in a common, most difficult pursuit: the perfection of one's craft. For more information about the program, visiting writers, and financial aid, write to Director, Creative Writing Program, Boston University, 236 Bay State Road, Boston, MA 02215 or visit our website at www.bu.edu/writing/.

Application deadline is March 1, 2009.